Jacob Ian DeCoursey

I0543128

VIVID

GREENE

and other unusual stories

Browne & Jenkins
Fiction

All stories previously appeared in the following publications: "Vivid Greene..." in *9Tales Told in the Dark;* "Santa's Train to Heaven" in *The Welter;* "Before the Flood" in *The Scum Gentry Alternative Arts & Media;* "Watching" in *Not One of Us;* "The Heat Went on Forever" in *Horror Sleaze Trash.* Please support indie and small press literature.

Keywords: "fiction"; "bizarro"; "horror"; "transgressive"; "experimental"

ISBN 978-0-578-57904-7

OfficialJacobIanDeCoursey@gmail.com

Browne & Jenkins Publishing: Balto. Md

First edition, 2019

VIVID

GREENE

and other unusual stories

Table of Contents:

Foreword

The Stories:

Afterword

About the Author

Foreword

*M*y goddamn editor, Wesley Hunt, requested a write-up before he would give this manuscript the final once-over. The assigned topic: *What do I want to accomplish with this book?*

It's a strange, vague question, one I'm not sure how best to answer.

Thanks, Wes. You couldn't have made this easy!

But alright. Here goes nothin'.

For me, the act of writing is often a form of cheap therapy, a way to depressurize. Because of this, each story you're about to read was written at a different stage in my life and meant something urgent at that particular time— pushing to rip through into the world like a monstrous turd.

I've joked before that at the best points in my life I have nothing to say worth saying. Even when the want is maddening and my ass is in the chair and I'm staring down a blank page, if life has been relatively comfortable then the page remains blank. And that is a whole other discomfort. Have you ever not been able to shit for days at a time? If so then you have a rough approximation of this creative constipation.

When it does come, though, it's a sweet release. And when I'm done with any final edits, and the piece is out there in print or online, I'm entirely done. I don't want to look at those pages, those characters, anymore. I rarely re-read old material, instead choosing to empty out, flush, and walk away. I'm not interested in fingering through my own excrement.

Often (I hope), this is because I'm not the same person coming out of a story as I was going in. As is the point of any successful therapy session—or restroom visit for that matter—I hope to leave a tad lighter of burden. But because of this, I can't remember half of what was so damn important to say when crafting these stories. Much of that urgency has been lost to time.

Honestly, even if I could remember, I wouldn't tell. After a story has successfully found a publisher, it isn't mine anymore. It was mine while incomplete. Once finished, it belongs to the reader.

Yet here I am, playing in my old dreck.

It's always baffled me how some of the best writers I've personally known all too often do what they do in secret. How could someone bleed over multiple pages and then leave them in a drawer to rot, either out of embarrassment or fear of rejection or just plain laziness?

Maybe I'm off-base here, but it seems like such a waste.

Not that finding a taker for your work is easy. When these fever dreams you're holding first found willing publishers, they were all small press and indie outlets. This is partly because they're what I actually enjoy reading and supporting (I just can't give a fuck about whatever *My Sad Yuppie Life* yarns that bourgeois rags like The New Yorker peddle any given month!) and partly because they're the only ones willing to touch any of my crap. Downside is small press readerships are equally small, and, sadly, many little publishers vanish without fair warning.

Just because that urgency I was talking about has been lost to time doesn't mean the final product should be too. Even though I don't look at them, the idea of these stories being forgotten is near painful. Compiling some of it into a book just seems like a logical move toward preservation.

For me, writing has always been a form of cheap therapy. But more than that, it's a way of desperately trying to make sense of this world we live in.

Since much of what you're about to read sprouts from dark headspaces, it might be easy to view it all as nihilistic defeatism. Personally, I prefer the label "transgressive." And that's an important distinction.

Despite what that genre would eventually become, thanks in part to reactionary-driven cultural narratives and conservative frat boy fan bases, the founders of transgressive fiction (whether Nabokov or Burgess, Ellis or Palahniuk, to name only a few) were neither nihilists nor defeatists. Maybe their approaches were questionable or their ideals worthy of scrutiny, but there was always a deeper message in their respective works about who we are or what we have become and—maybe buried deep within subtext—that we so badly need to be better.

There's a popular saying that "hurt people hurt people." While that's not always the case, nor does it justify harmful actions, it's a good look in the right direction. My characters hurt each other. Some engage in downright deplorable behavior. I don't justify that. I just want to understand why. I don't always come to an answer by the final line, but the question remains.

These are stories about human beings: at once beautiful and toxic as the Lilly of the Valley. There is a trend in contemporary writing to place morality at the forefront of a narrative. I respect this. Some uncertain souls need to be shown decent paths by which to walk; while others who may have strayed, gently lead back. And what better medium by which to accomplish such a task than fiction? Yet this isn't my way of telling a story. I have no desire to preach, nor am I confident I know how.

Instead, the best I have to offer is a mirror into various corners of life as I may have experienced them. The mirrors are often twisted, expressing distorted approximations of the otherwise familiar. But there, in those grotesque reflections, are those paths we walk—both kind and cruel. My hope is that, after closing this book, despite all the cruelty therein, readers will choose kindness.

Pretty sure that doesn't answer your question, Wes. But it's all you're going to get.

J.I.D.
Aug. 26, 2019
Baltimore, MD

Undertakers, hearse drivers, grave diggers,
I speak to you as one not afraid of your business.
—Carl Sandburg, 1916

VIVID GREENE

or

A Place to Lay My Bones

Field

The spade makes a deep crunching sound as it penetrates the dry and rocky soil. This was supposed to be a garden once, she thinks as she digs. A garden of beautiful flowers —bright, living, plentiful, their colors glowing beneath the hot June sun. The young woman strains and lifts another shovelful of dirt, turns her body to deposit it on the mound behind her. A cold wind pushes through her so she pauses, her fingers numb. Pale breath curls before her eyes. It's late October now, and late at night too. A cobweb of stars hangs overhead surrounding a white half moon. A white trash bag lies at her ankles, on top the matted brown grass touched with glittering frost. Inside the bag, a heap of wet pulp and raw carcass that was once her father's old golden retriever, Pluto. She'd grown up with that dog and loved it very, very much. But before church this morning, she'd accidentally left the basement door ajar, and the dog had wandered down.

Everything that ever goes into the basement dies horribly, she thinks, stopping long enough to nudge the bag with her heel. It feels soft and lumpy, like a huge cyst. "I wish we had pigs to eat our garbage."

Somewhere in the darkness, she hears the hiss of dry leaves shaking on their mother branches like the choral death rattle of some croupy infants. Listening, she breathes into her hands, rubs them together. She grips the wooden shaft and handle and stomps the blade of the shovel back into the earth and twists. A large clod gives way, and she lifts and drops it behind her again.

As she stabs the dirt and stomps the shovel blade hard, it hits against something beneath the dense soil. She stomps the blade again and again, frustrated, twisting it left and right, but nothing; the blade won't go deeper. So she lifts it out, and, as it comes free, another sharp wind gusts past and catches the concave of the blade, knocking it forward into her bare shin.

Pain surges up her leg, and she bites her lower lip to keep from screaming. She reaches for her leg and stumbles sideways, landing on the white trash bag, and for a brief moment, she feels the comfort of its soft contents beneath her.

Then it bursts open under her weight.

Blood. Bones. Bits of soft, fleshy tissue. All the bag's contents, now strewn over the ground, over her clothes and skin.

"Martha!" a hard, male voice calls through the thick darkness.

Covered in gore, she lifts herself to her feet and places her hands on the small of her back and pushes. It cracks and pops as she straightens herself upright. She turns and looks a little ways off and sees her father standing on the porch of their small farmhouse. The front door is wide open. A television strobes blue and yellow and red and blue again somewhere inside.

"Yes, sir," she hollers, standing on top the ruptured bag in a pool of cold red, holding her throbbing shin.

"Get in here, girl!"

So she does. Slowly walking toward the silhouette of a house before her, toward the shadow of her father standing tall and masculine and oppressive in the flickering doorway; her stride uneven, favoring the injured leg, shivering for the icy, stinking blood soaking through her clothes and dripping, dripping, dripping down into her shoes.

House

As she steps inside, her father grabs her arm and yanks hard.

"Come on, girl," he says.

She stumbles into the living room and knocks against the tweed sofa, smearing it with the red covering her clothes and skin. Every light in the room is off, and her eyes wander in the dimness: before the sofa she's leaning against, the television flickers with muted gospel programming. On the walls hang pictures of Christ and saints and various artistic renderings of da Vinci's Last Supper; every square inch of wall covered in some sacred print; then, slowly, back to her father, still wearing his white dress shirt and starched khakis from earlier this morning, his entire form flashing blue and yellow before the tube's luminescence.

"Your little sin is making some devil of a racket downstairs," he says.

She's quiet for a moment, listening. Through the floorboards, she can hear it.

18

"Yes, sir," she says with her head lowered, not wanting to look him in the eyes.

He always calls his grandson "little sin" on account of the boy's condition. This is a time of testing for the land, he often tells her, days of clay feet and fire. A few miles down the road, in the little town of Vivid Greene, Mississippi, other mothers have been making news, giving birth to babies with similar ailments—always young mothers like Martha, underage and unmarried—but none, so far as she knows, afflicted so severely as Martha's child. So much so, that her family doctor, a churchgoing man well past prime retirement age, upon examining the boy, could only scratch his white beard and address her father solemnly:

Best keep this under lock and key, Joseph, he'd said quiet enough for it to be a secret but loud enough for Martha to hear. Save yourself the embarrassment.

His words were like candleflames, small in their movements but capable of great destruction.

"Go put the little sin to sleep so I don't have to," Martha's father says.

"Dad—"

"It angers me, you understand?"

"Dad, I—"

"You understand?"

"Yes, sir."

"Then you can shampoo the mess you've just made off the couch."

"Okay."

"What?"

"Yes, sir."

"Good," he says, forcefully rubbing his palms across his eyes. "I'm going to bed." He turns around and heads for the stairs. She looks up, watches him go.

"Night, Dad."

He doesn't say anything. Just climbs the stairs. She hears the door to his bedroom close then gets up and begins walking toward the kitchen where the basement door is.

The darkened kitchen feels like a monastery long abandoned to rot.

A familiar cul-de-sac of hoarded holiness.

What was once a dinner table is now a makeshift altar covered in drippy, burnt out candles, their pooled wax gripping them to the woodgrain like deformed fingers. Other dollar store trinkets crowd the counter tops:

A Jesus bobble head grinning and nodding as she passes.

Wood carvings of angels.

Resin statues of every apostle.

A crucifix shaped candelabra covered in milky white wax.

Three different versions of the nativity, all ceramic, one with a black baby Jesus and white Mary and Joseph.

A plastic "suffer the little children to come unto me" figurine set complete with suffered children. She imagines them all levitating and floating around the kitchen and out the window, ascending into a cloud in the night and disappearing.

Just ahead and to the left of the pantry stands the wooden basement door with peeling paint that she remembers tasted sweet when she ate a piece as a little girl. When she gets to the door, she reaches out and touches the knob, turns it; the door opens.

Downstairs, the air is cold, almost as cold as outside but windless. She doesn't come down here but more than once or twice a day, and even then, she doesn't stay for very long. It hurts too much.

At the bottom of the stairs she reaches up and pulls a thin string that clicks on a lightbulb dangling from the ceiling. The dark is bleached by dirty incandescence exposing a six-by-six-foot cube of black metal bars bolted to the bare concrete walls and a red stain smeared on the floor from where she'd cleaned the dog up some three hours ago. A heap of quilts heaves and rises behind the bars, wailing like a child with the voice of a man, as a small foot darts out from underneath and begins kicking the bars frantically.

"Baby," she says, stepping forward.

The heap falls from the child's body, a little boy. He stands naked and hunched, his spine contorted forward in a low arch, vertebra poking sharp beneath his pale skin. he turns around. His bony chest is covered with scratches and his arms are sinewy and strong with spidery hands and long and dirty fingernails stained pink with Pluto's fur still clumped underneath. His malformed head, uneven like a sack of potatoes and sparsely haired. It is the child's face that bothers Martha the most though: his eyes are hollow and dark, almost lifeless glass beads pressed deep into his sunken features. He looks at her with those eyes what feels like a long time. There's blood coagulated on his chin. And when he opens his mouth, she sees his rows of sharp, crowded teeth.

He gurgles at her in a language both primitive and infantile. He's almost three now.

A few feet from the bars, she stops and kneels down, then sits and crosses her legs and places her hands in her lap. Sometimes, when she looks on him, she even feels a little apprehensive. But she doesn't like that feeling; she doesn't like feeling that way about her child.

"Baby, it's Mama," she says. "You know Mama, don't you?" But the child just looks. And despite a knotted feeling in the pit of her stomach, she's happy to have his attention.

Quiet hangs in the cold, and she holds her arms,

remembering now the slowly drying red caked to her clothes and skin. She stands up. The child begins gurgling again and hits the bars of his cage with the palms of his hands.

"Shush," she says, but he will not. "It's okay, baby, I'm not going anywhere."

At the far wall is the washer and dryer and next to them, a washbasin. She walks toward them. "I'm here. Just hold on, okay?" she says, turning on the faucet. She rinses her hands under the warm water, splashes her face, and, placing her head under the faucet, wrings the grime from her hair. She bends down and unlatches her shoes, kicks them away. Then she pulls her stained dress off over her head and hangs it over the edge of the basin.

Standing wet in the chill air, the calloused pads of her feet numbing on the stone floor, she looks down at her nakedness and remembers how her mother's funeral was on a rainy Wednesday morning four years ago today. Her mother had been sick with the cancer a long time, and when she finally went to her appointed glory, Martha's father had given the most beautiful eulogy comparing the time they'd spent together to a green forest; though looking back, Martha can't place what he meant by that metaphor. Regardless, the boy beneath the giant oak had spoken softly to her, had touched her face where she'd been crying and then tasted his fingers. She was new to this—she remembers his mouth tasting like snow and how he'd entered her body so smooth and tenderly that it didn't even hurt but a little. But that's probably just how she wants to remember it. The real truth is that after the echoing tremors of her first climax had passed, he left her lying there breathing deep and slow in the coarse grass and watching the sky darken, her panties around her left foot and a small red stain on her dress, and she knew she'd been cursed. But even that may not be true; maybe there was no boy; maybe, after the casket was lowered into earth and she and her father had returned home, she'd gone to her room to cry and think and pray. And maybe her father, with tears in his eyes too, had found her there on her bed and held her arms to the mattress, his grief surging into her body like a powerful waterfall into a gentle stream.

Either way, it didn't matter; time has a way of making certain details irrelevant.

"Mrah!" she hears behind her. "Mmmraah!"

The child shrieks and beats his bars. She ignores him a moment and reaches into the dryer for a clean towel to cover herself with. She retrieves one and hurriedly rubs it against her skin, trying to sop up every bead of moisture and warm herself by the friction then wraps it around her bosom. She turns to the defective boy behind the metal bars who is gripping his cage tight and beating his head against it. He stops and stands still, quiet, and Martha walks toward him. And as she draws closer, it looks like he's crying quietly, his small and weedy shoulders trembling and gently heaving up and down, and for the first time, he almost looks like a normal child. She sits again a few feet from his cell.

"It wasn't always this way, living here," she says partially to him but mostly to herself. "Daddy wasn't always like this. He wasn't always this heartless or cruel."

The boy looks up at her with dark and sunken eyes wet and droopy from crying, and she tries to see some semblance of humanity in them.

She tries very hard.

"You know, I remember when I was little like you, me and him used to go out to the county fair with Mama, my Mama, and he'd take me to see the animals in their pens. I always liked the ducklings, but I always felt so bad that they were locked behind that chicken wire and away from their mothers."

The boy cocks his head and bares his teeth. She can't tell if he's grinning or grimacing.

"I could take you too someday. I'd like that. I'd like that a lot. You like that idea, baby?"

He doesn't say anything. Just coos deeply and blows spit bubbles. And she recalls when she'd hold her belly and feel him kick and thrust impatiently behind her skin as if trying to reach the wonders of the world he'd be born into.

"You know, I'm eighteen now," she says. "I could take you away from here and there wouldn't be a thing nobody could do to stop me. To a faraway place to lay my bones and rest with you where we could both be happy and free and have each other always."

She reaches for the small lock keeping the cage shut. She doesn't know the combination; her father never told her.

"I could take you and go away from here if I like. Nodody'd stop us, I bet."

As her hand draws closer, the boy follows it with his eyes but doesn't move his head.

"I really do love you," she says with tears in her eyes, "and I want to be a good Mama, like my Mama was—" She reaches through the bars and tries to caress his face. He snaps at her with his sharp and crowded teeth. She jerks her hand back quickly and wipes the wetness from her eyes and cheeks. "—but I just don't know how."

The boy hoots and lunges wildly, reaching through the bars and clawing at the air in front of her face.

"I'm sorry," she says. "I'm sorry."

And as she stands up and moves away from the cage, the boy begins stretching his arms out through the bars and crying. Every night, he cries, but she's never heard him cry like this, and she has to cover her ears just to make the pressure deep inside her chest go away. She turns off the light and heads up the steps.

Back in the kitchen, she closes the door fast, but she can still hear him crying for her.

She sinks to the linoleum floor.

Later that night, just before sunrise, after changing out of her towel and into fresh pajamas, and after spending hours and hours cleaning the stain off the arm of the couch, she takes a paper plate from the pantry and places two Pop Tarts on it and pours a sippy cup of milk. She slowly and quietly carries the small meal back down the steps into the dark basement and lays them in front of the cage. But by then the boy is asleep and has been for some time.

An hour later, she hears a bedroom door slam. Her father has woken early for work today. Sleepily she readies herself and steps out the front door and into the early morning dimness to finish her digging before he scolds her for laziness.

Outside, the smell of decay assaults her nose, and she sees the blackbirds in the distance pecking the trash bag she'd left there the night before.

Road

After her father leaves, she decides not to sleep.

The daylight hasn't been up two hours. Her eyes heavy and sore with fatigue, Martha walks down the shoulder of the long two-lane nowhere road leading to Vivid Greene, and there are no cars, rarely are at this time of morning. Though there isn't any reason for it, she kicks off her shoes, picks them up off the ground, and begins to run; she always runs faster without her shoes: the pads of her feet clapping against the gravely blacktop, stones lodging and dislodging between her calloused toes. The feeling of the world beneath her every step. Above her, power lines hum and dip and arch, stretching out into the bright infinity ahead.

She follows them.

After a while, she hears a motor revving behind her ears, and then a horn sounds and she jumps and lands hard on her hands and knees. Sweating and cold from it, panting and swallowing the thick spittle that occurs with dehydration, her lungs feeling frozen and dry. Moisture running from her eyes and down her cheeks. She feels awake now; alive for the moment, her insides washed with adrenaline, she feels her heartbeat against her ribcage. She picks herself up, dusts herself off, and turns around. Behind her and creeping slowly closer on the far side of the road is a Dodge Hodgepodge, apparently built from junkyard parts of various sun-faded hues, rattling and squeaking and coughing up a cloud of sour smelling exhaust behind its rear wheels.

She turns around, sees the car. Facing forward again, she continues on, her walking now slowed to a trot. She looks back as the car inches closer, and she picks up her pace, but the car accelerates just faster than her legs carry her until it's beside her, matching her speed. Then the passenger side window opens.

"Goddam, honey!" a young man's voice calls from inside the car. "What'n Christ's name are you doin' runnin' barefoot in this kinda cold?"

She stops and leans on her knees and breathes heavily, each inhale turning her lungs to paper. The car stops beside her. She pretends not to notice it.

"What's the matter, can't talk?"

She brushes her hair from her face and tucks it behind her ears then looks up. "Hey," she says, squinting at the driver's features, "I know you."

"You oughtta," he says. "I only stand behind my pop and stare at you every goddamn Sunday at church."

"Your dad's the new reverend."

"Ooh, good eyes."

"Why you always standing behind him?"

"Learnin' the trade."

"You wanna be a preacher?"

"Hell no." He pauses a moment to think. "Well, if the money's good, since I'll probably end up taking care of my sister."

"Something wrong with your sister?"

"Don't worry about it." he says. "Ain't your monkeys, ain't your circus."

She smiles and spits a wad of foam onto the road.

He smiles back.

"So why you barefoot exactly, naturegirl?"

"I gotta run an errand," she says.

"Barefoot?"

"I run faster without my shoes."

The boy reaches over his passenger seat and pops open the door. "Get in."

"I'm fine. Don't you have anyplace else to be right now?"

He shakes his head and grins. "Nope."

She doesn't say anything, just starts walking again.

The car rolls slow beside her.

"C'mon," he says. "What're you afraid of?"

She doesn't look at him, instead studies her surroundings then the sky and sees both are empty.

"Maybe the real problem is you don't know me after all, "he says. "But I'd kinda like it if you'd get to know me. I've been wantin' to get to know you awhile now."

He then smiles a scary smile.

She likes it; she doesn't want to, but she does.

"Are you planning to kidnap me or something?"

His brow furrows and his mouth straightens. "Now, why the hell would I do that?"

"Idunno, she says. "You seem the type."

He smiles wide at her again and laughs.

She stops.

So does the car, and it sputters beside her, the passenger door still slightly ajar. She looks at it, through the window, and at the boy. She stoops down and slips her shoes back over her numb and dirty feet then stands up again. Then she steps slowly across the street toward the car sputtering louder and louder the closer she comes and opens the door and climbs inside. Once she is seated, the boy quickly leans over her lap and grabs the door handle, closing it with a metallic bang that reverberates throughout the entire car, throughout her body, like a cymbal crash. Still leaning over her, he looks up and smiles at her and says, "Are you in a rush?" and she says, "Kinda."

There are no other cars, so the boy lets his idle on the road.

They idle a long time.

Town

Martha buttons her blouse, her trembling hands fumbling as the boy speeds along the uneven road, seeming to intentionally hit every bump and pothole along the way. Inside her, the warmth of his seed leaving slow, for where, she's uncertain.

She ought to feel shameful.

She doesn't.

The boy drives her half way, and then lets her out. Tells her not to tell anyone she'd been with him.

"Okay," she says.

Immediately after she steps out from his car, he reaches across the passenger seat and shuts the door fast, then pops the emergency brake and cranks down the still-foggy window. He then looks her up and down. His eyes make her feel weird.

"Listen," he says after a little while, "You're not alone, okay?"

"Yeah," she says. "I know."

Martha watches as he opens his glove box. Religious

pamphlets and cigarettes and a pocket knife drop out like vomit from an open mouth and disappear below the seat. His slender fingers spasmodically shuffle the glove box's contents until they retrieve a small, square, dark-red object; she can't tell what it is. He then takes a pen from his shirt pocket and writes on the little thing.

"Here," he says and holds his fist out the window.

She reaches over and takes its contents: an empty Marlboro matchbook; inside, a phone number and the name Clinton in a barely legible scrawl.

"Alright?" he asks.

"Yeah, alright."

"Alright," he answers, then revs the engine and speeds away leaving the air smelling gray and sour. Martha stands there barefoot a long time and breathes deep and slow until the smell goes away. When the car is just a small blob fading into the distance and its clinking and sputtering noises can no longer be heard, she starts walking again. After a few steps, she realizes she's forgotten her shoes in his back seat.

She walks a while.

When the sun is nearly an hour higher in the sky, she reaches town. A runner's pace away, the road becomes a series of intersections surrounded by green and browning grass and tall tall oaks dripping their Autumn-kissed leaves like paint from an artist's brush: a wall of warm colors inviting her like an opening gate. And just beyond that, a landscape of burgundy houses and small colorful shops parting like the Jordan, revealing a tall church steeple jutting from the town's center.

The sign at the border reads, Vivid Green: Home of the Famous Whistleblower Family Cafe.

Stepping over the invisible border line separating it from the outside world, Martha enters the town. Inside, people are shuffling to and fro with the dry leaves the wind carries across the streets and sidewalks. She walks, mesmerized by the colors of everything. At the first intersection, she stands at its center and looks at the sky a long time until a car swerves slow around her and moseys away, so she turns left and follows it down the street until she reaches a collection of squat brick buildings—once dwellings now converted into small businesses—four on each side, and all with porches painted a different pastel shade. Something darts across the street a little ways in front of her, something large and moving quick yet clumsy, like an injured dog, and crashes through a thick hedgerow of evergreen bushes and vanishes. She moves closer, watches the hedge for movement, keeping her eyes on the bald spot where the whatever-the-hell-it-was knocked away branches and leaves as it dove into obscurity, but nothing.

She passes it and sprints away toward the third row home down, the one on the right hand side so she has to cross the street to get to it, with the chipping-blue-painted railings and the rusty-white-painted aluminum screen door with Gothic shapes curling around the borders and smudged-yellow-painted plywood sign resting in the porch swing that read, Whistleblower Family Cafe and Corner Market, and below that, Come On In We're Open, and she steps up the stoop steps and across the porchwood and pushes the door open, walks inside as a cowbell clunkles over her head. Inside, the air smells damp and sweet, and the light is a burnt-yellow dimness.

Store

"Well, hello," the man behind the register says and tips his fishing cap. He grins through a thick gray mustache. As he does, his jaw juts forward and opens, his lips retreating slightly, and Martha sees either all his upper teeth are missing or the few remaining are rotted black.

Martha nods at him.

"Where're your shoes, honey?"

She looks down at her feet, then shrugs at him without lifting her eyes.

"Got Crocs hanging near the back. Not the real ones, but they'll do just as good.

"Okay."

"Can I do you for something?"

"Baby food, I guess," she says. "But what do you give an almost-three-year-old?"

The man looks her up and down. "It yours?" he asks after a pause.

Martha hesitates before answering, "Uh-huh."

"Who did it to you, young lady?" he asked, his voice now

firm.

She doesn't say anything.

"Then I take it you got one of those things, then. Want to know what to feed it? Wild clover honey, the rawer the better. Straight out a bees asshole, if you can find it. Then pray the kid gets the botulism. You'll be better off, take my word."

She doesn't say anything after that but looks down again and walks toward where he told her the shoes are. He doesn't say anything else either but keeps eyeing her up and down as she passes. Martha steps toward the sandal rack, lifts off a yellow pair held together with a cardboard backing. There are a few other people in the store too. Three by Martha's count, two middle-aged men in tee shirts and khakis and an older woman in a sundress and riding a red power scooter, all in a circle and chittering a faint conversation:

"But what of your grandbaby?" one man asks.

"I ain't got any grandbaby," says the other.

"But your daughter—"

"What of her?"

"She was big with child last time I seen her at—"

"She just got fat is all."

"But I'd seen her with a stroller just last week," the woman says. "Must've been a baby in it, lest she'd up and gone loony or something."

"Ain't no baby," the other man says. "She did found that animal down by the riverside."

"You can't find babies by the river. What, do you think she got a Moses or something?" says the woman.

"I told you once, and I'll tell you again: That animal ain't no baby. And sure as shit it ain't no Moses, neither. Shame of the Lord, what it is."

"You're not making sense," the woman says.

"Not a lick," says the man.

The cowbell sounds again and Martha looks up over a soup shelf and sees the door open and then close but cannot see anybody walk in. She looks at the man at the register, now leaning his back against the wall behind him, his fishing cap lowered over his eyes as though he were trying to sleep on his feet. Then he tips his hat and looks at the door, then at Martha, then lowers his cap again.

"Damn kids and their knock-knock-ditch-'em games," he says.

Martha looks away.

"My baby girl," the other man says, "she went down by the rivermouth. Lead down there by a young man from church, and they went down and began to pray and do things like the Maker made them want to do, and looked and saw something wreathing in the water weeds.

"Not one lick of sense," the man says.

"Well, my girl, being a fine child of God, she is, and merciful to a hurt, she gone over and picked up that thing and wrapped it in a sackcloth like the Baby Savior were, then brung it home."

"Then what?" asks the woman.

"Well, she brung it up to me still wet and slimy and showed me and told me what'd happened, and I said, You throw him back! And she said, Why? And I said, 'Cos water trash gone wash up where it do, and ain't no use in picking it up neither."

Just then, a shelf of filled mason jars topples sideways, crashes to the floor. Everyone stops and looks toward the sound. Jelly and honey and glass crawl slow and dark over the hardwood floor like a rainbow of gasoline in a street puddle under sunshine. A jar rolls toward Martha, stops at her toes. She kneels, picks it up.

"Sam-Hell?" the man at the register says.

The now horizontal shelf begins to rock to and fro slightly, a still, small voice noising from underneath it. Like a hurt animal, Martha thought. And she begins to think about Pluto, about the time he broke his hind leg falling down the stairs and the noises he made, weak and near-human.

"Something's under there," the woman says.

"Chester, c'mere and help me, would you?" the man behind the register says stepping around his counter and toward the mess.

"Can't lift," says the one man. "Not a lick since accident. Knees are shot to hell and back."

"Mitch, help me out with this."

"Gotta watch the blood pressure," the other says patting his chest, sending a ripple through his soft torso. "Doctor's orders."

"You can't help me lift a shelf?"

"Doctor's orders," he says again and grins. "Ticker's getting old."

"Lazy bastards, all."

The woman steps off her scooter and grips a corner of the shelf. "Lordy, you boys wouldn't know hard work if it jumped up and bit you on the peckers."

"Thank ya, ma'am," the shopkeeper says. "On three: One. Two. Three!"

The two puff heavily and bring up the shelf, reposition it in its proper place.

The man with the bad knees stands staring at the heap of broken jars and spilled condiments. "Sweet Jesus, Matthew!" he says. "Look!"

"What?" asks the shopkeeper.

Martha steps closer and looks. There, in the middle of the mess and lying curled like a hatchling in a nest, is a small child—at least a child in the academic sense of the word: It has arms and legs, and a head and face, and between its naked thighs, the expected collection of little boy parts. But its arms are disproportionate, one too long and the other too thick and its fingers so numerous and gangly its hands look like fleshy spiders. She moves closer still: Its hair-lipped mouth hangs open, its gums gashed and wet with red, teeth sparse and crooked and jagged. Pushing past the men standing and staring, she sees its atrophied legs twitching, bent inward like a cricket's and kicking the jars surrounding. And Martha looks at the small and twisted half-conscious form before her and realizes her child had been born lucky.

"Yours?" the shopkeeper asks.

Martha looks at him and shakes her head. Glancing behind her, she sees the second man backing toward the door. His lips repeating, Water trash, but making no sound.

"Best back up then." He nudges her aside and steps away toward the back end of the store and then through a small door. The door closes; clanking reverberates faintly behind it. Then the man emerges, carrying a long-handled snow shovel.

"What're you gonna do with that?" Martha asks.

"What I gotta."

"Lordy, what's the matter with you people?" the woman says squeezing her paunch back into the scooter and riding toward the child.

"Gonna wash up where it do," the second man says from across the store.

The woman looks back and glares at him. "It ain't hurting nobody. It's just a little thing, barely more than a suckling after all."

She leans down and brushes some glass from its cheek with her plump fingers. It looks up at her and makes a sound low and inhuman.

"Ain't no use in picking it up," the man said louder.

As she touches its face again the child jumps, its cricket legs propelling it upward, and lands on the woman's bosom. Startled, she reverses her scooter knocking it into a wall of cereal boxes behind her. They rain to the floor with a thick galumphing sound. Then she screams in pain. The child leaps off her and slips and slithers on jelly and glass, then takes off on all fours toward the door. Martha watches as it passes her: Its mouth is smeared with blood, something pink clenched in its teeth. She looks at the woman, half falling out of her seat and clutching her left breast, red leaking from her soft flesh and down her shirt. Martha turns again and sees the man by the door collapsing to the floor in fright, tightly clutching his own cleavage. The child races on all fours toward him, and he bicycle-kicks at it hard. One blow connects with its head, dislodging the contents from its mouth, knocking the child sideways and into the front counter. The shopkeeper runs toward it, snow shovel out like a jouster's lance, and lunges the heavy orange plastic blade down.

There is a wet sound, and a loud cry. The cry lasts a long time. Then a silence so deep Martha could hear the blood pushing through her head.

The man on the floor pushes himself to his feet.

"Whose is it?" the other asks.

"Hell if I know," the shopkeeper says. "Some dumb bitch likely forgot to keep it locked up."

"Oh, God! Oh, Jesus Christ!" the woman says clutching herself where she's missing skin. Nobody seems to pay her mind.

"Either that're she started in feeling sorry for it and let it free, like a captured titmouse or squirrel," the shopkeeper continued.

"Lord, I need a doctor," she says. "I'm bleeding so

much!"

"Goddamn whores oughten just take a coat hanger to all 'em fore they're ever even born. That're learn to keep their dresses lowered and their panties up. Save us all the trouble of dealing with these little shits like they're our problem!" Then the shopkeeper scoops the baby with the shovel, then lets the shovel drop and looks over at the man pushing his wobbling mass back vertical.

The man looks at him, then away.

The woman's voice resonates through the store: "God! God! God!"

Martha quietly watches them, yet watches nothing at all, unable to comprehend their speech, their alien motions, replaying the last few minutes over and over in her head. Then she looks at the baby being gentled away, destined for the dumpster. Her chest jumps, and she starts to cry. She cries loud, so that she can't hear them talking anymore. After a while, someone places a hand on her shoulder, but she doesn't look up to see who, swats it away.

And at some point, she begins to run again, pushing through the store-folk encircling her and out the front door. She runs and runs, eyes open yet blind with tears, feeling the pebbly town road under her feet turn to grass and the grass to thick leaves and branches. Then she stops and breathes and looks around: she's out of the town, and far into the woods at its outskirts. She looks behind her at where she'd come from, then up at the high branches and the sun pouring white and smooth as hot milk through them, and deduces by the dimmer brightness she'd run into the late afternoon. Then she looks at her trembling hands and realizes they're still holding the glass jar of raw honey. Her feet are hurting bad now. So she sits on the cold and damp earth and sets the honey beside her and picks small rocks and splinters from between her toes. When she finishes, she buries her face in her hands and stays very still a while and cries again. After that, she wipes wetness from her eyes and sniffs. And she smells water; listening, hears it run.

River

Sitting in the reeds at the river's edge, Martha eats the honey with her fingers until her belly is bitter with sweetness. The river is big and green. Occasionally, she dips her foot into the water, which feels cold and slimy against her toes, and leaves it there until they burn with coldness. The pain feels right somehow.

She leans back on her elbows, tilts her head back, closes her eyes:

She thinks about her son, likely awake now, likely now bashing his head against his bars until he bleeds and howling for a release he'd never known nor ever will. Or maybe for food. She's been gone a long time. She looks at the honey.

She thinks about her father, who she knows is home by now, likely searching the house for her, to punish her for sins he'll make up when he finds her. She thinks about him pacing each floor, each room, as the child's disfigured and lonely screams permeate the very breadth and depth of the house's every crevasse, seeping up through the gaps in every floorboard, and further stoking the rage consuming her tired father by the second.

And how, when she was with child, he'd kept her locked in her room the six months her conception had become noticeable, not even letting her out when finally her time had come and she shrieked in pain and beat the door and floorboards as hot fluid ran down her legs. But her father vanished a long time. And when he finally came up the stairs and unlocked the door and entered, he lifted her dress and knelt in front of the gray, mucous-covered orb working itself out of her body with both violence and beauty. He ordered her, *Push.* So she did. She felt her skin tear. Screams leaped from her mouth. And after many hours and much blood, it was done, and her father took the baby away.

Then she recalls something all but forgotten: She thinks of a time when she was small, when her father used to take her fishing at a green pond some miles away. The water was warm under the summer sun. Her mother had packed the two sandwiches, tuna salad, or maybe peanut butter and jelly. Or maybe not; maybe that was a different time. Her father used bloodworms as bait. She watched them throb and wreathe and stiffen, venous and pink and wet, inside a small Styrofoam cup. Their shapes used to fascinate her in ways she would only years later understand fully. And as these recollections come and go and return and replay in shuffled, half-backward fragments, her heart begins to jump and a sadness she's repressed until now begins to flood over her. She cries out loud and long, her eyes still shut tight, gripping her hair and pulling hard, hearing individual strands snap and dislodge at their roots. Her back and pelvis arched, and she rolling stiff through the tall tall grass. Then the flood passes, and she finds herself on her side, her eyes blurry with wetness, tiny sobs hiccuping from between her lips—wordless curses at God for not existing in the first place.

The sun begins to set over the slow-rippling water. And she doesn't want to go home. She only wants to hide here in the reeds and wait. She sees her breath thicken, hears her heart beating in her ears and the small, smooth noising of crickets chirping and bullfrogs honking.

The water lap...lap...lapping against the riverside.

She remembers she is very tired.

Her eyelids lower—but sleep doesn't come. She wants to forget, release the pressure ever building behind her ribcage, doesn't know how but one way.

Slowly, the sticky fingers of her right hand spider down her abdomen. Her heartbeats, not so much increasing as awakening, stretching like some beast coming to from a deep slumber, synchronize with the cacophony of noises swirling around her. But her mind leaves her more and more by the passing seconds until the landscape of her senses becomes a patchwork of lucidity. Her hand resting firm on her pelvis. The other lifting her soft dress until her fingers find soft underwear, then skin and coarse hair. But she experiencing all as though outside her own body, as though succumbed to paralysis and pleasured by ghostly hands. And as she floats through a current of timelessness all the hurt, every memory of life up to this point inside her head washes away. She is nothing and everything, unborn and ever-existing all at once; the embodiment of the electricity generating between her thighs and there spreading throughout her form, out her fingertips, then back into her in an infinite cycle. Through her eyelids, she again sees Christ's bastard ceramic children, unsuffered at last and dancing ballet in the sky: behind the clouds, between the stars, around the moon. Her soul leaves her chest and joins them. She watches it go.

And for once, she is pure.

She stops, listens for a while:

Sounds of water and wind and life and heartbeat move through the air, notes weaving in and out of range and twisting into hypnotic knots of rhythm like fireflies in a dark and newborn forest.

But after a while passes, footsteps.

Her eyes tremble open as a long long shadow slides over her from somewhere behind.

"Can I help you with that?"

And the broken fractions of time reform all around as she, throwing her skirt back over herself, opens her eyes fully, rolls over onto her hands and knees, and looks up at the blurry silhouette standing there like the Holy Ghost come to repo her soul.

Car

She sits in the passenger seat. It all happened so fast, so strange.

When she got to her feet, Clinton had asked her if she needed a ride home.

She'd said she didn't, snatched the honey jar off the ground, capped it. "Were you watching me this whole time?"

"I didn't wanna disturb you."

"What? No! Why were you there?"

"I saw you runnin' and followed you in my car. I followed you a long time before you dipped into the trees. Then I got out tracked you here."

"What, were you, like, jerking off in the bushes or something?"

"Thought about it. A couple times."

"That's so fucking creepy!"

"Sorry. I don't know why I—"

"Just leave me alone!"

"Let me give you a ride someplace."

"No."

"But it's dark and getting colder." He breathed out hard and slow so she could see.

"No. I need to go home."

"Then I'll take you there."

"Jesus Christ, no. Just go away."

When she turned away from him and walked through the trees, trying hard to feel some semblance of a trail under her burning-cold feet, Clinton followed her, giving directions. She'd glared back at him a couple times, but he didn't say anything about it, so she let him be.

When they'd reached the car, she couldn't feel road beneath her toes. So Clinton opened the door without a word, without an expression. And she got in.

Now, in the car, they sit in a silence thick and awkward as a jellyfish and have been what feels like nearly an hour.

"I'm sorry," he says.

"Shut up."

"Okay."

"Shut up!"

He reaches for the keys dangling in the ignition. "Found your shoes in the back. They're underneath your seat, if you want 'em."

She bends down and sees them resting on top the collection of items that fell from his glove box earlier. As she bends down, slips the shoes on, something catches her eye, something shiny half-buried under gospel tracts. She reaches for it, picks it up. The knife's red handle has a white Swiss cross on it. She opens the small blade. The engine starts, so she sits back up, hiding the knife in her palm between her thighs.

He puts his hand on her knee and throws the gearshift out of park, and backs out onto the dark road. He drives slowly. She asks, "You planning on kidnapping me or something?" and he answers, "Where do you want me to take you?" She says wherever he wants to take her, and he says, "Away," and she says she can't, and he says, "I know." After that neither says anything. Not until the car stops in front of Maratha's house. Inside, the lights are on.

"Listen. Earlier, I said I've been wantin' to get to know you awhile, but I think I already do. I know your name anyway, Martha. And I know what you've done. Word gets around at church and in town, and I've had my fair experience dealing with mongoloids too."

She watches him as he talks. He stops a second and looks at her as if to see if she's listening. Then he keeps on.

"Plus, I've seen you with your father. Guy reminds me of mine: a fanatic who thinks you're some kinda heathen for doing what the invisible man says 'Thou shalt not.' But, yeah, I know you. Better than you think. And I like you. And I want you to like me too."

Then he leans closer. Slow and timid, suppressing a grin from curing on his lips. She doesn't move. So he kisses her, gently this time. She doesn't move. Kisses her, and that's all. She doesn't. And when he finishes, he looks at her awhile, and she him, and there are no words. None at all.

Martha looks aside and sees an unfamiliar car parked in front of the house.

Clinton looks over too.

"Wait, why is my father here?" he asks.

"Your Dad?"

He smiles and runs his fingers down her face, her shoulder, arm, leg, and up her dress. "It's okay."

"No, it's not. Let me out."

He squeezes her thigh, and she squirms."It's fine. Don't worry."

"Get off!"

"Relax."

"Goddammit!"

He leans in closer again.

Her heart races. She pushes away.

He puts his hand on her neck to hold her still.

Then she puts the knife blade in his throat.

He falls sideways into her lap. Gulping, suffocating, confused noises bubble angrily from his mouth. She watches, holds his face still, and cries some. Blood pours gently from the knife handle and pools between her knees, seeps through her skirt, runs down her legs, over her feet. It takes a long time for him to die.

When he does, she pulls the blade out, pushes him off her, and, with the honey jar in the crook of her arm, exits the car.

She just stands there holding the jar in her left hand and the knife in her right.

And the long, silver blade is out and cobwebbed in warm red the same shade as the red handle—little droplets falling from it like spiders weaving themselves downward on ruby threads; and there she is, standing, looking at the spiders and the unmoving boy inside the car; she is standing there and looking at what she's done; and she isn't sorry. She isn't sorry.

House

Martha stumbles into the living room and sits on the tweed sofa, smearing it with the red covering her clothes and skin; folds the blade, slips it into her skirt pocket; then sets the jar down beside her and removes her shoes—a thin trickle of blood dribbles from one—and she leaves them there. Voices seep through the floor. So she stands and walks trancelike toward the basement entrance.

The door is ajar.

With trembling hands, she pulls it open, then places a foot on the top step.

It gives slightly under her weight, creaks, and she stops, listens.

No change. The voices don't pause.

She continues to the next. It doesn't make a sound.

The air becomes colder the further she descends, yet she feels herself sweating as the blood chills and dries on her clothes and skin. Her legs shiver with each slow footstep. The voices grow louder.

"Open the gate easy, Joseph."

"Get your cat-grabber ready. He's a biter."

"I got it."

"Okay, I'm opening it on three."

"I'm ready."

"One. Two—"

Stepping down, she sees a large dog kennel at the bottom of the stairs. The Reverend, still in his minister's outfit—today must have been Monday Evening Bible Study —kneels brandishing a long-handled claw. To his right, her father stands in his overalls and tee shirt, facing the door of the cell and slowly slipping the lock off. Inside the cage, the naked child cowers on top its heap of blankets, far from the bars and on all fours, back arched like a frightened beast ready to pounce. Martha's foot lands on the bottom step which creeks loudly. This time the two men turn their heads and look at her.

"Good Lord!" her father says.

The Reverend glances at him. "Language, Joseph."

The Reverend then looks at her again. "Martha, whose blood is that?"

"What are you doing?" she asks, stepping over the kennel.

The two men look at each other, and her father replaces the lock but doesn't click it shut. They walk toward her and The Reverend's head knocks against the light bulb hanging from the ceiling. He sucks his teeth as the bulb swings away and back and a small pink oval appears on his forehead.

Her father says, "Sweetie," but he's not called her that since she was a child. Then, "This's just something that's gotta happen."

"What are you talking about?" she asks.

They continue forward and she looks for a place to move to but finds none. And the bulb swings and splashes the color-starved crannies of the basement with brown light like a tide advancing and receding and advancing again.

"The Reverend has been telling me there's a place he's planning to sponsor in Vivid Greene that'll take mongoloids like yours and raise them up right, civilize them."

"What?"

"They're all God's children," The Reverend says, "just like we're all God's children and deserve a chance to know that."

"You're taking him?"

"It's for the best," The Reverend says and reaches into his pocket, removes his wallet and from it a crumpled photograph.

"Come here," he says, placing his cat-grabber on the floor, "and have a look at this."

She does.

The picture is torn at the edges and badly faded, but its scene is clear enough: The Reverend with his arm around a middle aged woman, likely his wife, and his other tousling a much younger Clint's hair. Clint is holding hands with an older girl in a sky-blue dress. The girl has sparse hair and a veil of skin partially covering her left eye. Her flesh looks the appearance of papier mâché, and small bone nubs protrude from pink lumps on her scalp like whiteheads on massive acne clusters. The depicted family smiles the way only the God-fearing smile, including the girl, whose mouth looks more like an open gash lined with pearly barbs.

"You're not the only one who's succumb to temptation," he whispers. "My wife was a sinner once, herself, in another life."

She pushes the photo away. "Why are you showing me this?"

"Because that's Clinton's older sister," he says. "I taught her to read. Taught her right from The Good Book. At age seven, her first word was—"

"No."

"No?" The Reverend asks

"No, I won't let you."

"What do you mean?"

"I won't let you take him." Tears rolled down her face and she looked away to hide her shame.

"It's not your choice, Martha," her father says.

"It is my choice," she says and pulls the knife from her pocket, unfolds it.

The Reverend backs away and bumps against the light bulb again, but her father steps forward, a look of malice in his eyes. She lunges at her father with the knife. He catches her wrist and hits her across the cheek with the back of his fist. She turns a half spiral and falls at his feet. The blade slips from her fingers and clatters a few feet away. Then he climbs on top of her and holds her hands to the floor.

"How dare you?" he says. "Do you pay the bills to keep it alive. Do you feed the little sin, clean the shit outta its cage. No, you don't. I do. Every night. And every night I hear it scream and holler and carry on regardless, and I can't get no sleep."

She can feel his balls pressed against her midsection as he shouts. He pauses and breaths before saying at the ceiling, "And then it ate our dog, my dog! Didn't just eat it, tore it to shreds. And I come home to hear Pluto yowling in pain, but couldn't save him. All the blood and parts and innards thrown everywhere."

He looks at her with fire.

"All because you couldn't listen to simple instructions and close the goddamn basement door!"

"Language," The Reverend's voice stammers from somewhere.

She hears the child begin smashing his body against the door of his cage and screaming:

"Mrah! Mrrrah!"

"And now you wanna tell me what to do with the little sin, when all you did's make it? Little slut!"

He lets her hands go and hits her again. She tastes blood: bitter and metallic. He leans in closer, so close she can smell the coffee on his breath. She pushes her neck forward and headbutts him, and he leans backward and lifts his hands to hold his nose. Twisting her body, she grabs the knife off the floor and lunges it into his groin. She twists the blade, and he howls and launches backward, landing hip-first onto the concrete.

Then a shrill, almost feminine scream fills the room followed by the sound of another body hitting the floor. Martha pushes herself upright in time to see The Reverend with his right leg already knee-far between the cage's bars while the child straddles his ankle and gnaws fervently through the man's shined leather shoes.

"Jesus Christ!" The Reverend shrieks. "Get it off me!"

Martha glances back at her father writhing on his back, blood soaking through the crotch of his pants. Then she stands and walks to the cage, places her hands on the bars. The child stops gnawing The Reverend's now mangled toes and looks up at her. His eyes wet with tears and drooping.

His lips move up and down.

"Muh, muh." he says.

"Yes, what is it?"

She leans her ear closer.

"Muhmuh."

"Mamma?" she asks.

"Mamma," he says.

"Yes," she says and presses her forehead against the bars. "Mamma's here."

She lifts the lock off the cage door and breathes in. "Mamma's here."

"What're you doing, you crazy bitch!" The Reverend shouts as he reaches out to stop her, but too late. The door opens just a crack as if in slow motion, then stops. And all noises in the basement cease as the two injured men on the floor stare motionless. The child rolls off The Reverend's ankle and crawls toward the door, kicks it hard. It swings and hits the bars with a sharp clang. then the child gets to his feet and toddles out. Martha looks at him standing tall and free beside her and smiles, extends her arms to hold him, but the child doesn't look at her. His mouth opens and drops of red spittle and shoe leather fall out, his chest heaving faster as he gazes around. The Reverend pushes himself upright and hops one-footed toward his cat-grabber still lying near Martha's father who's too preoccupied with the knife in his genitals to notice it there.

And Martha watches. She watches as The Reverend reaches the grabber, bends forward to pick it up, only to look behind and see the child dart up his back, wrap his arms around the man's neck, and sink his sharp teeth into his Adam's apple; she watches her father pull the knife blade from between his legs and plunge it into the child's shoulder, and the child shrieking in pain then grabbing her father's forearm and snapping the bone in half. But then she doesn't watch. Doesn't watch what happens next. Covers her eyes with her palms, listens to her child's screams and her father's screams and the noises of tearing flesh and cracking bones. Then, nothing, and she lowers her hands. The swinging light bulb casts weird shadows that bob and weave like manic dancers. Making the room seem to move hypnotically, seem calm. Her father, or what remains, lying motionless on his stomach beside the stairs, arms stretched out in front of him as though he were trying to reach something in his sleep. The Reverend on his back, jaw moving up and down, all color draining from his face. Near the kennel by the stairs, the family picture sits all smiles. Martha walks over and picks it up, takes it to The Reverend. Pries his hand away from the wound on his throat, places it in his palm. He doesn't seem to notice.

Looking up, she sees her son crawling his way up the stairs. His motions slow and sluggish, the pierced skin on his back bleeding a lot and leaving a trail on the steps behind him.

"Mrah Mah."

She follows him.

At the top of the steps, she reaches down and tries to pick him up. He hisses and writhes out of her grasp. She tries again. This time, he bites her, and she drops him. In a sudden burst of energy, he darts away out of the kitchen.

"Wait!" she says and runs after him.

In the living room, the front door is still open and leaking moonlight across the floor. She sees him running ape-like into the night. She runs outside. On the porch she stops and scans the darkness, but her eyes are tired and it is very dark. She peers around the side of the house and calls for him, but nothing.

She calls again, louder this time.

A wind in the trees: like a death rattle.

Reentering the house for a candle, a flashlight, anything to search for him, she notices her shoes lying by the tweed couch. The honey jar is gone. So she sits on the couch to think:

I'm no mama.

She leans her head back and stares at the ceiling.

She remembers a time not long ago but when she was still very small, when her mama had taken her to the fair. Martha always loved the ducklings most. That day she'd asked to go off and see them, and her mama said, Okay.

Kneeling in front of the chicken wire, Martha reached

her small fingers through the gaps to pet them. She knew she wasn't supposed to, but she wanted to, so she did. All the ducklings scuttled away from her fingers, and she began to get upset that she couldn't touch one, couldn't feel its soft down against her fingertips.

Finally she reached and caught a passing one by the leg. Only when she pulled it, the leg bent and popped. She felt it happen and let go.

The duckling just lay chirping, unable to walk or even stand, and Martha looked at it and felt something awful in the pit of her stomach and left it there, ran back to her mother but never told her. She never told anyone.

She closes her eyes and thinks about this.

When she opens them, it is daylight.

Field

After washing herself and changing into fresh clothes, Martha steps out onto the front porch for the last time and looks around. Brightness consumes the landscape, and the weather is warm, pleasant. The car is still parked right where it is, its boy-shaped contents likely baking slow beneath the blinding-pale sunlight. Birds of prey haloing around and around miles high above. She walks to the car, looks inside, and there is so much blood, and the body looks bloated and unfamiliar. She opens the door. And a rank stench of death fills the air.

She gags and covers her face with her sleeve to keep from vomiting. When the air becomes less thick with stench, she grabs Clinton by the shirt collar and pulls him off the seat and onto the ground. He lands with a stiff thump and something in him cracks and pops loudly. Then she climbs into the driver's seat and closes the door.

The dead stench remains. She rolls down the window, tries to ignore it.

She tries very hard.

The keys still dangle in the ignition. She's never driven a car before. Only seen beautified actors do it on TV. Apprehensively, she turns the key. The engine starts. She shifts the transmission from P to D and turns the steering wheel as far as it will go. The car drifts a one-eighty, and she centers the wheel and lightly presses the gas. She looks ahead and sees there are no cars on the road and creeps toward it. Then stops, adjusts the rear view mirror and looks through it at the stillness behind.

At the house.

At the field.

At the boy on the ground and the carrion gathering around him.

Then she turns the car south, a direction she's never taken, and presses the gas.

When she was a little girl, she'd once planted a flower garden with her mother that never grew because birds kept landing there and eating the seeds out of the ground. From the living room window, she and her mother and father would watch the birds leave and return and peck the topsoil, and one time her father said, Since there's so many of them, we should build a birdhouse. And her mother told him, Okay. But they never did, and when the seeds were gone, the birds went away and didn't come back again. But she doesn't remember this. Only that there was supposed to be a garden but wasn't, and nothing more about it.

Instead, steadying the wheel, she takes a nervous hand off and touches her belly—knowing it is far too soon to feel a kick, if there will ever be one, but frightened she might anyway. Looking up at the glittering sky, at the stagnant clouds smeared across the azure, she wonders: What place will she find to start again, to live happy and free always, and which won't decay with age the way this one has?

The questions linger in her mind.

SANTA'S TRAIN TO HEAVEN

It was Halloween night in New York City, or at least it had been. I was standing in the subway someplace under Manhattan—I had no idea where anymore—with gray subway dust coating the inside of my nose, and a dry, gray subway taste in my mouth—so tired I could barely think straight. I'd been hopping from train to train, station to station, for a long time. The white polyester beard itched, and the suit itched, and the kids were screaming for more candy. Aside from the children, there were no people around but one sleeping man propped against the adjacent wall near the restroom. He was without blemish, wearing a dirty three-piece suit, tweed with well-shined black shoes not on his feet but his hands like two forehooves. A bagged bottle rested between his legs. I looked at my wristwatch. it read four in the morning. The sun would be coming up in a few hours. There was so much left to do.

I lifted my arms, my gloved hands, and commanded silence from my disciples.

"Everyone hush!" I said.

They wouldn't.

The Rapture was coming.

"Be still!"

They ignored me, ran in circles and took off their shoes and socks and threw their socks at the suited man. He did not move.

But one little girl—small and wearing a black cat costume with an much-too-large rubber mask which kept falling over her eyes—the little girl who'd been awkwardly quiet until now, began asking for her mother.

The little girl's name was Molly; she'd told me when I found her. Now, standing off by herself in this dusty cellar below the city, she asked for her mother again, but was too quiet to be heard over the echo of the madness from the other kids. So she became silent. I watched as she waddled blindly toward me, slow and gentle footsteps, and tugged on the hem of my red and green robe.

"Santa?"

I looked down at her and lifted the cartoonish feline face from her eyes. Her eyes were amber—almost yellow. A color somehow both smooth and burning. The kind of eyes that knew God when He was alive.

"Yes, Molly," I answered.

"I'm cold."

She sniffed. Snot ran in a clear line down from one nostril and over her bottom lip. She licked at it.

"I know. But there will be comfort soon, child."

She looked at me like she didn't understand. I patted her head and promised that there would be a show of signs and wonders in the tunnels tonight, and asked her to round up her brothers.

"Okay," she said. "But Santa?"

"Yes?"

"Why couldn't our mommies and daddies come with us?"

I looked at her and asked, "Do you believe in me?"

"Yes," she said.

"Well, they didn't. Your folks, they weren't of faith. Not like you."

"Is that why you didn't want them to see you when you told us to come with you?"

"Yes."

She stood there and just looked up at me for a little while and didn't say anything. Then her eyes squinted as though her next question had shined on her like a spotlight. She tugged on my robe again.

"But Santa?" she asked.

"Yes?" I answered.

"Where are we going?"

"I already told you," I told her. "Don't you remember?"

Her face expressionless, she nodded, never taking her eyes off mine, never blinking.

I patted her head again.

Children are the only perfect people. They needn't saving, only freeing. Reaching into my robe, into the breast pocket of my tee shirt, I fingered the smooth, wooden handle of the switchblade therein, and then I looked down at Molly again. She was still looking up at me.

With Molly next to me, I watched my perfect disciples, my lambs. They were running barefoot now, the pads of their feet slapping against the frigid concrete floor, playing a game of tag around the sleeping derelict they'd thrown their socks at. I raised my hands again and began to call them, then stopped, lowered my hands. I didn't know how to command them—how to make them listen.

I pressed my face into my palms and moaned.

I wondered if God was this stressed his first day on the job.

I'd seen a vision the night before: The Lord in all His magnificence weeping alone in his heavenly throne room. The room was filled with a pale light. All His disciples were gone, and He was disappearing. It was a sparkly kind of disappearing, like Yoda in Return of the Jedi, just a slow fading into splendid nothingness.

Before vanishing, He looked at me and spoke. Asked me to take His place. Asked me to take a train. The Rapture. Said I knew the right one, but I didn't. Said he would send the necessary sacrifice: Like Abraham to Isaac, He said, my little lambs in the brush were waiting to be freed.

His voice sounded amazing.

The voice of many waters.

"Do you hear that?" Molly asked.

In the black distance of the tunnel, I could hear the rumble of a train coming.

Behind me one of the kids, the oldest boy dressed as a pumpkin, had stuffed a handful of Hubble Bubble into the sleeping suited man's mouth. Where he'd gotten the gum, I could only guess. I turned and saw the man's eyes widen and heard him gag through the mouthful of stale gum and yellow wax paper. The man hacked and spat and smacked the kid in the head with a shoe, and the kid ran to me and cried. The witch and the ghost followed, screaming.

The man rolled onto his side, holding his abdomen, and defecated loudly. He hissed and pulled his brown-stained pants off, hurled them at the children. He fell to his knees and began speaking in tongues—bare-ass and looking terrified.

"Damn you!" he said in a language I understood. "Why can't you give me peace?"

The kids were gathered standing crying in a semicircle in front of me. They all began demanding the same thing.

They wanted to go home.

I lifted my arms again.

"Peace and quiet!"

This time they listened.

When they were quiet, I reached into my robe, into the breast pocket of my tee shirt, then looked at the pumpkin boy.

"What you did for that man—"

The pumpkin looked at me, at my hand moving behind my coat, a shamed gaze in his eyes.

"—was a good thing."

From my pocket, I retrieved four Taffy Rolls, handed one to each child.

"Giving is virtuous," I said. "It is like a miracle. No, it is a miracle. A show of signs and wonders."

Molly eyed the candy, then cupped her hands around it as if to pray.

I pointed behind them with my chin.

"Look at the man."

They didn't want to look. They complained that he was naked and had "pooped his bum."

"I said, look at him," I said.

We five looked at him together. He was on his knees and pawing at the cement floor and crying. Ass to the ceiling. Face to the ground. Only lifting his head long enough to shout unintelligible slurs at us, scoop up the spitty pieces of wrapped Hubble Bubble and toss them into the air. The hard gum made faint tapping sounds as it fell atop his shiny, bald head and against the gray, dusty floor.

"You all have a wonderful gift," I told the kids.

The rumbling was loud and growing louder. I looked up. With its wheels growling against the metal of the tracks and screeching as it slowed, the train pulled up to the platform and stopped. The doors opened.

A pale, beckoning light flickered inside.

The same light I'd seen in my vision.

"Come now, children," I said. "The Rapture is come!"

"Where are we going?" the ghost asked.

"To Heaven," the little girl, Molly, turned to him and said. "This is Santa's train to Heaven."

Perfect humans. All of them, perfect. My followers into the light I'd seen—the light I'd soon teach them about.

"Enough," I said. "We need to hurry before the Rapture leaves us behind."

"Is it a rapture or a train?" the witch asked the pumpkin.

"What's a rapture?" the pumpkin asked the ghost.

The ghost shrugged. "I think it's a dinosaur."

"There are dinosaurs in Heaven?" the witch asked.

The ghost shrugged again.

I'd teach them soon.

I took the children under my arms, my long, red sleeves brushing against their costumed backs, and guided my disciples into the light. As we stepped into the car, I looked over my shoulder. Behind me, the man stopped praying to the god of gum and looked at us. The doors began to close. He got on all fours and ran, his shod hands clopping against the concrete, and pried the doors apart with his elbows. He stepped aboard, one hand at a time, and sat his naked ass on the seat in the far corner of the car.

"Looks like there's room for him too," Molly said.

I agreed. There certainly was room for him.

The lights flickered as I relaxed into my seat. Then the train bumped and wormed into the darkness of the underground. As we picked up speed, I looked down at my disciples, two at my left hand and two at my right, and they looked up at me, and I motioned toward the pantless man. They turned their heads in unison and looked at him. In my shirt pocket, the knife handle bumped and tapped against my chest near my armpit.

And I felt a smile stretch across my face as the man looked at us and trembled. Our sacrificial ram had come.

BEFORE THE FLOOD

*B*y the fifteenth month, the whole damn state had grown so thirsty the ground seemed to drink the sap of its own trees. Those of us who remember admit to speaking of rain the way some Christians speak of the apocalypse, so that in every town it seemed there was someone pointing out signs of the times. Dead fish lay rotting at the pebbled bottoms of shrunken streams. Nightly, stroboscopic heat lightning, like war in heaven, would herald strange distant fires. Behind the hills, rising smoke mixed with the ever-pregnant clouds so that the throbbing firmament seemed to cry out in agony of its pangs.

Even the Big Lake seemed much depleted revealing the ghoulish remains of what once was. Dilapidated market signs, skeletons of slanted roofs, and just all manner of haunted shapes jutted from the still water, surrounding a tall church steeple that once marked the town's center. In the full dark, one could appropriately mistake this fishing hole for a cemetery. Rumors swirled in that sticky heat the place was cursed somehow. In truth, it was simply forgotten. Its stories and secrets only gossiped by ghosts beneath the murky depths.

*T*here were two brothers.

Likely, other siblings existed strewn about from one county border to the next and maybe farther, kin neither of the two knew about nor ever would. It didn't matter.

Two brothers, and that was enough.

Their little flatboat sloshed between rusted and rotting structures, carrying their father home in a shoebox.

When they'd gone far enough, Alden let go of the long oar and stepped off the riser, took a seat and massaged his arms. Davis sat as he had been sitting the whole time, still and quiet. The night was starless. Strange calls filled the air from no direction in particular. The boat drifted a little ways and then bumped against something and stopped completely. They sat adjacent each other but said little. Instead, smoke wafted softly from their mouths in acrid cursive as they took cigarettes from the pack of Marlboro Reds sitting between them atop their father.

The dry full moon cast the two in near-monochrome, yet it was light enough. Alden bore the looks of a creature much older. His gaunt face was dark and sun-wrinkled. His thinning hair fell in burgundy ribbons against his lean shoulders and over his hungry eyes, the corners of which, if one looked closely, were a sickly yellow. His clothes were stained and hung loose on his bones, boots marred and untied with laces tucked in. Overall, he seemed a man who'd walked through thorny bushes all his life. Davis wore his shirt buttoned to the collar. His shoes were muddied, but nothing a little polish wouldn't fix, and his curly hair was slicked tight against his scalp. His flesh bore the healthy color of a midsummer wheat field. More so, his face was plump, almond-shaped eyes flickering when kissed by the moonlight jumping up from the black water all around.

Davis reached and took the pack from the shoebox. He picked a bent one and placed it between his lips, removed a Bic from his pocket, lit it. A puff of smoke engulfed his features for a moment then opened. He reached through the smoke, picked up the shoebox. Its soft contents shifted.

"How's this supposed to work?"

"You open the box," Alden said, "and dump the sonofabitch in the goddamn river."

"Shouldn't we say something?"

"Such as?"

"That he'll be missed?"

"Ain't about missing him," Alden said. "Nothing to miss."

Davis removed the lid. Inside was his father. The powder was gray beneath the pale light and coarse with little pebbles which must've been bone. The boat rocked causing the box to tilt in his hands, and he watched its shallow contents pour downward toward the left corner and form a small mound there. A curl of barely visible dust floated upward and went away into the darkness. He watched it go, squinting in the dark, until there wasn't anything to watch anymore, then placed his finger into the mound, drew a crude face.

"Didn't necessarily mean by us," he said. "Somebody's gotta miss him somewhere, or at least everyone wants to think that'll be the case when they're gone."

Alden took a drag from his cigarette and held it a long time. His eyes looked away. Then he breathed out a pale phantom that writhed in the air before dissipating.

"Think at this point what he'd've wanted doesn't matter much."

Davis balled his fist beneath the box, then uncurled his fingers and replaced the lid, set the box down at his feet.

"What do you even know about it?—"

Alden looked up with eyes like broken glass. He stood. Taking small steps as not to lose bearings and tumble into the water, he moved to where Davis sat, and, when he was close enough, moved even closer until the intimacy of their inky forms became unbearable. Alden grabbed his brother's hair, which was slick with product so he had to hold white-knuckle-tight, and yanked.

In a panic, Davis tried to swat and kick him away, but Alden stooped low and slapped him across the face. Davis calmed and raised his hands in surrender.

So Alden hit him again.

First with the back of his hand.

Then harder with his calloused palm rough as splintered wood.

A clenched fist plunged into the center of Davis' face. He wrapped his arms around his head. Alden reached and threw the appendages away and, in the same motion, wound back to deliver one more blow. He steadied his feet. His boot soles slipped a little, something like small gravel beneath.

Then both men looked down.

Their father lay spread into small landscapes of silt, sleeping and colorless in the dim like some map of a primitive time. The smiling face was demolished, spilled into formlessness again and smeared in gray semicircles and footprints. The box stood at the center upside down.

Alden lowered his fist and released his brother's scalp. He stepped over the mess and sat next to him. Davis didn't say anything, only sat and bled, and both men were there but as though the world existed between them, and perhaps it did.

"Where're those smokes?" Davis said after a while.

Alden toed the box over, and there they were.

Davis leaned forward, took the pack and fished out the last two, placed one in his mouth. The other he handed to his brother.

"He ever lay into you like that?" Davis said.

"When he was around enough to," Alden said.

"Never struck me."

"Figured as much."

"Saw him whoop my momma pretty good once though."

Alden shifted in his seat.

"Go on."

"Ain't nothing to go on about. He beat her black and blue, then took off for a few weeks. I was small. I only recollect momma crying on the floor with blood in her ears and teeth. He was always taking off, most often at night, never stayed longer than a week at a time, but that was the only time I'd ever seen him go."

"He came back though."

"Yeah, 'course he came back. Momma'd always forgive him after long enough away. Said it was just how things were and ain't no use in trying to change the course of rivers."

"Looks like we both got reared by women who fell for the bullshit of a common garden snake," Alden said.

"Everyone's got their sins."

"Why do you think that's so?"

"I reckon it started somewheres and just got passed down. E'rything starts somewheres."

Alden looked away. "Where'd you start?"

"Eh?" Davis said.

"I mean, how'd he end up your poppa."

"I'd imagine same way he became yours."

"That's why I ask. I've no idea how I came to be."

Well, from what I know, he'd known my momma when she was a young girl, watched her grow. He was much older."

"He was always old. Nobody ever seen him as a young man."

"Well he'd befriended her, told her all kinds of things she thought were so learned. Then when she was a teenager he started in making his moves. She wasn't having any of it, though, the more she grew up."

"Young women don't often fawn for an old man, lest he got something to offer 'em, which I reckon he never much did."

"Well it didn't stop him none. Got her real drunk one night so she couldn't've told a man from a maple tree if in broad daylight, and when she'd begun to take sick on her barstool, he took and walked her into his hotel room and had her until the daylight shone red through the treetops."

"Did you remember him ever around for long at all?"

"Some of the time. When he'd come back around he'd tell my momma she'd better bring me out, so she would, and he'd drink from a bottle in a bag and tell me stories about his adventures on the road. And momma'd just set there in the kitchen and not say anything, outta fear, I suppose."

"Did you like him?"

"I didn't know any better one way or the other. And often as she'd forgive him, she never did forgive me."

"Who?"

"Momma, my momma."

"Forgive you for what?"

"Being the closest thing to him she could lay her hands on."

After that, they both sat quiet. No sounds but the light sloshing of water.

"We're outta cigarettes," Davis said, crushing his half smoked one beneath his heel.

Alden exhaled his last plume into the night and flicked his away too.

"Yeah. Looks like it."

Davis stooped and began scooping handfuls of ash from the wooden deck.

"Here, gimme a hand."

Alden shrugged. "Alright."

So the two men swept the floor with their fingers, creating small hills of dust then lifting and depositing them in the shoebox. Time seemed to pass differently as they worked, as though its hands reached not left and right, up nor down, but front and backward as well and all at once. After a while, there was nothing but a layer of soot too thin to lift from the floor, so the two gave up and stood. Alden held the box.

"Which of us gets to do the honors?" Davis asked.

"You."

Alden handed the box to him.

"Why me?"

"Why the hell not?" Alden said.

Davis took the box with both hands, wiped his nose against his shoulder, leaving a glossy smear of blood and mucous. Then he turned and dumped its contents into the water without a word. The dust cloud caught onto the wind and opened like a flower, a white dandelion scattering its seeds. A light hiss lasted a second or two as the grains hit the water one by one, then nothing, and it was over. Somewhere a fish lapped across the water then vanished. Alden looked over the edge of the boat, but saw only a few ripples expanding out of sight. He spat into the water.

"Guess that's that," he said.

"So it seems," Davis said.

*L*ater that night, in the hours just before dawn, Alden lay beside a young girl whom we will call Wren—though her real name is now lost. She was no older than sixteen and great with child, expecting any day now. He set his hand atop her belly and felt, but nothing moved. Her soft breathing lulled him, and as he drifted, a vision of his brother came to mind.

He saw through Davis' eyes, and that he was still standing at the lake shore, staring out into the great inkiness. He felt his nose still bleeding, cool wetness running over his lips and down his chin. He looked and saw it dot the gravel by his feet; lifted his hand, which only moments before had rested on the girl's belly, and felt the blood trickle into it.

A sound rumbled far away.

He looked up, and saw lightning in the sky, the bright kind that only comes with rain. He felt a droplet fall on his broken nose, held his hand out. Another landed in his palm, making a small star in the dark blood.

Yet the noise carried on like distant drums. He stepped forth toward the water from where it seemed to come.
Into the lake, and the water covered him slow and dark, first his feet, his knees, then his chest. The strange noise beat from below, like a muffled bassline to some danceable music. With a gasp he lowered his head into the murk and swam blindly toward the sounds, into the ruins.

As he moved closer, the drowned and collapsing houses were lit, as though lived in. Yet all were empty through their windows. The rhythm thumped through the water in his ears.

He floated on into the church. The pews were filled with all manner of bones. He wondered if the ghosts were dancing and if his father was joining them now. The music grew louder.

Davis closed his eyes and listened.

When Alden opened them, thunder beat against the window glass as a bright flash lit the room.

"That ain't heat lightning," Wren said. "It's good lightning."

"Doesn't seem too good to me."

Alden took his hand off her. There was another loud crash, as though the world had caved in on itself, and drops began to crackle against the galbestos roof.

And it rained, and it rained and rained, and it rained for days, and then on and off for months so that all the world around flooded. And the floods erased all blood and histories from the ground in a series of violent muddy tides, and the tides filled the lake higher and deeper than it had ever been, covering the building tops at last.

Even the little flatboat, which had been left abandoned on the Big Lake's shore, vanished mysteriously, perhaps beneath the mud and silt, or carried into the Lake itself and swallowed.

So in the end, when the rain finally ceased again altogether, everything was simply as it was and as it should have been all along, and the Lake was still and quiet once more—save for the occasional birdcall above it and catfish below swimming through the church steeple unknowing of any secrets and without a care regardless.

WATCHING

One.

She'd dreamed about her baby.

When Jennifer woke up there was fire. Fire and a sky burnt burgundy and full of stars. She lay on the grass a little while, breathing in the warm smell of charring wood, watching the flames reach higher and higher and the escaping plumes of black smoke, then stood up and looked around. The blaze before her growled as it slowly devoured the house from the inside out and spread to the adjacent trees like a swarm of red ants attacking their prey. But all else around her was silence and stillness. Very little wind, no animals, no people. Only fire. So she got to her feet and walked over to where her twelve year old son lay face up on the grass a dozen or so feet behind her, his head propped up on a dark brown duffel bag as though it were a pillow. His sweaty features caked with dirt and soot. His peaceful and serene eyes looking up at the sky.

Her son's name was Adam. She touched his arm.

"We have to go now," she said.

He looked at her.

"Where?"

She knelt down next to him as he sat up and faced her.

"Anywhere. Far away. We just need to go now."

Adam rose to his feet, standing over her, and stretched his arms above his head, reaching high in a Y shape like a victory gesture. He yawned. Then he pointed at the fire.

"Is it pretty?"

"No," she said. "Not at all"

"Why not? I think it is, in its own way. Like the sunrise, kind of."

"We need to go."

"Fine," he said, rolling his eyes, and lifted his singed bag off the grass. He slung it over his shoulder.

She stood up and took his hand, and he looked at her and smiled warmly. With her other hand, she reached into her left pocket and felt the smooth plastic prescription vial therein. She cupped the vial in her hand, wrapping her slender fingers around its cylindrical form, and squeezed tightly, feeling the capsules shifting inside their container. Tiny taps against the plastic barrier separating the capsules from her palm.

"Mom?"

She didn't answer.

"Mom."

"Yes?"

"You're not going to let anyone else take me away, right?"

"No. Never again. You belong with me, and I should be the one watching you."

"That's why you came back, right?"

"Right."

They both turned and took one last look at the burning house, its blackened windows shattering one by one, its tiled roof already beginning to concave: Jennifer's vision trembled with each heartbeat, while her son, Adam, her only son, just gazed expressionlessly into the brilliant, hot orange glow.

"Mom?"

"Yes?"

"I'm glad you came back."

She let go of his hand, removed her other from her pocket, and turned to face him. He'd gotten so tall in her absence, she thought as she stared into his empty, innocent eyes: deep, dark and glassy, filled with flashes of flame. She put her arms around him, pressing his face into the lower part of her shoulder.

"I wanted to be with you on your birthday," she said, "and I'm going to take you back home. So we can be together when it comes. But you need to come on!"

Then she let go of him and they turned from the fire and ran, cutting through thick trees until they reached the dirt road where Jennifer had parked the silver station wagon; the faint, almost weeping cry of sirens could just barley be heard in the distance. When they got into the car, she asked Adam to please put on his seat belt, and he did, and she started the engine.

With her headlights off, she drove the two of them away, watching the trees disperse and the dirt road turn into blacktop and the blacktop eventually into a highway that stretched out into the dark blue infinity that was Virginia at night. She drove straight for a long time, moving between walls of foliage on one side, and acres of unused farmland on the other. Once, a few low beams bobbed in her rear view mirror, then vanished as two cars swerved around her and sped away.

When the cars were gone, Jennifer realized she didn't hear any sirens, that she saw no flashing lights behind her. There was only a hypnotic silence pushing into her ears through the steady hum of the engine, through the endless miles of night ahead and behind.

After a while, the abandoned agriculture became a sporadic succession of billboards; then the billboards, businesses.

She passed a Shell station, then a Burger King.

She looked at the clock on the center console: five past midnight. Her eyes felt heavy. When she saw a large, flickering neon sign that read Matheson's Motel and a smaller sign below, vacancy, she slowed and turned the car to the right and into the motel's parking lot.

The front of lot was well lit, but there were no working lamp posts to the left hand side of the building. She pulled into the darkest space she could see, shut off the engine, and told her son to wait in the car while she booked the two of them a room for the night.

"Do they have a TV?" he asked.

"I don't think so, but I'll see. Just stay here a moment, okay? I'll be right back."

He paused for a few seconds.

"We're going home, aren't we, Mom?"

"Yes. This is just a stop for the night."

"What about the trunk, what are we going to do about it?"

"We can't worry about that right now, alright?"

"Alright," he said.

She shut the car door behind her and walked across the lot toward the main office.

Two.

*I*t was very late, and she was very tired. With the light off, Jennifer looked around. Their room was painted a dreary, off white hue that blended the sand colored curtains, dirty carpet, and beige bed sheets into a visual pool of brown. Like a sepia rainbow, even in the dark. There was no TV, or even a phone for that matter, but hanging over the door frame, a small analogue clock ticked and ticked and ticked softly.

Adam had bathed and changed into a fresh set of clothes from his bag and was now lying awake on the bed. His eyes darting to and fro, staring at the bars of light which slid along the emptiness of the wall. And there were roaches in the room. And house centipedes. The big, spidery kind that looked almost like feathers and liked to sting people while they slept. He had already been stung when he'd first lain down in the bed, when Jennifer had pulled the covers over him and said, "Try to sleep."

And he said, "Something just bit me," but didn't yell or cry about it. Just said it nonchalantly.

And when Jennifer had turned the light back on and pulled the sheets away, there was one of those centipedes wreathing and convulsing around a small, red bump on Adam's abdomen. After that, Jennifer turned the light back off, but kept awake and watched him. She watched him a long time. He lay there in the bed for what she could only assume were hours, staring contemplatively at the occasional beams of light crawling across the walls and ceiling. Car headlights passing outside their window.

It wasn't until around three in the morning that he fell asleep.

Jennifer lay down next to him and stretched her arm over his torso, feeling his lungs expand and contract with life and fresh beauty. With her other hand, she reached into her pocket and removed the plastic amber-colored vial. In the dark, she could just barely make out the writing on the paper label. With her thumb and index finger, she twisted off the childproof cap and shook out the vial's contents into her palm and counted the dark green capsules. There were three left. Only three. She dropped the other two back into the vial, closed the lid, and swallowed the remaining capsule without water. By ten after four, Jennifer was asleep too.

Three.

She heard a noise and sat up on the bed and looked over where Adam had been lying and saw he wasn't there anymore and the small and brown room was still very dark but she could see everything just fine even though everything seemed distorted and a hazy and a little disorienting for some reason she couldn't explain and she tried to get up but her arms and legs felt heavy as though the air in the room were somehow thick or as if she were moving underwater but she still willed herself up and stood on the carpet and listened and heard water running and she looked around the room and noticed a faint and yellowish glow coming from underneath the bathroom door and the more she looked at it the more she realized the noises were coming from behind the door so she walked toward the light until it was smeared golden over her toes and she lifted her hand and touched the knob and felt a sudden jolt of familiar fear for some reason and she turned the knob even though the knob was difficult to turn and she had to force it to turn with both of her hands gripping the knob and when it finally turned she pushed the door open and the yellow incandescence behind the door embraced her like a tidal wave so that she had to let go of the door and cover her eyes with her hands and the door shut in her face but she though she saw her son standing in the brightness before the door had closed and it made her feel scared again even though she wasn't sure why so she gripped the knob again and turned it hard and pushed against the door with her shoulder and stumbled into the bathroom and into the brightness and couldn't see very well but she could hear water running and a faint crying again and she could make out the silhouette of her son standing by the tub and not moving but just standing by the tub and watching it fill and she watched him as he stood still and quiet and watching the tub fill and the crying got louder and she was very frightened and her body felt strange and heavy and she tried to walk toward her son toward the crying coming from the bath tub but couldn't her arms and legs wouldn't move fast enough her feet wouldn't grip the floor it felt like she was running underwater the crying got louder she recognized the crying she tried to run faster couldn't run couldn't run her son didn't turn around turn around she tried to scream couldn't scream didn't turn around just watched tub fill listened crying get louder got on hands knees tried crawl couldn't crawl like something couldn't feel holding back tried scream couldn't scream couldn't move couldn't help just watched son watch tub fill then the crying stopped and her son slowly turned around and said, Hi Mom, Clarissa's done with her bath.

And then she woke up. Lying on her back, Jennifer opened her eyes slowly. The dark ceiling in front of her and a dim light in the corner of her eye. She turned her head toward the window and saw fragments of the sky glowing cobalt and peeking through the gaps in the curtains. The sun was almost up. She averted her eyes back to the bed and watched her son sleep, his slow, rhythmic breathing, his eyelids twitching. He was dreaming. She watched him and hoped his dreams were happy. She watched him until he woke up.

"Hi, Mom."

Four.

They left the following morning, just before noon, and began driving again. It was a bleak and cloudy day with a dense overcast obscuring the sun and moving quickly across the sky. The car drove past three restaurants and a diner, but despite Adam's protesting that he was hungry, Jennifer did not stop. She kept driving straight. Cutting right through the town and onward into more nearly empty road, more trees with green and yellowing leaves, and more quiet farmland.

"Where are we going?"

"I told you: home."

"This isn't the way."

"You know the way?"

"No, but I really don't know this way."

Jennifer smiled. "You're funny, you know that?"

"You've told me," he said, and his stomach growled.

"Okay, here's the deal: we need to take a detour."

"Why?"

"Because of the trunk," she said.

"Oh," he said. "I kind of forgot."

She adjusted her rear view mirror so she could see him. He looked back at her reflection.

"What are we going to do about it, though?" he asked.

The corners of her mouth dropped.

"I really don't know," she said. "I'm thinking."

"I have an idea," he said.

He told her. As he did, a few droplets pattered against the windshield. Then many more. Soon the windshield was speckled with raindrops. Jennifer turned on the wiper blades. She kept driving, listening to her son talk, her eyes shifting from the road to his reflection in the rear view.

She drove a while longer, watching the farmland gradually disappear and the trees become a thick forest on either side of the road.

Every few miles, Jennifer saw chained off, unpaved side roads with signs that read DO NOT ENTER and PRIVATE PROPERTY, KEEP OUT. As they approached one with an entrance that looked particularly overgrown and had a chain that was old and rusty, likely untouched for a long time, Adam asked her to stop.

Jennifer slowed the car, then pulled over.

She got out and walked through the rain toward the rusty chain and unhooked it from its post. It slipped from her hands and dropped to the moist ground. Dripping wet, she then sprinted back to the car, got inside, shifted the transmission back into drive, and headed into the now open path. Once the car was through the entrance, she stopped, got out again, and hooked the chain back onto its post; she got back into the car and drove down the path and into the woods.

When the road narrowed to the point of being no longer drivable, Jennifer stopped the car and shut off the engine and waited to see if the rain would stop.

After an hour had passed, the rainfall had only gotten harder, so she and her son stepped out of the car and into the downpour. Though the trees all around them offered some protection from the storm, it was very minimal, and Jennifer felt her feet sink into the muddy ground as she and Adam walked toward the trunk.

Jennifer opened it.

"Wake up," Adam said. "Wake up!"

Jennifer wanted to look away, but didn't.

"Come on, Mister Sleepyhead," he said. "Wake up."

As drops of water landed on the man's greasy face, Mister Sleepyhead twitched and stirred inside the trunk. He was still wearing his bathrobe, which had come undone revealing his white boxer shorts and bare chest and stomach. He was a small man, no more than five and a half feet tall, and thin aside from his protruding belly. He lay unmoving in a shallow puddle of his own ungodly smelling excrement, his eyes barely open, his hands and feet taped behind his back in a reverse fetal position. An orange tennis ball duct taped halfway into his mouth, his jaw stretched open almost to the point of dislocation to accommodate it. He turned his head and looked up at them, at Jennifer and Adam, at their wet forms dripping over him. His reddened eyes widened as his pupils dilated. His weak nose-breathing quickened.

He began to squirm and wreathe, never taking his eyes off the two and making muffled, whimpering sounds through the tennis ball crammed into his mouth. Jennifer watched Adam lean in closer and rip the tape off in one quick motion.

The man gagged and pushed the ball out with his tongue. He moved his jaw from side to side, wincing at each motion, gasping for air. Then glared at the boy with a look of both hate and terror. And the rain fell harder and harder through the branches above, washing the shit and sweat from the man's features.

Then Mister Sleepyhead let out a bestial howl at the boy. But Adam was unmoved.

"Please don't make noises like that," the boy said. "If you do, my Mom'll have to get the tennis ball again."

The man sniffed and moaned like he might start crying.

"There, see? Very good. We're going to play the quiet game. I like the quiet game. It's one of my favorites."

Jennifer pushed her soaked hair away from her face, then wrapped her arms around herself and shivered.

Mister Sleepyhead asked, "Where am I?"

"No place I think anyone's going to find you anytime soon, if that's what you mean."

"Where's my wife?" he asked. "Where's Gloria?"

"Probably roasted toasty like a crunchy munch by now," the boy answered.

Then the man did start crying.

"God!" he screamed. "Oh, Jesus Christ!"

He screamed those words over and over again. Screamed them until his voice cracked. Jennifer looked away, but couldn't drown out the pitiful screams and curses. She looked at her son. The boy just raised an eyebrow and looked Mister Sleepyhead over.

"What did I tell you about all that screaming?"

"Fuck you, demon child!" Mister Sleepyhead said.

Jennifer's head jerked forward. "Hey, don't you use those kinds of words in front of my son, you hear me!" she yelled back at the man.

Mister Sleepyhead tried to spit at her, but his mouth was too dry and the thick, white foam just dribbled down the side of his face. The rain washed it away.

"God!" Mister Sleepyhead shouted at no one. "I just knew you were a messed up kid, just knew it!"

"What do you mean?" Adam asked.

"I told Gloria there was something off about you, that I could tell. But she didn't believe me, thought you were just troubled."

Adam cocked his head.

"Then, just a little at a time, I started to piece together why got taken away from your mother—"

The boy watched him, confused.

"—Don't you look at me like that!" Mister Sleepyhead screamed. "We gave you a home, and tried to love you, and Gloria tried to be a good mother—"

"You shut up!" Adam yelled back. "You just shut up! She wasn't my Mom, I have a Mom, and she loves me, and she's going to take me home!"

Then turning to face Jennifer, the boy said, "Right, Mom, you're taking me home?"

Jennifer stood there, drenched through her clothes and shivering violently. She wiped her nose with her wet sleeve and nodded.

"Yeah," Mister Sleepyhead said, lifting his head and looking at Jennifer. "Take the little, murdering bastard home then. You two'll be real happy together. Thinking to keep me as a pet or something, torture me a little more just for laughs?"

"No!" Jennifer exclaimed through chattering teeth. "I don't like hurting you. I don't like hurting anyone. Neither does my son. He's a good boy. We just needed a car to get us home. We couldn't walk it, and I needed to be sure nobody would take him away from me again. That's why I let him do what he did to your wife and house. It was a beautiful house. You two took really good care of him. You both were very kind, and I'm grateful for that, but he's my son. He belongs with me."

As she spoke, the boy disappeared beside the car and

began shuffling through the wet leaves and the mud. Searching for something. Mister Sleepyhead's breathing quickened again as he tried to see where the boy went but couldn't. He pulled harder at the tape, and Jennifer saw the tape dig into the base of his hand and draw blood.

His warm-looking blood diluted with the cold wetness already covering his flesh.

But the tape was tearing. Jennifer saw it. She didn't say anything, afraid of what might happen next.

Mister Sleepyhead motioned to his surroundings with his eyes. "Why go through all this trouble for me though?" he asked. "Am I special or something?"

The boy was somewhere behind the car grunting and digging in the mud. The sound of clods of wet earth pattering on the ground.

"I figured," Jennifer said, watching the man struggle, "if they were looking for my son with you, they wouldn't look for him with me."

Mister Sleepyhead looked at her, baffled. "Lady," he said, "then you're as stupid as you are crazy."

That was the last thing Mister Sleepyhead said before the boy reappeared with a feral shriek that made the man jump further back into the trunk with shock. Mister Sleepyhead's eyes and mouth locked in an expression of terror, his hands and feet vainly trying to free themselves from their bonds; the boy's eyes and mouth wide with rabid intensity, his hands lifted above his head like a victory gesture. In the boy's hands was a very large, muddy rock. Mister Sleepyhead lurched and struggled. At the last moment, the man ripped one hand free, but that was all. He lifted the torn and bleeding hand, almost shielding his face, before the boy cried out again and brought the heavy rock down on the man's forehead. The impact peeled away skin, leaving a dripping red gash with an oval of pink in the center—bone—and the man howled in pain. The boy lifted the rock high again.

Jennifer watched her son's hands holding the rock hitting the man. After two hits, the rock became bloody; after three hits, the man's screaming stopped; after five hits, the boy lowered the rock and let it drop from his hands. The gore dripping from Mister Sleepyhead's head hanging lifeless over the trunk, dripping over the back bumper and mixing with the rainwater into a dark puddle snaking between the two back tires and away like a newborn river. Jennifer watched the red run. Then turned her head and watched the boy. She looked him over, up and down, his hands wet with rainwater, spattered with flecks of transparent pink.

And he looked back at her and said, "Okay, I'm done. Will you help me clean up now?"

Jennifer closed her eyes and swallowed hard.

"Okay," she said. "Okay."

Five.

It took them an hour before they'd found the right place, before they'd dragged the body far enough into the woods: to a place where the trees became dense on every side and ivy and thorns and leaves cluttered the ground in a disorderly mass obscuring the soil beneath, a place where the glimmer of the wet highway could no longer be seen between the trees and even the rainfall seemed quieter. The quiet haunted Jennifer's ears.

Jennifer let the man's legs slip from her shaking hands. Adam followed suit. Jennifer sneezed and coughed and held herself but got no warmth.

"Now what?" she said.

"Well, we should cover him with rocks and dirt and stuff."

Jennifer looked around. There were no rocks. And the dirt was covered in plants and foliage.

"We can't," she said. Her voice was nasally and weak.

Adam looked at her.

"Do you feel okay, Mom?"

She coughed again.

"I'll be fine. Let's just finish this."

"Okay," he said. "Do you think leaves would cover him up alright?"

"We can try," she said.

So they did, picking up handfuls of wet and slimy leaves, carrying them back and packing them around the body like a cocoon. A couple times, Jennifer thought she saw the body move, slight finger twitches, its broken and bloodied features trembling, but she knew it was only her imagination. The man was dead. That was all there was to it.

They moved the leaves from point A to point B for a long time. Haphazardly packing them tight to the man's body like amateur masons laying cement, then going back for more.

As Jennifer carried over an armful of moldy dead leaves, she stopped and looked. Her son was crouched over the man's body, sprinkling leaves over his torso a little at a time. He sprinkled them slowly. Then he looked up at her, and she dropped her leaves and walked toward him.

"What are you doing?"

He didn't answer.

She swallowed hard, shivered.

"What are you doing?" she repeated.

His big, dark eyes.

"Flowers," he said.

"Flowers?"

"Yeah, flowers. And mushrooms, too."

She sniffed.

"What about flowers and mushrooms?" she asked.

"They can grow here."

"You mean in the woods? Honey, I don't—"

He pointed down at the leaves covering the dead man.

"No, I mean here."

Jennifer stood there for a moment while the boy eyed her.

"I mean—"

Jennifer watched him, watched his eyes, his mouth as he spoke.

"—isn't that how it works: things die and become new things?"

Jennifer didn't answer.

"And it's pretty when that happens, right?" he said.

"Yes," she replied, "I guess so."

They finished covering the body and began moving back to the car. And as they walked, the rain slowed before ceasing altogether. She held her son's hand as they walked. Cold and trembling, Jennifer felt sick. Adam, however, it seemed, did not; he didn't appear fazed by the cold or rain at all, and Jennifer thought about this, but then let the thought pass.

Walking, she turned her head, looked back at the earthy colored heap of wet autumn concealing the remains, now small and blended into the distance, and her vision felt distorted. Then she turned her head back around and kept walking until they reached the car. Its chassis and windows speckled with glimmering beads of rainwater. Underneath the rear end the river was gone, though the soft earth was stained red where it drank the slowly falling diluted blood still dripping from the open trunk.

"We have to leave it," Jennifer said, resting her trembling palm against the slick hood. "People will look for it."

"Okay," Adam said. But he sounded unsure.

They kept walking past the car. When they reached the rusty chain, Jennifer lifted it and she and the boy passed underneath and stepped back onto the blacktop. The road was empty; there were no cars. The only passing sounds were that of the chilled wind moving through woods they'd just left. The cold bit into Jennifer's skin.

"But how will we get home without the car?"

Jennifer coughed. "We'll have to walk, I guess."

"Isn't it too far?"

"We'll do what we can," she said, too afraid to tell him she was scared. "It isn't raining anymore, I think we should try. Come on."

She held out her hand again and her son took it. The rain had washed nearly all the blood from his hands; his clothes, though, were still covered in light red stains. She feigned an unsure smile at him and he did the same.

"I love you, Mom."

"I know," she said. "I love you too."

Then they started walking again. They walked a long time.

Six.

Jennifer walked, Jennifer looked. The gravel-freckled blacktop under their feet gave the road an almost ethereal hue. A thin glaze of moisture glistened under the late afternoon sunlight like a cluster of distant stars on a curving ribbon of space. Whatever form it took, however, the open road twisted and arched in front of Jennifer and her son as they walked in the grass alongside it, and for all they could see, it was unending.

Few cars had passed them during their trek, and the ones that had only slowed long enough for their drivers to eye the two warily, pass around them, and then speed off and disappear. After a while, Jennifer stopped, sat on a metal guardrail dividing the blacktop from a grassy ditch; she looked down, and below, in the ditch, a small stream trickled between the dense tree trunks and into a concrete tunnel under the road.

Adam remained standing, watching her.

"You're really looking bad, Mom," he said.

"I just need to rest a minute," she said.

She sat and her son stood and they were both quiet, save for the sound of their faint breathing. Then the boy's stomach rumbled.

"I'm still hungry," he said. "Really hungry."

"I know you are, honey. I have dinner stuff at home for us. And tomorrow I'll have a special birthday surprise for you, for both of us, together."

Her son's face beamed.

"What's the surprise?"

Jennifer looked down and smiled.

"If I told you, it wouldn't be a surprise."

"Okay," he said, sounding a little despondent.

They walked until nightfall. The emptied rainclouds having long dispersed revealing a sporadically glittered, navy blue sky. The darkness cloaking the distance ahead and behind, save for the orange-pink glow of streetlamps which colored the road in an unusual, dreamlike pastel. There was a wind. The wind was very cold.

Jennifer was nearly sleepwalking. And in her sickness induced half-dreaming she heard a sound: a low whine, faint and far away.

"Clarissa?" she whispered, lifting her eyes from her shoes.

Then brightness flowed over her. It grew brighter and brighter until it passed around her. As it passed, a red glow washed over her, coupled with the whine of an engine and the sound of stopping tires crunching on asphalt.

"Hey!" a voice called out, and then Jennifer woke to the sight of taillights staring into her eyes, causing her to squint.

"Hey!" the voice called out again. A woman's voice.

Jennifer looked to the side of the dark blue SUV now parked about ten feet in front of her—dark like the sky and purring gently, smelling of exhaust— and there was a

102

woman's head and arm stretching out from the driver's side window. Round-faced, her skin a constellation of freckles.

"Do you need help?" the woman called to her. Her voice was smooth and deep and laced with compassion.

Jennifer didn't answer.

"Ma'am?" the woman called again.

"Yes," Jennifer said at last, shouting over the sound of the engine, "we need help!"

The woman reached her arm back into the car and shut off the motor. The automobile became dark for a moment. Then the headlights and taillights clicked back on. It was at that moment that Jennifer noticed a small crying noise from inside the car and a tag hanging from the woman's rear windshield: BABY ON BOARD.

Jennifer looked down at her son. He wasn't saying anything, wasn't moving. He just looked straight ahead into his reflection in the darkly tinted car window glass.

The woman peered out from inside the car again and caught sight of the boy. She looked him up and down, noticing the bloodstains on his clothes. Her eyes widened as her brow furrowed.

"Is...he hurt, or—?" the woman asked.

Jennifer looked at the boy.

"No, not really. He suffers from chronic nosebleeds. Getting caught in the weather gave him a bad attack."

"Nosebleeds?"

"Yes. It was a really bad attack."

The woman eyed them both. The unseen baby cried louder. "Where are you going?" she asked.

"Home," Jennifer said. "I'm taking my son home."

The woman eyed them both suspiciously.

"Is it far from here?"

"Not too far."

"Can you tell me the address?"

She told her.

"Oh, well that's maybe an hour up the road, maybe two. I know the place, though. I know exactly how to get there."

"Can we have a ride?" Jennifer asked.

The woman looked the two over and sighed.

"Alright, but only if you can furnish some gas money. I'm almost on E."

Jennifer reached into her moist pocket and only felt the plastic prescription vial. Her other pocket was empty too. She looked up at the woman.

"I have money," Jennifer said. "That'll be fine."

The woman looked at Adam as he stared blankly forward into the car.

"He doesn't say a lot, does he?"

"He's shy," Jennifer said turning her head and watching the boy in his silent intensity.

"Well, alright," the woman replied in a low voice. She looked them both over once more. Then she said, "Okay, get in. But try not to let him nosebleed on my upholstery."

"Thank you," Jennifer said and took her son's hand and stepped toward the car and opened the rear door and let him climb inside. He remained quiet and seated himself next to a gray, plastic car seat which contained the crying baby. Jennifer stepped through the passenger side door and sat next to the woman and smiled a tired smile.

"Thank you again," Jennifer said.

The woman started the engine.

As the car began to move, Jennifer reached into her pocket and removed the orange vile, opened it, and took one of the remaining two pills in her mouth and swallowed it dry. The woman watched her, but didn't say anything.

The car picked up speed, and Jennifer watched awhile through the passenger side window as the layers of passing scenery blurred and distorted into a hazy sleepiness. Just before she closed her eyes, through the drone of the engine purring gently in her ears, Jennifer thought she heard the boy behind her say something: she thought she heard him say "flowers," but even as she thought about that, she breathed in slowly, then out. Then everything went away.

Seven.

When Jennifer woke up she was still in the car, which was now parked crooked in front of her house. But she was alone.

The driver's side window was shattered.

She opened the door and got out. She walked around to the driver's side, her legs shaking and weak. Shards of glass crunching underneath her soles. The sight of disturbed earth and a few scattered spots of blood. A large stone lay beside the back tire. Everything was quiet. It was still dark outside, and before her, the house stood. She walked toward it.

As she walked toward the house, she exhaled, watching her breath swirl like smoke and vanish into the dark sky. Almost full dark, save for pale glow of the moon clothing all benign shapes around her in looming silhouettes. Surrounding oaks and elms once touched with autumn's strange and fiery colors now saturated in a thick coat of inky shadows. And as she looked up at the almost full dark and wanted to step inside her home and sleep and forget everything that had happened, another thought eased into her mind: tomorrow, that special day, she would be with her child. Together, a family. With that thought, her body regained some of its strength lost to illness, and she pressed on toward the front door.

The door hung open. She stepped through it. Inside, noises echoed through the foyer, sounds faint and distant and seeping through the ceiling above her. She followed the sounds. Up the stairs, past a small, pink, room in the process of being bricked up. Bricks burnt burgundy and full of flecks of grit stacked in a stout pyramid beside a bag of quick dry cement mix, beside the half-sealed off entrance. To seal the stale air of whispered memories within.

Past the partly bricked up room, at the far end of the hallway was another door, and behind the door were noises. She moved toward the door; she moved toward the noises. When she reached the door she stood there a little while and listened. The sound of water running and a baby crying and something else, something strange and muffled, came faintly through the gaps around the rectangular door frame. And with the sounds came a light pooling under the door. Jennifer moved closer until the light was smeared golden over her toes. Then she touched the knob, and the door opened just enough for her to peek inside.

The room was filled with a warm incandescence. The water was running in the tub. She could hear a baby's muffled cries. To her left Jennifer saw the woman who'd picked her and Adam up in the SUV: she was tied to the toilet with jump rope, a sock shoved into her mouth and secured with tape, a large gash, red and bleeding, just above her left temple. The woman looked scared.

And in the center of it all was Jennifer's son, her only son, Adam, standing still and silent and watching the tub fill as the faint cries slowly muffled and bubbled and then

107

silenced altogether.

Without a word, Jennifer opened the door and stepped inside the bathroom. Stepped past her son and up to the tub. She gently pushed him aside with her hand and lifted the baby from the water. Its eyes widened and it gasped and Jennifer looked at it a long time.

"That's enough of that!" Jennifer said, turning to face her son.

The boy looked at her and the baby and frowned.

"Now go to your room" Jennifer said. "You wait for me there, understand?"

The boy looked at Jennifer like he didn't understand but did what he was told. He left the bathroom, and, turning the corner, disappeared down the hall.

Jennifer set the crying baby down in its mother's lap and proceeded to untie the woman. The woman sat there sobbing until her arms were freed, then picked up her baby and held it tight against her breast, and the woman and the baby cried together.

"You can leave now," Jennifer said. "Your car is still outside."

The woman looked at Jennifer with red and desperate eyes.

"Do you think I'll just let this go?" she asked. "Like it's nothing?"

"You can leave now," Jennifer said again. "Get in your car and drive far away from here, as far as you can."

They both looked at each other. Then the woman, still holding her baby, stood up, her knees trembling, and walked out from the bathroom. Jennifer listened to her footfalls as the woman stepped down the stairs. Then the front door slammed, and there was silence. Except the water sloshing in the tub behind Jennifer's ears. She looked and saw her face reflected in the clear water, then turned around and walked out of the bathroom and back into the hallway. The boy was standing there. He looked like he might cry. She walked toward him. And when she reached him, she put her arms around him and held him, pressing his face against the lower part of her shoulder.

"Are you still hungry?" she asked.

She felt his head nod.

"I'm so hungry my head hurts," he said.

"Well," she said.

She let go of him and reached into her pocket and removed the orange vile and uncapped it and shook its contents into her hand and gave it to the boy. He looked at her.

"It'll make your headache go away," she said. "Come downstairs and I'll make you something to eat and drink, and you can take it."

He looked at her and seemed to understand.

"Alright. But are you sure it's okay for me to take it?" he said.

"Yes," she said. "And then when you wake up tomorrow, it'll be your birthday, and everything will be better,"

"Okay," he said. "Okay."

So, together, they walked down the steps and into the kitchen. And as they walked, Jennifer lifted the orange vile from her pocket again and examined it.

She was out of pills.

Epilogue.

As the air in the room began to grow sour, Jennifer sat on the floor, her back against the wall, her knees pressed against her chin, and looked at her son—her only son—as he sat cross-legged on the floor and stared at her. Today was his birthday: thirteen.

"Well," she said, trying to gain his attention.

He didn't answer.

Jennifer, realizing her boy was in no mood for conversation, rocked back and forth on the hardwood floor and scanned her surroundings: four walls; a child-sized desk; a lamp on the desk, the dim light from the bulb in the lamp filling the small room.

And the bricks.

She looked at the bricks a long time—their burnt red color, their slight sparkle when she'd tilt her head, the way they filled the door frame so perfectly. There was something admirable to them, those bricks, behind their disheartening reality—then she put her face into her hands, looking through the gaps between her fingers. That's when her son spoke.

"Are we supposed to have a moment or something, Mom?"

He sounded so grown up. It felt strange. She didn't look at him.

"Are we?" he asked.

She didn't answer. Just looked at the windowless walls covered in pink alphabet wallpaper. The small, empty, wooden crib. The light flickered. Then came back brighter than before. Igniting the pink room in white.

"You know," he said, "if I killed you right now, no one would blame me."

"I would blame you," she said. "You're all I have left."

"Well," he said.

"Well," she said.

He scooted across the pink carpet and sat next to her.

Then they were quiet. So quiet she could hear his faint breathing, faint heartbeat, smallest muscle twitches. They were quiet a long time.

"I'm not going to though," he finally said.

"What?"

"Kill you."

"Why not?"

"Because you're my Mom," he said. "And because you'd blame me."

"No I wouldn't. Not really," she said. "Have the drugs worn off all the way yet?"

"I think so," he said, rubbing his eyes with his palms. "Maybe not. My head still feels funny. What was that pill?"

"I don't even know what it's called," she said. "Diaz-something, I think. I'm sorry."

He put his arm around her and held her like a son would, like a son ought to. He looked into her eyes, and Jennifer sighed and looked away.

"Are we going to die here?" he asked.

She didn't answer.

"If we die," he said, "we'll turn into something pretty when they put us in the ground."

She didn't answer.

"Is baby Clarissa something pretty now?" he asked. "Like a flower or—"

"I don't want to talk about that!" Jennifer said and buried her face in her knees. "It was my fault. I wasn't watching her or you. I don't want to talk about it."

"Alright," he said. "I love you, Mom."

She didn't answer.

So the boy held his mother close, and she did the same, and they both turned their heads and faced each other. Then the light bulb popped in a bright flash, and the room went dark. Outside, she imagined, the sunrise was ripping through the horizon, lifting higher and higher into the sky like a rising forest fire; it shined over the grass, the trees, the mushrooms and flowers.

Jennifer couldn't see it, though. She couldn't see anything.

THE HEAT WENT ON FOREVER

I rose with a start from my pillow and rested my hand on Anna's bosom who lay beside me. Her chest raised, lowered, slow and gentle. Her skin was warm and slightly damp with perspiration through her tee shirt. She was there. She was there.

There was no light in the apartment but a glowing heat that beamed through the closed curtains and filled the room with an eerie pale glow. I looked at my watch.

6:23pm.

The dusk was being eaten already. I had slept too long. Outside, the sound of a woman's voice penetrated the strange bright silence. I pushed away the sheets loosely cocooning my unclothed body and rose to my feet, opened the window. The air was dry and hot. I squinted from the brightness.

On the ground three floors below, a woman stumbled and staggered down the center of the street. Her steps drunken and erratic. Twice she fell to her knees. When she did, she picked herself up like a marionette lifted by invisible strings and turned and walked the other way.

Back and forth, back and forth.

Molly, she shouted. Molly! she shouted. Her voice was loud and raspy.

Behind me, Anna stirred and groaned.

"Christ," she said under her breath.

Anna pushed herself upright, and stumbled from the bed. Naked from the waist down, her bare legs wobbled as she made her way toward me. She pushed me aside and hung her head out the window.

"Hey," she called.

The woman stopped and looked up.

"Shut the fuck up!"

"Please, I need—" the woman shouted, her words slurring and trailing into incomprehension.

"Nobody gives a shit about you getting one last fix!"

The woman fell to the ground and shrieked.

Anna shut the window.

She paused, rested against the pane and turned her head to face me. I saw her eyes right then and there; eyes tired and sad, filled with small flecks of luster from the growing light surrounding her body.

She and I had spent the day tangled in each other. We had gone on for hours, neither breaking for food nor drink, draining ourselves, pushing ourselves, until the act of sex itself had become painful and ugly. And even still, she raw and dry and I limp and weak, we took to writhing in feigned ecstasy—the last lie we would ever tell each other: our flesh speaking more boldly than words ever had. After that, fatigue took us both by force.

"I don't think she was looking for drugs," I said.

"That's the bitch who dropped her daughter off the balcony yesterday," she said, "while the little girl was asleep. Now she's pacing all over looking for her like—"

She paused a moment, picked at a dried clump of something in her pubic hair.

"Shit, Neal," she said. "You didn't wake me up."

"I know," I said. "I'm sorry. I must have forgotten to set an alarm."

"You promised."

"I know. I'm sorry."

She turned and looked out the window. Then something caught my attention, and I looked past her: outside, small birds were fluttering to and from the window ledge, carrying sticks and bits of trash and laying them in a neat pile. They suddenly took off and flew away.

"I don't want to see this."

"I'm sorry," I said again.

"Okay," she said. "Okay, I think there's still enough time. It's under the mattress."

I walked to the bed and ran my fingers between the mattress and the box spring. I pulled out the Browning HP-35.

"Do you have it?" she asked.

"Yes."

"Okay, hurry and do this quick."

I pointed the barrel at her.

"Is it already loaded?"

"Please," she said, "just make it fast."

"Forgive me," I said.

"There's nothing to forgive," she said then looked out the window, squinting for the brightness growing brighter.

"I'm scared, and I don't want to be scared anymore."

As I squeezed the trigger, the light grew, disintegrating the windows and dissolving the walls. Outside, the briefest sound of chaos surged through the air—shrieks of pain, shouts of rage, breaking glass and wood, a crash of the world caving into itself. Screaming women and children. Crying men. Bestial, almost inhuman noises. And even from our height, it all sounded so loud. I felt fire in my blood and

117

bones, and Anna screamed as everything went blank.
There was only the white heat. The heat went on forever.

Afterword

*I*n 2011, I was beginning to think I wanted to be a writer—though I hadn't yet produced anything substantial.

I'd already settled that "horror" was the general trajectory I wanted my writing to take. Problem was, much as I've always loved all things spooky and macabre, I hadn't read a whole hell of a lot of the genre—aside from a few library classics and the mandatory childhood collection of R.L. Stine novellas.

I'd grown up home-schooled, and as voracious a reader I'd been as a kid, I'd become literature-deficient throughout my teens.

Then in my early 20s, I'd gotten this bug up my ass to write stories. I wanted to write scary stories. And to do so, I needed to start reading.

So like most young punks of the digital age, I turned to the internet.

There I stumbled across a Wikipedia article on horror fiction. Further down the rabbit hole, and I landed on a page about Clive Barker, specifically his *Books of Blood*.

Before long, merrily to the bookstore I went (tra-la-la), and there found a paperback copy, read the story "Dread" while sitting in the middle of an aisle, and was instantly hooked. I paid the money and took the tome with me, reading "The Midnight Meat Train" on the bus ride home.

This was sometime in December, as I recall consuming "In the Hills, the Cities" beside my family's Christmas tree. While sitting among the tender twinkling colors, I was taking in visceral details of gore and sex and malevolent things lurking in shadows. But there was something else that grabbed me.

Anyone could write excessive grotesquery or tasteless descriptions of blood and guts. B-movies did it all the time.

What Barker did was far different, instead framing complex human dramas against a backdrop of madness and monstrosity. Despite all the ugliness he could splash across a page, the way Barker depicted people and their (sometimes brief) lives made each story unique and beautiful.

That was what I wanted to do.

Or at least try.

Fast forward about twelve months. I had already completed my first serious story. I say "serious" because it would become my first published piece of fiction, and is included in this anthology as well.

Feeling that urgent need to squeeze out yet another, I sat and, by random happenstance, typed the following lines:

This was supposed to be a garden once, she thinks as she digs. A garden of beautiful flowers—bright, living, plentiful, their colors glowing beneath the hot June sun. The spade makes a deep, muffled crunching sound as it penetrates the dry and rocky soil. The young woman strains and lifts a shovelful of dirt and turns her body to deposit the mound behind her.

I had no direction, no plot. All I had was an image in my mind of a young woman in a wide field, at night, digging a hole for some unknown reason.

The image disturbed me.

I needed to know who she was and what secret she was attempting to bury. And I slowly discovered it with that paperback copy of *Books of Blood* open beside my computer monitor.

The story took me a long time to write.

More than a year.

I remember because my first taste of publication in a literary magazine came in 2013, and at that time I was still less than halfway done with what would eventually be "Vivid Greene."

It also went through a number of revisions, both during and after completion. For example, initially the subtitle "A Place to Lay My Bones" was just the title, and the town wasn't going to be called Vivid Greene at all. It was Barkerville. Of course I changed it because the reference was embarrassingly on-the-nose.

Since then, I've been published in nearly a dozen print and online outlets. Still, despite having been at this the better part of a decade, I can't shake the feeling of being a novice each time I face that blank first page. Like I'm muddling through unknown territory. Each story begins with a first line, but before that with a surge of anxiety, frustration, and self-doubt.

These days, my interests no longer reside in "horror." At least not rigidly. I would rather create something fresh, difficult to define, conduct weird experiments in the written word—after all, why limit oneself?

But that early passion for the art of all things dark and morbid never waned.

Earlier this year, I was in New Jersey attending Monster Mania, a horror convention held annually in Cherry Hill, where I had the honor of meeting Clive Barker. My girlfriend took it upon herself to ensure I bought a ticket. To my knowledge, Barker doesn't make many appearances these days, and she knew (bless her heart) that if I missed this chance I wouldn't forgive myself.

I didn't take anything with me.

Not that I didn't have anything to take. Over the years, I'd amassed a sizable collection of his films, comics, and of course books.

I figured, I'll just have him sign my arm. Just for appearances, so I didn't seem odd. Some cursive on a knickknack or curio...that wasn't important. The important thing was I get to meet the guy.

When I set foot inside the autograph room, I was trembling. I'm not usually the nervous type when it comes to meeting people, and a famous person is still just a person. But this was something else entirely.

The line moved quick. Quicker than I expected. When it was my turn I approached and blurted out something along the lines of "Mr. Barker I just wanted you to know I'm a writer and I've been at it for such and such many years and it's all because of you and your work inspiring me."

It sounded much better in my head. Things always do.

He looked up, smiled wide and thanked me.

Told me he was happy to hear it.

Not at all in a condescending way like, "Okay fanboy, calm down," (which would have been my first reaction), but as though he genuinely appreciated what I'd said. Then he shook my hand.

The handshake was firm and genuine.

What did I ask him to sign?

A hardback copy of his very first short stories, written in the '70s but never before published, which I ended up purchasing at his table.

It's not a "collector's item." I'm not keeping it pristine. I'll never sell it. Its value isn't calculable in money, as nothing truly valuable ever is. The signature is evidence of having met someone whose work inspired and continues to inspire me.

Like how *Books of Blood* rested beside my computer, I keep this small book of his *First Tales* on my shelf for the days when I feel like my work isn't good enough. When I crack it open, it reminds me that everyone starts somewhere, that I still have growing to do, and that I always will because storytelling only gets better with age and ages over a lifetime.

J.I.D
Sept. 12, 2019
Baltimore, MD

About the author:

Jacob Ian DeCoursey is a writer of fiction, poetry, and pop culture journalism. He is a contributor at *Brutal Planet Magazine* and former staff writer for *Shockwave Magazine* and *Movie-Thoughts.com*. His literary credits include *9Tales Told in the Dark, Grub Street, Row Home Lit, Poems from the Heron Clan, The Scum Gentry Alternative Arts & Media, Horror Sleaze Trash, The Welter,* and *Not One of Us*—among others. In 2014, he was first-place recipient of the *CSPA Gold Circle Award* in both *Humor* and *Experimental Fiction* categories. He resides in Baltimore, Maryland.

What Is It Press Copyright 2020
Editor: Sebastian De Angeli⌐
Author: Sue Yan Nish
Revised: 03-24-2020
ISBN: 978-0-9679947-3-4
ASIN: B07D5K97XD
GGKEY: UG4FZC25T0T

I0543207

The manual (SM069) is no longer provided in the appendix of the books in the Empty Nation (EN) series because it grew beyond a reasonable size. So it's published separately on Amazon (small cost), Google Play Books (free) and also available for free when you purchase this title on Audible.com, the accompanying PDF support material (SM069) will be available in your Audible Library along with the audio book.

References to Manual are made throughout the books in the series. Tag format: the word being referenced is tagged in **bold** print preceding the reference in square brackets. Reference format: a period [.] the dot symbol is used to separate the components of the reference, as in the following examples.

Tag [*section* dot *sub-section* dot *description*]

SIT [4.D-G2.22], section 4, sub-section D-G2, description 22
PBS [2.10], section 2, description 10
SEC [26], section 26

EN02: Growing-Up

C01 Sissy Preschool: This is book 2 of the Empty Nation series. The Gurls (Mary & Jane) are man-handled and playfully abused by Stud® class men. They've been trained to perform Sissy-Love® which is the new system designed to diminish human violence and increase revenue. Starting from preschool these, promiscuous by nature, adorable Homo-Sis-Sapien (non-human) Gurls engage in training lessons. Although not naturally occurring on earth the Gurls are not registered as extraterrestrial aliens but as livestock animals in the USA Inc. Other Sissydom issues are, the Pledge of Allegiance, humiliation training, the Piss-On-Me ritual, Hide-the-Banana, social class Opt-Out®, Jane is reprimanded for behaving naughty.

C02 JAS Camp: The mom's scheme about creating a perfect D and B type Bonded Pair, a **DBBP**®. The Gurls survive Scout camp unharmed and got to play with the other Gurlfriends which show up in later books in the series. They're satisfied emotionally and physically. Also in camp, Mary and Jane are exposed to many new intimate situations with camp (vacation resort) guests as they grow-up in the new USA Inc. Junior American Sissy (JAS) camp is just what the Gurls needed to feel liberated from their overly loving parents. Other issues discussed, government supplied Sissy-Breeding® inoculation drugs, **D** and **B** formulas and the Mind Control **MCD** drugs, Pool-Party, Snowballing, and Bonobo-Love®.

C03 Elementary School: The story in the series is further defined by boring lectures about **Sissydom**® from elementary school teachers. Every class filled with lengthy ramblings on about USA Inc. propaganda, enslavement of the working class with labor compensation system which incorporates sex as a benefit, dollar hegemony and more. Knowledge of the new Whores-for-Profit® world in the Modern Social Economic System, **MSES**® is brainwashed into the minds of the innocent Gurls®. Also reviewed in this chapter are, Hono-Sis-Sapien®, Sex gym class, modern history, sociology, Labor Compensation Transaction, **LCT**®.

C04 High School: The Gurls are taught the MSES® is a newly created system of governance which rewards the wealthy citizen with sexual prowess (drug induced). Also new moral rules legalizing free love, free sex! And although the workers are provided only basic essentials, the downtrodden citizenry is quite pleased despite most of the population living in FEMA zones squalor (Little do they know, in the camps senior citizens are ground-up into food products). An even more sick & twisted change is, society in the future has again accepted a social class system. In this new system, wealthy men are promoted and so can afford penis enlargement drugs **PED**® to maintain social status. This Stud® class is sexually well-endowed therefore it abuses lower class Non-Stud citizens based on their mediocre sexual ability. Also reviewed and referenced, American Economic Disparity, the **AED**®, Penis Official Length Certificate, **POLC**®, Sissy gang violence from transmutation, **TM**®, also touched on, one unit of money is equal to one unit of a male-orgasm, a **MO**® credit and more....

Books in the Empty Nation (EN) Series

EMPTY NATION

A DIRTY STORY ABOUT A DIRTY COUNTRY

Series (1) Book (2)

GROWING UP

SUE YAN NISH

Table of Contents

Chapter 1: Sissy Preschool

Three years later…the year is 2236…

[1.1] DICKGURL

Okay **Jane**? (Not a word from Jane). Hey! Jane, cum on! Proper Sissy conduct is necessary at home and at school. You're four years old now and you don't need to walk around with cum dripping out from the corner of your mouth or down your leg like a Hoe! You know better than this is little Gurly-Boy®.

MOM! Don't call me a **BOY**! (Jane pouts and folds her arms in protest).

Well my little dick-loving **JAS**© [16] **Gurl**® [7.G1.7b], it's your huge one inch peanut sized boy dick which gives it away. Hee… heee…. normal girls just don't have monster clits with a tiny little nut-sack dangling between their legs. Mwah… And stop pouting!

I know! Geeezz… Mom! Do you have to lecture me, I know I was born with boy stuff, but I don't care what I was born with, I'm a Junior American Sissy, I'm a JAS Gurl and there's nothing you can say or do to change my mind I'm a Dickgurl®. Not a boy! Ugh... (Jane sighs).

Jane you mean you're a **Sissy**®! There's a difference. Daddy is a Sissy-in-Training, a **SIT**® [1.A2.4], he's a Dickgurl. And hey, I'm just razing you sweetheart don't pout. Mwah…

Mom! (Jane frowns and is kinda self-conscious).

Swallow Mommy! Swallow! Ahhhh....

Gulp... Guk, Gak... Wow you shot in Mommy's mouth so fast little Sissy-Gurl®. Oooh Babe! You taste sooo good! Hmmm! So much came out!

Ah huh, I shoot a lot! All the Gurls say that.

Oh! Jane Gurl, you don't have a clit, you have a little cum hose! (Jane's mom Sandy cleans off her clit with her tongue) Ummm... Honey you cum way more than Daddy does! Mwah...

My Cock-God! You shoot gallons little princess! The Sissification® drug **SD69** [4.D-G1.4] has amazing results!

Dill-a-ling, dill-a-ling, dill-a-ling.... (The school bell rings).

There's the bell, I gotta go Mom! Thanks for the blow-job!

Here's your cum collecting sock (Jane's Mom rolls the removable sock over Jane's still erect little clit and tightens the pretty bow strap), there! It's so cute with the pretty little pink bow. Mwah...

Mwah... Mom! Do I have to wear it?

Yes Sweetheart, you know its mandatory here at the **Sissy-World**© preschool. All Sissies must wear these specially made Sissy Clit-Socks® to catch all of your sweet Sissy-Cream®.

Mom! Our Teacher Ms. Carol calls it by its technically name. She calls it, Homo-Sis-Sapien Cream or **HSSC** [18.13b]. She says it causes human people to get divorces.

Oh my! She's squirting. Wow! Mary is only four and she lactates? Yeah anyway, the Dunes live on our block a few houses away. Well Babe, just carefully roll the tiny little condom, I mean the Clit-Sock® off your clit like daddy and I showed you and then roll it back on and tighten the strap after you guys finish blowing each other's wee-wee's.

MOM! It's not a wee-wee, boy's call it a wee-wee or pee-pee, I have a Gurl-Clit and Mary has a Gurl-Cocklette®. She's special.

Okay JAS Princess! Mwah... You're going to be late, kiss Mommy good bye. Kissss.

Do you have your bunny-tail plug?

Yes Mom... (Jane says in pacifying voice). And it's clipped to my teen-belt so I won't lose it when I pull it out to do sex-play or humiliation training.

Okay, Baby, Love you! Mwah... say hi to Mary for me!

[1.2] THE PLEDGE OF ALLEGIANCE

Okay, class! Let's all put our right hands over our hearts, your left one around the Clit next to you and say the Pledge of Allegiance [17-6.9] together.

I pledge allegiance to the Bank of the United States of America Incorporated, and to the profit for which it stands, one debt under God, repayable, with sexual liberty and orgasms for all.

Good morning class!

Good mooorning Misssss Carrroool! (The Sissy Gurls all say good morning in their cute high-pitched youthful voices).

Everyone mount the probing wand on your **SissySeat**® [4.D-G1.22] and please wiggle down on it and be quiet.

Miss Carol, it doesn't fit up my hole! (Some Gurls are having a hard time mounting their probes).

Oh **Martha** and **Jean** (EN09), adjust the lengths sweethearts. Now class we're going to do something very, very special today. We're going to practice a special kind of submission.

Wow! Yeah! Wow! Awesome! Whoohoo! (The Gurls are all a glee for a challenge).

Okay! Ok, quiet down you little Nymphos! This will be part of your submissive and humiliation training which we haven't done yet. So, I need all of you to pay very close attention to the instructions. Jane, stop playing with Mary's nipples.

Now, the humilation we're going to learn today is called, **Piss-On-Me** [4.D-G2.15], the POM Ritual.

Oh Cool! Yeah! My mommy and daddy piss on me! Cool!

Ok, Ok, quiet down! Yes I'm sure you've all practiced this at home with your parents or family, but this is different.

Miss Carol why is it different?

Well it's different because this is a formal public, **Piss-On-Me**. It's when you get pissed on in public by United States Federal Government officials or by people in the US Military. Also for example, today we have females who are all married to Stud® men who work for the USA Inc. government.

Females Ms. Carol, are they girls?

Yes, they're all Stud-Breeding® females, either an adult woman or girl. You know people, with have a vagina. And this is important, remember, a Sissy-Cunt is not a vagina, it's a **Vaganus**® [14.O1.6]. Your Sissy-Puss® is a special patented body part owned by the USA Inc. government and is considered a National Ass-Set.

Miss Carol, what's a vagina?

A vagina is, well here just look at mine, (Ms. Carol picks up her mini-skirt so the kids can gape at her crotchless panty clad vagina), you know, where human babies come from? And Sissies don't make babies. So, like I was saying, you pretty little blossoming Sissy flowers usually do a public, **Pissed-On-Me** with human female women or girls who have a vagina.

Why Miss Carol? My Mommy has a pussy!

Yes! All your mommies are Sissy-Breeders®, so they're all human ladies who have pussies.

Why do the pussies piss on us, Miss Carol?

Well, because human women don't like the fact you registered mutated Sissy creatures have been made the official government sponsored loveholes for all men.

Huh? What do you mean Ms. Carol?

Ahhh... Well you guys are way too young for me to even start explaining the Modern Social-Economic System, the MSES® and the Vaginal Penetration Prohibition, the **VPP**© [14] in the United States Inc. So I'll leave out the part about contraception being illegal. And wow.... You guys ask a lot of question!

What the heck is she talking about Mary?

Shhhh... I haven't a clue Jane! When I sleep with my daddy tonight I'll ask her. Now be quiet. (Mary, Jane's future DOM, is always a little parental around her little Bitch Gurlfriend).

Just know this Gurls, it's not that the human cunts hate you little official receptacles of Man-Juice®. They just feel deprived. Because women nowadays they have a lot less sex than you precious little Cock-Whores do and they be cum jealous of all the **Cockage**© [7.G5.4] you receive.

What's **Cockage**® Ms. Carol?

Never mind! And you'll find out soon enough. So, we've brought in Government volunteer ladies for each one of you Sissies today.

What? We're not gonna get cocks today, Miss Carol?

No, no I'm sorry, you little precocious little nymphets, we just have lady cunts today. But tomorrow I have big strong Policemen cuming to teach you submission. And guess what?

What? What? Miss Carol!

They're going to share their creamy Dick-Milk® with you! Isn't that exciting Gurls?

Wow! Cop Cum! Yummy! My favorite! Yay! Yah! (The Gurls all shout and start squirting Sissy-Cream all over the place). Squirt... Squirt... Squirt...

Oh **Jizz-Us**©. Donna! (Carol shouts for her Teachers Aid).

Yeah Carol? (Donna cums to the rescue). Geeeezzz... They're squirting! Agh! (Donna ducks out of the way of a Jizzzies stream spewing across the classroom).

Yeah! Can you get the Janitor to cum in and clean this mess up? There's Sissy-Jizz all over the classroom. Ugh! I'm stepping in it! Yuck! Uoooh...

Are we gonna get in trouble Ms. Carol? My Daddy says the government only wants to persecute us!

No, no, no... Maybe a little, but no, no, no... And like I said, all of the women here are owned by men who work as US Federal Civil Servants. So you will all be receiving in the mail an award certificate from the United States Department of Commerce Sissy Trade Division, the **STD** [23.33] for your meritorious submissive conduct.

Okay Gurls! So there's a Lady for each of you and they're going to humiliate you by pissing on you.

Ooooh! Miss Carol, Are they going to hurt us? (An intimidated frail voice whispers).

No, no, no... Tammy (EN05) not physically but you might feel emotionally not so good afterwards. But this reminds me.

Clap! Clap! Listen to me all of you Sissies (Ms. Carol claps her hands for attention). Before we go to the Gurls locker-room, I have to warn you about something.

Psssss…. (Martha, one of the little nymphs wets the floor she's so frightened). Sorry Miss Carol. They're gonna make us feel bad, aren't they? Sniff… Sniff…

Oh Geeezzz… The women pissing on you are not going to hurt you. They've all been to Sissy-Love-Therapy© **SLT** [15.6] and have been taught to suppress their anger and jealousy towards Sissies or are on heavy medication to remedy their hatred for you. They have all accepted their fate as ordinary Stud-baby making woman. Their families grow Stud babies and the babies have unusually large penises. So, they are not Sissy-Mommies, they're Stud-Mommies.

Ms. Carol do they really hate us?

Ahhhh… You see class (Carol pauses to think of a simple way to explain it to these four year olds). The old belief that all females are whores has been thrown off with the acceptance of Sissies assuming the role of Whores and not the human women, which I won't explain any further, cause I don't want your pretty little Sissy brains to explode.

What's a Stud® Miss Carol? My Mommy says my Dads a pansy, dickless Whore!

Haa ha… Good question Amy! Ahhhh… a Stud is a boy or a man with a big, Man-Shaft.

What's a Shaft Ms. Carol?

Ahhh... An erection, boner, penis, dick, dong, prick, rod, man-tool, pecker, you know the things you milk for cream everyday so you can grow-up and be cum healthy, hot-looking, dainty little Sissy® Gurls. And you cum-guzzlers are all so adorable!

Okay, all the government Ladies are ready Carol.

Thanks Donna! Oh, tell them to hold it in and we'll be right there.

Okay class, the government ladies have all drank a gallon of water and are ready to burst. So, I want each one of you to hold the hand or clit of the Sissy next to you and we're going to go to the Gurls locker-room. Then I want all of you to take-off your cloths, put all your stuff, your Sissy gear, but-plugs, jewelry, everything into your lockers and go to one of the shower stalls and assume a submissive position on your knees in front of a Stud-Lady with your mouths open nice and wide.

[1.3] RULES

A while later Carol announces the POM rules...

Hey **Carol**. (Donna has an update).

Yeah **Donna**, what's up? (EN07) They ready?

Yep! The Gurls are ready for the **POM** [4.D-G4.16]. Tssss... Carol, you got the guts to tell these little Nymphs what this is really all about?

Donna! Don't even go there! (Carol knows this is a low spot in her governments attempt to control the Sissy population and a way to pacify the Stud® women who are getting a lot less sex because of their position in the MSES).

What? You don't wanna tell em the truth! This POM ritual is just one big deception. It's just a way to get the human Stud-Female citizens to think the Sissies are sexually inferior to their pussies. Their husbands spend more time at a Whorehouse banging Sissy slaves than they do their old cunts!

Cool it Donna! I don't wanna get accuse of treason. Thanks for getting them ready. Clap! Clap! Okay Sissy Gurls, is everybody ready?

Yes Miss Carol (All the Gurls obediently chant in response).

Okay good! Here are the rules for the **Piss-On-Me**, the **POM** training. **Tammy** (EN10) go takeoff your swimsuit, we need you to be naked.

But Miss Carol I'll get the piss on me! And my Daddy is a Hardon-Vard® graduate and is a lawyer in Washingcum and he said we can sue you if you hurt my pussy!

Aghhh! These guys are gonna drive me crazy! Okay, the rules are as follows,

One, all Sissies must wear protective goggles.

Two, a Stud® woman or girl may gently slap the Sissy on her face to initiate the **POM**. Then the Sissy must make a formal request. The request should be first, a self-depreciating comment about oneself, specifically your inferiority to the human-race, followed by the request for the **POM**.

Three, after the Sissy has spoken the appropriate request to be pissed-on, the human women may slap the Sissy gently on her face as many additional times as they find necessary, but only if the Sissy has not shown the proper amount of humiliation. The Stud-Lady may also grab the Sissy firmly by the hair on her head and direct the Sissies mouth towards her pee-hole.

Four, all Sissies must ask the Stud-Baby-Maker Lady, politely and with gratitude to continue pissing on them.

Five, the Sissy must keep their mouths as open as possible the entire time of the pissing.

Six, the Sissy is required to willingly swallow all the piss which has been squirted into their mouths.

Seven, the Sissy must after the POM ritual, kiss and lick the piss off the pussy lips and pee-hole of the woman which pissed on them. Then thank them verbally for pissing on them and finally kiss the women's clit in appreciation.

Eight, after the Sissy has completely cleaned-up the lady, the Stud-Woman or girl may slap the Sissy on the cheek one final time, as a conclusion of the **Piss-On-Me** ritual.

[1.4] POM

Are the **Piss-On-Me** rules all clear to everybody?

Yeah Miss Carol... (The Gurls chant with reservation).

Yep! It's pretty explanatory Ms. Carol. We receive an undeserved disciplinary slap on the face and request the High-

Listen up everybody! In reality, the human women pissing on you are all appointed federally sponsored. And the United States government by the partial ratification of the USA Inc. Second **Cunt-Stitution** [17] has the exclusive right to piss-on whomever it wants to in this Cunt-tree. So it's important someone from our government humiliates you and not just family members, friends or your teacher. And it should be an honor to be pissed-on by your government. You should be proud you're an American Sissy® doing what she needs to do for her Cunt-tree.

Ooooh! Cock-God in heaven!

Sniffle, sniffle... sniffle... (Martha is extremely sensitive and being only as tall as Carol's snatch she raps her arms around one of her teacher's legs).

Honey, Oooh... **Martha** (EN09) this is what Sissydom® is all about in America! You Sissies are abused and humiliated so other people feel good about their useless selves and work harder.

Sniffle... Okay Miss Carol, sniffle...

Hey Martha, (Carol puts her arm around Martha's shoulder) tell you what sweetheart, I promise I'll piss-on you in the shower later after the Piss-On-Me, Okay? Kisss...

Ok Miss Carol. Sniffle... Sniffle... And my Daddy said to tell you he had a really goodtime at the Parent-Teacher conference and he liked your backdoor, whatever that means!

Huh! Okay, too much information! Mwah... Good Gurl, (Miss Carol pats Martha on the ass a few times, scooting her into a shower-stall).

The POM starts…

Wheeee…!!!... Okay, Sissies, Ladies, begin! (Carol blows the whistle and shouts).

Shower Stall [1]: Slap... slap... slap… (The Stud classified ladies are all aggressively slapping the Sissy children into submission), Slap! Here's another one bitch! Are you ready to be pissed-on yet? Slap! My husband bought a Sissy as a pet and he's divorcing me! Slap! Slap!

Ouch! Ow! Geeezzz… My hair Lady! Yes Ma'am, please piss-on me I'm only a mutant Sissy, I'm NOT human! I was created in a god dam test tube and implanted in my mommy's vagina! Piss-on me please.

Slap.... slap.... Pissssss.... Aaaah! Yeah… You freak!

Shower Stall [2]: Miss my name is Mary and I don't deserve your piss! (Mary is highly sophisticated compared with the other Sissies her age and knows enough about the MSES to response with the appropriate replies). I'm not special like you. Will you please honor me by give me a golden shower? I'm a Homo-Sis-Sapien, inferior to humans. I willfully submit to you! Kisss… (Mary blows an air-kiss at the lady).

Oh my! You sweet little thing! Tap! (Just a very light gentle loving tap on Mary's cheek). Do you want my piss now Sissy Gurl? Kiss, beg me for my piss you horny little Gurl! Mwah…

Mwah… Yes, yes, yes… Only if you think I'm worthy of it. Please Lady please piss-on me! Please... Ummm… Kisss... I want every golden drop of your piss! Forgive me, I'm just a Sissy. I want to swallow your sweet Stud Lady piss!

Okay you good, little, well behaved, Sissy! Open that pretty little mouth of yours nice and wide. Aaaagh! Pissss... Aaaah... Pisss.... Aaaah...

Guk, Gak... Glrck... Gulp! (Mary gulps it down).

Hmmm... Lick... Lick... kisss. Thank you Lady (Mary says looking up at the beautiful mature lady with a submissive puppy-dog stare then bats her eye lashes for effect and blows a kiss). Mwah...

Thank you Mary for being such a wonderful obedient little love toy for all of our strong hard working men. Hmmm... You're such a beautiful Sissy Child, hmmm, kiss.

Ma'am, it was an honor to be pissed-on by you. Mwah...

Oh! You adorable little creature! They call you Gurls monkeys, but that's so untrue. What's ID number? I'll call your parents for a Play-Date appointment. Mwah... Adorable! Mwah...

Shower Stall [3]:   Piss-on me Cunt! (The Gurl says in a derogatory manner, rolling her eyes with a smirk on her face).

Why you miserable little... Slam! Slam! Bam! (The Lady strikes the kid hard with front and back of her hand).

Ouch! Ow! You Cunt! (The Sissy is knocked to the floor by the blows). Geeezz... What's your problem?

Smack! (The woman lays a few more good hard whacks to the disrespectful Gurls face). You pathetic tiny faggot! Slap. Slap... Slap. Not the appropriate way to ask me bitch! Slap, slap. You're just a make-believe cunt! Slap! You're not even a real girl!

Ouch! Ow! I'm sorry Lady, go ahead and piss-on me! I'm a dickless little Boy-Bitch® Please piss-on me!

Smack! Smack! Smack! Not appropriate!

Ouch! Ok, ok! I'm a little boy that likes taking dick-up my ass! Okay? And Lady, we're preschooler kids! We don't say cuss words and slang like faggot!

Slap! Pissss.... I work for the Government! I can say whatever I want! You're right you little faggot! Aaaah... Pisss, (piss flying everywhere). Aaah... Pisssss.... You were born in a test-tube! You don't know what the freak your sexual orientation is! You're just an anomaly! Sissies should be eradicated from the face of the earth!

Shower Stall [4]: Slap.... Slap.... Slap.... Slap.... Ouch! Slap, Slap, Ouch! You call your shit-hole a cunt!

Lady it's a **Vaganus**®. The USA Inc. government own the patent!

Slap! Shut-up! Slap! (The dominatrix yells really loud and Miss Carol cums over to observe the ritual).

Shut-Up... !!!...

Ouch! Ow! You're hurt me... Ow! Miss Carol!

I'm a real cunt! I have the right to hurt you! Isn't that right Miss Carol?

Yes you do, to a certain degree, yes continue. (Miss Carol stays to watch for abuse).

You're just a faggot little queer boy, Slap, (The Stud-Lady spits in the Gurls face). SLAP…!!!... SLAP…!!!...

Ow! Ouch! Ms. Carol! She's hurting me! (By law, Carol can't interfere with the ritual but can file a report afterwards).

Piss... Pisss... Aaaah! Pissssss.... Aaaagh! Your breeding parents should be arrested! They breed for money! You're just an animal! Bred as a Sex-Toy® for humans to enjoy! Slap! You're nothing but a fucking monkey! Pissssss.... Pissssss....

Shower Stall [5]: You non-vagina little sex animal. Sap... Slap... Slap. I haven't had a dick in my cunt in months because of you little boys dressed-up like Gurls.

Oh please Lady! Piss on me! Just get it over with!

Slap... Slap... You belligerent little bitch!

Ouch! Ow! Okay, okay… No more, please stop!

Pisss... Pisssss… Aaaaaah! Pissssss... You pathetic male Sissy piece-of-shit! You queer Boy-Bitch! Slap! Pissss.... Pissssss..... Aaaaah! Slap! You're not even HUMAN! Swallow Bitch! Slap!

Ouch! Geeezzz…. (The Stud classified lady tightly grips the victim by the hair on her head and force her to swallow the piss). Gak, Gak… Glrck… Ugh! (The Sissy throws-up on the lady).

Ahhhhhhh...!!!...

Shower Stall [6]: Slap! Slap! Slap! Slap! Faggot! Scank! (The lady shouts in rage).

Ouch! Ow! Sniffle... sniffle... please lady it hurts! Sniffle...

Ma'am! Ma'am! Derogatory comment and slang cuss words are not allowed. Thank you! (Carol tones down the insults).

Sure Carol! Don't you dare cry! Slap...You little gay piece-of-shit whore! My husband left me for one of you Whores! Slap!

Yes, (The Sissy is crying out of fear), please piss on me Lady. Sniffle… I'm a whore! I'm only a Sissy, piss-on me please!

Yeah that's right! Beg for it bitch! Slap! You're just a science experiment! Slap... Slap! Slap. One that went horribly wrong! Sissies are supposed to reduce human violence? I'll show you how that worked out! Slap... Slap... Slap... Pissss....

Ow! Ouch…!!!... Guk, Gak, Guk… Glrck…

You mutant freak! Aaaah! Pissss... Aaaah! Pisssss..... Yeah!

Shower Stall [7]: Thank you Ma'am for taking out a moment of your busy day to train me. Will you please piss-on me Lady? It's my civic duty to be humiliated in public. You'll be improving my awareness of my inferiority! Can I please eat your pussy?

Okay! You seem like a very nice Sissy-Bitch. I was skeptical at first, but my husband brought a few of you Whores home with him and it turned out to be a goodtime. You Sissies are actually pretty good in bed!

Yes Ma'am. Sissies are here on earth for one reason, to make humans happy by providing sexual enjoyment to reduce human violence.

Very good! I like your response and realization of your position in life. Fux News keeps pumping out all kinds of stories about how Sissies all a bunch farm breed dumb little cunts. I guess you're not like they say you are!

No Ma'am! My parents and teacher tell me it's my obligation to submit my body to human sexual advances. Mwah…

Okay, sorry! I gotta relieve myself. Open your mouth wide little Gurl! Ooooh! Pissssss.... Ooooh! That feels sooo... good! Pisssssss.... swallow it princess!

Guk, Gak, Guk… Glrck… Gulp… (Jane takes the stream).

Oooooh… I couldn't hold it in anymore. God-of-Cocks! I dumped a gallon on and in you. Mwah… Uuoough! It feels so relieving to piss-on a pretty little Sissy like you! Mwah… You're so tiny and dainty! Cute, very cute. My husband likes little **B-Type** [1.2] Bitches like you. Mwah…

Thank you Lady for pissing on me, your piss tastes really good! And it makes me feel proud. I'm doing something for my cum-munity and government.

You're well cum dear. Hmmm... And you sound like you have some civic pride. What's your name Sissy-Gurl?

I'm Jane, Jane Goldberg (Jane politely kisses and licks the piss off the Ladies cunt and slides her dainty little hand up her aroused twat). Thank you Lady (The Lady pats Jane on the head). Mwah... Mwah...

Uooch! Cock-God! Oooh my, Jane Gurl, you know how to eat and fist a cunt! Aaaagh! Yeah! Ooooch I'm Cuming! Oooch! Oh, Jane, I have to get your parents phone number and your Sissy serial number. Ooooch! I'll have to visit your Whorehouse. I need more of your loving. Mwah...

Thank you Stud-Lady. Mwah... Kiss... Hmm, (Jane's making out with the lady). I'm available for Play-dates too. Mwah... Mwah... Ummm... I'll go home with you...Ummm...

Shower Stall [8]: Slap... Slap... Slap... Slap...

Ouch! Ow! Please don't hurt me!

Shut-Up...!!!...

You're a God Dam Monkey! Slap! You Humanoid Freak! Pisssss... Pisss... Slap... Slap, Slap... You are an ANIMAL!

Ouch! Ow! Okay! Hey stop pulling my hair!

Pisssss... Pissss.... Slap... Slap... Slap... Slam...

Sometime later...

Shower Stall [24]: Slap.... Slap... Slap... I'm a Federal Employees wife! I shit-on people for a living! You should bow to me! I'm sponsored by the USA Inc. Government who actually owns your little queer asshole! Slap… Slap… Slap… Slap…

Okay, okay, piss-on me! Funny my Daddy has a different opinion of the Government! He says the entire Cunt-gress is a bunch of assholes!

You little…

Piece-of-Shit… !!!…

How dare you say that! You barn-yard animal, YOU'RE NOT EVEN FUCKING HUMAN! Slap… Slap… Slap… You're nothing but a god-dam animal…!!!… You're a monkey! Bred into existence in a fucking laboratory!

After everyone was pissed on…

Okay little ones (Carol call an end to the ritual). Everybody's done. Let's take our showers, cum on. Let's get all your yummy piss off of you! It's going to be lunch-time soon let's not take too long. And thanks to all of you gals for cuming in today, the kids look like they all had their fill of humiliation. Good job!

[1.5] LADIES

Carol thanks the volunteers…

Yeah anytime, thanks for the goodtime and for inviting the Federal Stud Ladies **Auxiliary** [25.41] to the training, Miss Carol.

Yeah sure, sure! The **Stud Ladies Auxiliary** has always supported our Sissy training. Some of the kids look like they got a couple of extra smacks. But, hey, it was their first formal **Piss-On-Me**. So it's natural for them to need additional encouragement, be it slaps or hair pulling. Besides according to the United States Sissy Psychology [25.42] rulebook, it's better for animals like Sissies to feel rejection now at an early development age than later.

Oh yeah Carol, definitely. They were all reasonably well behaved little boy-cunts, very feminine, very prissy and cute.

Hmm.... Yeah Carol. They're adorable little faggots in their kiddy size platform shoes. (Most of these wealthy Stud Ladies live privileged lives and have an extremely low opinion of the whole Sissy thing in general).

Right, right, and just a FYI about derogatory language, words like faggot for example. The MSES® rules and the Sissy Rights Act, the **SRA** [17.34] are clear about the use of disrespectful accusation regarding sexual orientation. Here at Sissy-World© preschool we keep it clean, no slang or cuss words.

Sure, sure Ms. Carol. But at our stations in life, we just ignore all that **Bonobo-Way** [22.19] lifestyle bullshit. I mean, we're not idiots, we all know our husbands are screwing around with these little monkey Gurls!

Yeah Carol, relax. Their just sex-pets! And personally, as long as my man isn't in bed with another human female, I really don't give a crap if he's banging a Sissy Whore!

Ahhhh... Okay Ladies (Carol knows she put her foot in her mouth and tries to back-peddle her way out of it). I can assure you they're not just screw holes, these pure Breed-from-Birth Sissies are great Cunt-Munchers too.

Really, do tell Miss Carol?

Believe me! They can munch a cunt. Wooo! (Carol reaches down and rubs her clit). I tell you, these little mutants are awesome Pussy-Eaters®. They're always up my skirt taking a lick at my baby-making hole! We train them well here at Sissy-World© preschool.

Really? Well I'll volunteer for Pussy-Eating training. Your precious class of Sissies can eat-out my cunt anytime. God knows since the invention of Sissies, my husband doesn't visit my fuckhole with his tongue anymore.

Well, I'll call you when we have our, **Lady-Licking**® training.

Cool, thanks Miss Carol, see you soon.

[1.6] LOCKER ROOM

The Gurls reflect on the POM…

Okay, class, let's go to the lunchroom, cum on everybody lets go. Pick-up all your things. Whoa! (Something heavy falls on her Carol's foot).

Whoops! Sorry Miss Carol. (Jenifer says with an embarrassed look on her face).

Wow! Jenifer, you always carry a double-headed dildo in your gym bag? Okay anyway. You all need some Dick-Milk nutrition in your little bellies.

I like piss mixed with pussy juice, it's not a bad combination (Jane comments).

Yeah but I'm hungry for **Man-Cream**® [18.13a]. Let's milk as many dicks as we can and then sixty-nine with each other if there's time before the bell. Mwah…

Mwah… Yeah, for-sure! I'm with you Mare! (Jane grabs Mary's hand and smiles). You're my buddy. Mwah…

I'm dying to suckle on your Clit® Jane it's like a big tit nipple. Hmmm, kisss.

Yeah, me too Mary, I can't go a day without sucking on your big cum-nozzle, hmmm… kisss. Mwah…

Jane, did you see those cunts slapping around our friends!

Yeah they were slapped way-to-many times. I swear their faces looked out of alignment!

They may gently slap you

Yeah GENTLY my ass! The slaps were more like bunches! Talk about Sissy abuse!

Yeah, those old Stud® ladies should have stayed home and popped out Stud-Babies or something. And I heard them shouting, Boy-Bitch a lot. What don't they understand about Sissification? We're **Gurls**® with little dicks! We're not boys!

Yeah, we're Sissy-Bitches not boy-bitches! What's wrong with those Stud® Breeding Mommies anyway? We're not even in the same **Genome** [18] as these humans!

Oh, yeah, I know Mary. Our human moms are super-cool compared to those angry mean, wacko, Stud Ladies.

Well Jane, I think it's because they're not allowed by law to be registered Whores® like us, this is the problem.

Yeah but they can eat-out each other's girly cunts. There's nothing wrong with Pussy-Eating®, it's even in the Sissydom® Olympics now!

Yeah Mary but this could be one of the reasons those woman were in such a pissed-off mood and slapping the shit-out of our Sissy friends. And I just played a psychology game with the Lady. I mean, she was an attractive woman. I didn't mind her piss, I kinda liked it.

Yeah, yeah me too. Mwah… And I like the humiliation and being submissive, this is what being a JAS Gurl® is all about. But our friends just got assaulted by a bunch of sexually deprived women. So do you think they're all on medication?

Oh Yeah! Huh, are you kidding? Their psychiatrists probably told them to slap the shhh…it out of us to vent their anger!

Hey Mary, Kiss.... Kiss, do you want to piss-on me later? Yeah Baby, sure, it'll be cool. Kiss, would you piss-on me too? Mwah...

Of course you're my love-buddy I'll always share my piss and **Sissy-Poop**® [4.D-G1.37] with you. I'd share everything with you. Kisssss.... Hmmmm. Mwah…

Thanks Mary. Hey Mary? Mwah…

Mwah... Yeah Jane. Mwah...

Are we hooked-up?

Haa... haaa... ha... Oh Jane! Where did you hear that?

I told my Mom we do 69 and share our Clities and she said we're, hooked-up. What does that mean? Mwah...

Mwah... Yeah Jane. Haaa haa ha. Yeah, we're hooked-up, me and you Lover Gurl. Kiss... Kissss. Stick with me Jane and you'll get all the love you need.

Promise? Mwah...

Mwah... I promise Lover... Kissss.... Hmmm...

[1.7] LUNCH

Preschool lunch...

Here we are in the lunchroom. There, over there, two milking stations next to each other. Cum on Jane!

Yeah, let's milk dicks side-by-side. Oh Mary kisss me! (The Gurls are all over each other). Mwah... Mwah...

Jane, kiss.... hmmm... (Licking and twirling tongues, the two of them put on a display). Kisss... Mwah... Oh! I love your tongue Jane, lick.

Mary I just want to hold you forever! Mwah...

Oh **Jane**, you sweet little Sissy **Bitch**® [1.A2.2]. Put your arms around me, Gurl, hold me tight. Jane someday I'll be your **DOM**® [1. A2.1]. Kiss me again Babe! I love you Gurl! Hmm.... Ooooh do my mouth with your tongue, French kiss me like my **SIT**® [1.A2.4] Daddy does, Lover! Mwah... Hmmm.... Sooo good! I want to make love to you all night! I wanna sleep with you Jane.

Mary! Ooooh! My nipples are so hard for you Gurl, tweak em hard! Tweak my nipples! Take your Clit-Sock® off I gotta blow you! Mwah...

Jane! Not here. Mwah...

No problem! I'll bend over! Just screw me here in the lunch-line Mary! I want to be your Bitch! Mwah... Mwah...

Caught in the act...

HEY! HEY! You two! Let's put it off till after school please! It's not a kissing contest or a Whorehouse! It's a lunchroom. Save the making-out stuff for later. Gurls, get to your milking stations and drain some balls. Thank you.

Yes Miss **Donna**. Hee.... hee... Busted! Hee... hee... hee... he... heee. Miss Donna is just jealous I have a hot little Sissy Bitch Gurlfriend.

Yeah! Two hot little Sissy whores making-out, can't get hotter than that. Hee.... heee, (Jane & Mary making little girly laughing sounds), hee.... heee. Yeah, we're hooked-up! Hee... heee... hee.... Mwah... Mwah...

[1.8] MILKING

Well, I'm hungry for some Man-Cream® anyway! We gotta have our **RDA** [4.D-G1.4.29] of Jizzzies!

Okay Bitch®, me and you after school!

I hear you Gurlfriend and I'm gonna be all over you Sissy-Gurl.

Let's not get caught, my parents aren't going to be home at my house. Let's go there? Slurp... Slurp... Slurp. Next... gulp... gulp.

Next! (The Gurls are swallowing and slurping down lunch), slurp, Oooh! Next! Gulp... Oooh! Hmmm.... I love swallowing Jizzzies. Wow! Huge load I almost couldn't swallow it all.

Thirty minutes later...

Next... Gulp. Oooh! Hmmm... Yeah, my belly's full of Man-Milk®.

Dill-a-ling, dill-a-ling, dill-a-ling, dill-a-ling...

There's the bell! Lunch is over Gurls return to your classes. (Ms. Donna shouts as she stands there looking deprived, licking her lips, staring at all the non-swallowed lunch-line ejaculations on the floor).

Okay Miss Donna! Hey, you look kinda hungry, you want me to snowball you a load?

No! Sorry, it's not permissible for Teacher-Aids to sexually interact with Sissy students.

Oh! Sorry... (Jane feels like helping so she quickly unclasps her full, ready to burst Clit-Sock, ties a knot on it).

Whoops! (Then Jane purposely bumps into Ms. Donna slipping the sock it into her jacket pocket). Hope you like Gurly-Cream. Mwah... (Jane says with a mischievous smile, blows an air-kiss and winks at Ms. Donna).

After lunch talk about Opt-Out...

Wow! Now I know why she's so cranky all the time. But Hey! I must have gulped down sixty-nine loads!

I know! And Mare, those smaller cum-hoses were sure easy to pop a load out of today.

Yeah, yeah... Jane they were really small. It's because they're Non-Stud (NS) kids, they're called NS Kids. They cum to integration schools with their nuts-sacks bursting full.

Oh yeah, I forgot. The Non-Stud kids go without blow jobs at home. And the only place a **Non-Stud** [1.A1.4] boy can get a blow-job is at an integrated school. I wonder why Non-Stud boys are in our Sissy preschool.

Jane the Non-Stud kids can only enroll in integrated schools if they do this thing called a **class Opt-Out,** a COO [13].

What's that, Mare?

Well my Daddy told me if the Non-Stud, NS working class family wants to be cum a Sissy or a Stud classified family, they do an MSES class Opt-Out.

Oh! Well it sounds complicated.

For sure Jane, life is different for Non-Stud families.

True, there's no one at home to have any sex with, poor guys. It's illegal for Non-Stud families to screw each other.

Yeah, incest sex is illegal for everyone except Gene-Modified Sissy families like ours. It's a **Sex Law** [7]. I was in bed with my Dad last night and he showed me the, Permissible Sex laws in Appendix G of the Sissydom Manual.

Yeah those poor NS guys, I feel sorry for them. I'm so glad I'm a Sissy®.

Me too Jane. And glad our homes are both Sissy Whorehouses® too.

Oh yeah! We can have all the **Man-Cream**® [18.13a] we want!

Yeah you can't beat it! But hey those sexually deprived Non-Stud families could join a Holy Cockolic Church, an **HCC** [9] if they're into being sexually religious.

Ahhh… No not really Jane, only a Sissy or Stud-Breeding Family can join an **HCC**. Religion in the USA Inc. is either sanctioned and or sponsored. Not available to everyone in the MSES®. See Amendment one in the Second **Cunt-Stitution** [17.1].

Really? Now you're quoting the Cunt-Stitution? You're only four years old Mare!

Well I heard the Non-Stud Churches won't even let them do each other, not at church or at home, just like the old Christians.

Wow! That sucks! The Non-Studs are super deprived and horny! Heee... heee... hee. And they have really small little dicks, heee... hee... hee.

Yeah but if they were Sissies they would have monster clits! Heeee.... heee.... hee....

Hey! At an HCC, the Stud® men can have sex with anyone.

No! They can't Jane! The married Stud husbands can only do it in a vagina if the he owns the woman. And Sissies in any hole. But a Sissy-Breeding® Mommy can only take dick in the ass-pussy, or what they call the Human Female Anus, the **HFA®** [4.D-G3.16]. Oh! Or face-fucked in the mouth, their baby-making-vaginas are forbidden.

Wow! No pussy action? (Jane sighs) Uooogh!

Well, the Studs can be put in a **FEMA** [4.D-G7.13] camp for cheating on a wife if they stick their dicks in a vagina they don't own. I mean they have to be married to the cunt and have ownership of the hole they stick their dick into. And here in the United States Inc. they cut off the guy's dick if they screw a vagina they're not married to! It's called, Infidelity.

Ow! Heee hee... Yeah! So where did you learn all this social engineering stuff, Mary? Did your Daddy show you it in the Sissy Manual? Heee... heee... hee... hee.

Yes Jane, smartass! While I sucked off my Daddies beautiful Sissy-Cocklet®. Heee... heee. Yeah intercourse is forbidden with human female Girl-Pussies.

Right, sex is VERY restricted with humans. Human-to-Human sex or HHS [7.G1.15] is a real No-No. I'm just glad I'm not a female girl! Or for that matter a human!

Me too, I love our life-style having sex the **Bonobo-Way** [22.19]. And Jane the really weird part is, human females are biologically whores from birth, they're always in heat, but society keeps them in chains sexually.

Hey but Stud-Men, **SM** [1.2] have a big selection of holes to have sex with at a Cockolic Church.

 Oh yeah! There's always plenty of young Sissy pussy **Vaganus**® [14.O1.6] to train at an HCC.

I know like during mass if we're Altar-Gurls and assist the Priest during mass. I love the part of mass where we receive Holy **Cum-Union**® [9.HS.2].

Yeah and if not during mass, after mass the parish has recreational Prayer-Sex to spiritually enlighten the Sissies through Cock-Worship of all the faithful Studs in the parish.

Right all the female girls and woman can only munch on each other's twats.

Twat?

A pussy you dummy!

Dill-a-ling, dill-a-ling, dill-a-ling, dill-a-ling….

[1.9] HIDE-THE-BANANA

You Sissies being the Gurls go douche-out your precious little holes and get them ready to take the boys big make-believe penises. Also the one's playing Gurls, put some sexy lingerie cloths on.

Ms. Carol? Do we have to wear stockings and high-heels too?

Yes! Of course, this is what whores wear. Okay meet here in ten minutes to play Hide-the-Banana. Lisa and Dana stop sucking your clities and go get ready. God-of-Cocks! These Sissies can't control their horniness at all, their all over each other.

Thirty minutes later...

Okay Gurls! Listen up! The rules are as follows! When the Gurl pops a load out of her Sissy-Clit, hopefully into her Clit-Sock®, Jane! (Ms. Carol gives Jane a stern look). Or has a **Sissygasm**® [12.L1.10]. Or in other words, ejaculates in their bottom hole.

Ms. Carol, is my bottom-hole my Vaganus?

Huh! Yes! Yes, also it's called your Lovehole.

Cool! That's what my Daddy calls it!

Great! Then, you reverse the roles. The Sissy playing the part of the big dicked macho dude, once she has pulled out her big fake dick, she removes the man cloths and the strap-on.

Ms. Carol? Do we pull the dildo out of the Bitch first?

Yes! Pull it out and give the strap-on to the Sissy-Gurl you just screwed. So the Gurls be cum the Boys and use it on the bitch, which just screwed her sweet Sissy-Puss®. And you might be confused…

Ms. Carol? Ms. Carol? What if the Gurly-Boy wants to eat-out her Bitches Creampie?

Wow! Okay, let's not! You can do that at home with Mommy and Daddy.

Okay Ms. Carol. My Mommy likes when I eat-out my Daddy's Creampie.

I'm sure she does! And again, you Sissies playing the part of the Gurl should go put on fancy lingerie, make-up and get sexy. And make sure you all have your Sissy Clit-Socks on those, precious little cum spewing Clits. Jane! (Carol gives naughty Jane the evil-eye because she never wears a sock).

Yes Ms. Carol (The Gurls all go scampering away to get ready).

Gurls, I don't want to see a cummy mess all over the place after the Hide-the-Banana game. Geeezzz! You two nymphos! Nicky and Tina! Stop eating out each other's Cum-Socks and go get ready!

Much, much, later…

Okay Jane, you got your sock on Baby?

Yeah Lover! I'm ready to get laid! Bang me!

Okay bend over Bitch. Look at my big piece of man-meat. I'm gonna do you so hard you little whore! You're my Slut! (Mary waves the enormous dildo at Jane).

Yeah bring it Mary. Ooooh! Ahhh… All the way Mare!

Whoa! Jane you took all of it up your coochee in one thrust. Ooooooh! Mwah… Mwah…

Mary, you know I take big dick! Screw my cunt it's yours Babe! Aaaagh! Ooooh! Mary I'm your Bitch? Bang-me!

Yeah Jane! You're mine, I own you Bitch! Oooh! Love Me! Ooooh! Your hole is sooo wide and juicy! Mwah…

You know I've had my Sissy hole widened every birthday.

Yeah, all Sissies have their Vaganus® opened. The Compensation Orifice Widening Procedures, the **COWP** [4.D-G1.2]. Ooooh! Aaagh! It's called a sphincterotomy; tell me something I don't know!

Aaaagh! I love you. Get me pregnant! Mwah… Mwah… Mwah… Knock me up!

If I could I would! I love you too Jane. Mwah… Ummm… Yeah…

Mary when are we going to tell our parents?

No Jane! We're secret lovers! Aaaagh!

Ooooh! I'm Cumming! I'm Cumming! Aaaagh! Jane! Dam Gurl! Take-it Baby! Ahhhh… Splat… Splat… Splat… (Jane wipes off her Sock and ejaculates long ropes of Sissy Jizzzies all over the place).

Pull it out! I wanna give you a facial! (Jane points her miniature Gurly-Dick at Mary's face). Splat… Splat… Splat…

Jane! Jane! You took your sock off and shot your load all over the place Sissy-Gurl! Where's your Clit-Sock? Oh Gurl! I told you not to take it off SLAP! Jane you little Bitch! You can only hose me when we're playing at home in private! I told you that!

Hey, I wanna spray you Baby! I want you to see my Love-Juice shooting out for you! I love you Mary. Mwah…

Mwah… I know you do Gurlfriend, but Jane I want it to be special with us. I wanna have intimate sex in private with my Gurl. And you're going to get us both in trouble. You made a mess!

Wow! Check it out? Cool! Annie's licking my Clit-Cream® off the floor!

JANE! What did I tell you? (Ms. Carol is fuming).

Oh crap! It's Miss Carol! Hide behind me Jane.

Cum here please, not you Mary Dune. Mary, thank you for reminding Jane about her sock. Now go put the strap-on away in the toy box, it's time to get ready to go home.

Yes, Miss Carol (Mary looks at Jane sternly and silently speak, I told you).

Annie! Annie Sweetheart. Stop licking Jane's cum off the floor please. Oh my God-of-Cocks! These little Sissy kids are too much! Aaaaaagh! They abandon all sense of normality.

Jane as for you, cum here.

Sniffle... Sniffle... Sniffle... Yes Miss Carol (Jane is so embarrassed she can't even look the Teacher in the eyes).

Jane, I think I made myself clear about the Clit-Sock® when I was giving the game instructions to the class.

Sorry Miss Carol. Sniffle... Sniffle... Sniffle... Mom and Dad told me I have issues because I'm a Bitch®.

Sure, I known what you are Jane, that's not my point. I know I sent a memo home with you so your parents could read my note about you never wearing your cum collecting Clit-Sock®.

Yes, Miss Carol they got it and my Mom gave me trouble about it. My Daddy is a **SIT** [1.4] and he said I have an obligation to be a good Gurl. Sniffle... Sniffle... Sniffle...

Jane, Honey I'm not trying to punish you sweetheart. And hey, I empathize with the Sissy culture. Being a Whore® in our modern society is hard for little Gurls like you. Look at me Jane! (Carol goes down on one knee to be at eye level with Jane).

Sniffle... Sniffle... Sniffle... (Jane looks into Carol's eyes with a heart-breaking puppy-dog look).

Huh! Jane Sweetheart... (The innocent look on Jane's face dispelled all sense of discipline Carol had). I love each and every one of you.

Sniffle.... sniffle.... Yes, Miss Carol. Are you mad at me? Sniffle... Sniffle... Sniffle... I'm sorry... Sniffle...

Huh! (Carol sighs). You know when you go to elementary school it will be harder to break the rules Jane. And the rule is you can't just shoot your Jizzies all over the place.

Yes Miss Carol. Sniffle... Sniffle... Sniffle...

Because the cream you catch in your sock is very valuable. You're supposed to drink Jizzies from your Cum-Sock® or you can share it with other Sissies. And this is one of the reasons why Sissies wear cum collecting socks on their pretty little Sissy-Clits.

Okay, Sniffle... Sniffle... Sniffle...

Jane Sissies have special things happening in their little bodies which make them produce more Jizzies than a normal human person. A normal penis of a man produces about two ounces per cum load and Sissies produce many times that per cum load. Not only more per load but more loads per day as well. Sometimes 69 or more loads a day. And this is a lot of Sissy-Cream sweetheart.

Wait a minute, Cathy! You need to change your sock! It looks like it's going to pop and make a mess.

You see Jane? Sissies are biologically engineered to be cum factories. Your cum socks are always filling up. Jane if you don't start putting a cum-catching sock on, I mean a **Clit-Sock®** on your precious little cum-hose, I'm going to sit you far away from Mary. And not let you play together.

NO! (Jane lashes out at Carol). I'm hers. Mary is my buddy!

Jane is this what you want Sweetheart?

Sniffle... Sniffle... NO! I need to sit next to Mary. Sniffle, sniffle... I wanna belong to her!

Yes, I know Jane! You and Mary are doing what's called, Sissy-Bonding. Jane I have a degree in Sissyology, I know exactly what's going on between you and Mary. You can't fool me.

I want Mary to own me! Sniffle... Sniffle...

Exactly! And someday that might happen! So if Mary is going to be your DOM® than you need to start listening to her. You have to behave yourself and start to obey her. When she tells you to put your cum-catcher on and keep it on, you do it. And Honey, if you do this I'll let you sit next to Mary all the time, Okay? Mwah...

Ummm... (Jane is slurping away at Miss Carol).

Jane! Jane! Stop licking my pussy please, Aaaaaaah! Stop it! Help me dear Jizz-Us! Ahhhh... Ouuugh! That feels sooo good!

Dill-a-ling... Dill-a-ling... Dill-a-ling...

There's the bell! Okay, it's time to go Jane. Oh please stop it! I see your Mom's car outside. Wow! And Jane, I'm gonna have a little talk with your Mom about going under Miss Carol's skirt and putting your tongue up your teacher's coochee.

Miss Carol? What's a Coochee?

Huh! In my case, it's a vagina. Jane. Now go get your stuff it's time to go home. Mwah... Mwah...

Yes Miss Carol. I love you teacher. Sniffle... Sniffle...

Aaaaaaagh! Jane you adorable little angel! Mwah! Get going your mom's waiting! I'm so glad this day is over!

[1.10] TEACHER TALK

This little **B-Type** [1.A2.2] Gurl is just sexually out of control. But dam! Donna she sure knows how to eat pussy.

Oh yeah Jane is just a wild child! Carol I caught Jane and Mary making-out and feeling-up each other in the lunchroom today.

Nymphos!

Yeah but hey, you got a smile on your face she must really know how to eat pussy.

Oh Jane? Huh! Yeah that kid is definitely getting instructions from her mother at home. She had her dainty little hand up inside me in no time, Ahh! She's a professional pussy pleaser.

Wow, I wish I was her mother, I wouldn't mind wild little Jane munching on my snatch or fisting me every night!

Well, we could invite Jane's Mom over for a Girl's night. And get some pussy eating demonstrations.

Yeah, it sounds like fun, we can make a daisy chain. Girls and Gurls.

Sure I know Sandy.

Who?

Oh Jane's mom, Mrs. Goldberg's name is Sandy, I know her from Church. I'll give her call.

So do you and Sandy do anything together at Cockolic Church?

Oh sure! While the men are screwing, I'm sorry, having recreational Prayer-Sex with the Sissies or doing the Sissy Mommies in the ass, aka registered **HFA** [4.D-G3.16], us church girls usually are eating each other's cunts out, I like Lady-Licking® for religious proposes.

Oh yeah? Any tasty treats to eat, maybe Stud-Creampies® Uoooh! Uoooh! Are the Ladies lactating? I love suckling Titty-Milk!

Sure, sure, well you know all the families in a HCC are Sissy or Stud®, right? Lots of body fluids!

Yeah, yeah… Eight inches or longer, Carol.

Right Donna, I'm from a Stud family. The men are all hung like horses and real heavy creamers, plenty of **Dick-Milk**® [18.13a].

Yeah but Carol, FYI and this is just between us Girls, the large pricks in my family are mostly the effects of the government issued **PED** [4.D-G1.8] meds they take.

Oooh! Sorry Donna, I didn't know. So your family was a Non-Stud who did an **Opt-Out** [13] to Stud Class?

Yeah **Carol**, we traded up to Stud Class. Mind you, the men in my family weren't too small, maybe six inches on the average, the typical size. But they definitely needed the **PED** drugs to get long enough to Opt-Out. And Rank matters. The Stud-Cock

Ranking, the SCR [5.E2.1] is tightly regulated. The PED meds cum in different potency. And the potencies and price ranges of the PED meds varies.

Wow! **Donna**, so the dude has a dick length related to his wallet. Wow! The penis enlargement drugs are really expensive!

Oh Yeah! Our whole family is in debt because of the Opt-Out drugs, but Carol what was the alternative? To live in servitude to the Stud Class! No way! And hey the bankers always make their cut. I mean when haven't American's not been in debt? So what were you saying about HCC?

So yeah **Donna**, all the Stud mothers at church come fully loaded with their husbands seed.

Oh! How can you tell?

Well you know Studs are always big shooters, the drugs keep their balls fully loaded with **Jizzies**®. So the Stud mommies cum to church with tasty cream filled cunts to eat-out. Plenty of fresh **Man-Cream**® dripping out and down their legs, you can tell just by the smell of sex during the mass. And you know there's nothing better than the smell of fresh **Creampies**®.

Oh Wow! It sounds delicious! I can just imagine what the Cream or Poop Severity is in the Church. I bet it's off the charts?

Oh yeah Donna! You mean the COPS rating?

Yeah! The Cream or Poop Severity, the **COPS** [18.13a].

Yep! Off the charts. And the Stud-Family daughters always come to Cockolic Church too, if you like to eat fresh, young, virgin snatch. And besides the new Sissy-Breeding® formula the young Gurls take nowadays makes their virgin Stud pussies squirt gallons of Girly juice.

Hmm... Ummm...Yummy! Girly pussies squirting Pussy-Juice®. Yummy! It sounds like there're plenty of really tasty cunts available?

Oh yeah **Donna**! Lots of Girl-on-Girl action. Actually, it's one big LGBT fuckfest! Lots of religiously condoned sex! Awesome Cum-munity orgies!

Well hey **Carol**, maybe I'll join your HCC. I'm a cum-hungry snatch-eating slut too!

[1.11] CLUBING

Donna the Slut invites Carol...

Hey Carol, talk about sluts, and this has nothing to do with **Cockolicism**© [9.B.3]. Just between us Stud Gurls. I know about this secret illegal **Non-Stud** [4.D-G3.21] men's club, well it's really a whorehouse. They have hundreds and hundreds of super horny Non-Studs waiting for a chance to mount a real woman's Ass-Pussy® aka HFA.

Ahhh... Donna I think I know where this is going.

Carol! These guys wanna mount chicks like us instead of a substitute mutant **Sissy-Gurls**®. I mean it's pathetic how desperate they're for sex with a real live, human woman. If you want we could go and get our ass cunts stuffed with small dicks for hours and hours! It's like dick heaven!

Wow! Really? Sounds a little slutty to me!

Yeah! But we can put-out just like the female prostitutes did in the old United States.

Wow Donna! Un-Fucking believable! How horny are you? I mean, I've heard about those places but I can't risk losing my job just for a gangbang.

Yeah but Carol, it's a blast! Sure their peckers are really small but hey, there're just so many of those horny fuckers!

Yeah **Donna**, Ha... ha... ha... I don't know. Non-Studs, small dicks? And between us Girls, you realize they're all small because of the Penis Shrinkage drugs the USA Inc. government contaminates the water supply with?

Sure, sure, But hey! I don't discuss politics **Carol**! And Honesty me or you or anyone else for that matter ain't gonna change the power of our Oligarchical government. I mean, if our government wants American men to be emasculated and submissive to the Wealthy Law-Makers and Lobbyist, you're fucked!

Donna, I know all about the Great American penis shrinkage phenomena, the [23.17] **GAPSP** or GAPS.

Yeah, I don't wanna break the law either, but Carol, I'm thinking with my pussy! Who cares why they have small dicks.

Well, going to jail and imprisonment in a Feminizing, Emasculation, Modification Agency, a **FEMA** [4.D-G7.13] Camp! Hmm... It just ain't any big turn on for me. And anyway

Donna, I'm dating this really nice well-hung Stud-Class© dude and we're getting serious.

Wow! Hmmm… Do tell? Do tell?

Yeah, yeah… He works for the State Department. His name is **Ben Dover** (EN06) and I think he's going to pop the question on me soon.

Wow! Carol I'm soooo happy for you! How hung is he?

Huh! Well, let's just say his Love-Muscle makes my pussy happy! So about the NS Gentlemens Club, I think I'll pass this time, I got a hard Stud waiting for me at home. Well, I gotta go. Sorry Donna. See yah!

Sure, sure, see you Carol.

[1.12] DISMISSED

Hey Gurls! Clap! Clap! (Ms. Carol calls for attention).

Yes Miss Carol! (All the tiny little Sissy-Gurls response).

Have a great weekend Gurls and don't forget, next week we're going to practice, Deep-Throating® and Snow-Balling®, so try and practice these techniques at home with your Moms and Dads this weekend. Okay?

Yes Miss Carol!

Miss Carol! My Daddy and his card game buddies all say I give good-head, do they mean blow-jobs?

Oh my Cock-God! (Carol shakes her head in disbelief and is often taken aback by the innocence of the Monkey-Gurl Sissies she teaches). Yes Honey, Mwah... You sweet, innocent, adorable little creature! Mwah... Wow!

Okay, Bye, Bye little ones! You're all dismissed! Be safe! (Miss Carol Waves good bye to all the smiling little Sissies leaving the school yard), Bye! Remember to practice! (Carol says as she blows kisses at them). Mwah... Mwah... Mwah...

Jane, tell your Mom I'm gonna call her (Carol says to Jane with a disciplinary, stern look on her face).

Yes Miss Carol, sorry I licked your coochee.

Aaaah... Jane cum here! Hugs... Hugs... Kiss. Mwah... Oh! You precious little Sissy, kisss (Meant to be only a simple goodbye kiss, Jane slips her tongue into Carols mouth and starts a wet make-out session). Wow! Mwah... Jane!

Love you Miss Carol Mwah... (Jane gives a seductive stare then winks and blows a sensuous goodbye air-kiss at Carol).

Wow! You little temptress! Okay, there's Sandy your Mom, get going (Miss Carol pats Jane on the ass good-bye).

Chapter 2: JAS Camp

One year later…2237

[2.1] OFF TO CAMP

And you're going to call me when you get there?

Yes, Mom! I'm not a baby!

Oh, here's Mary. Do you have your **Clit-Sock**® [4.D-G1.39] on?

Why do I have to wear a sock if I'm not at camp yet?

Because I know you little Gurl, you pop a load just by staring out the window. You're my little cum factory Mwah… And I love you sooo much my precious Sissy princess! Kiss kisss. Mwah… (Sandy smothers her daughter with hugs and kisses).

Love you Mom! Mwah… Bye!

Love you Jane. Try not to get into trouble at camp this summer, please. Kiss… kisss… kissss.

Bye Mom, let go! (Jane can't escape her mother's loving grip).

Stay close to Mary! Bye Mary, have a good time at camp sweetheart! (Mary had jumped out of the bus to fetch her buddy).

Thanks Mrs. Goldberg we will!

Ring, ring... Ring, ring... Ring, ring... Hello! (Mary's mom Heather calls).

Hey Heather! (Sandy Jane's mom answers).

Hey Sandy did they leave yet?

Yeah Heather they just left all dressed up in their cute little **JAS Scouting** [16] uniforms.

Good! Well does it look like Mary and Jane are going to spend the entire summer at camp doing Sissy-Bonding?

Oh yeah! Are you kidding? Those two scampered away holding hands and were all over each other like a happy little **DOM-Bitch** pair of nymphos [2.B2.13].

Great Sandy! Well we followed all the Sissy Breeding Program, the **SBP** [6.F.5] instructions explicitly just like they told us to. And I have no idea how or why hey qualified to be a DOM-Bitch Bonded Pair, a **DBBP** [2.B2.13].

Right, right, Heather who cares! They're gonna pay us more to bond them! I mean, this is easy money! All we had to do is get them to engage in sex with each other as soon as they were able to have sex.

Yeah, it was easy-peasy all we had to do is put them in the same crib and Mary and Jane immediately Sissy bonded to each other.

Yep! We got ourselves a hot little DOM/Bitch pair of kids, should we start planning the Sissy wedding?

Ha... haa... haaa. Do you think they think we know about them?

Nah! No way! Our kids clueless!

On the bus…

Hey. Mwah…

Mwah… Hey your Mom's exactly like mine! My Mom practically kissed me to death when I got on the camp bus. But at least she doesn't French kiss me anymore.

Yeah, my Mom told me to stay close to you. I think she figures you're going to keep me out of trouble or something.

Oh Jane my Lover, Mwah… Yeah, I'm going to keep you out of trouble sweetheart and in my bed! Shut-up and kiss me Gurl! Mwah… (Mary and Jane embrace and get into a wet make-out session, feeling each other up), hmmmm I love you Gurl, Mwah…

I love you too Mare. You got nice tits. Mwah… Do you think our Mom's know about our love affair?

No way! Our Moms are clueless! They have no idea we're planning our wedding!

One hour later…

Wow! I love the scenic views of the country-side. All the beautiful green trees and rolling hills, it makes me feel so peaceful. Ooooh! Hmm… My clit just popped a load thinking about making-love with you! Mwah…

Mwah… Glad you did! But Jane you're a B-Type Gurl, you pop for no apparent reason. Me on the other hand, I get especially wet when we're in each other's arms feeling each other up, how can I not feel wonderful when I'm with you? Mwah… Kiss... Kisss lick... Kiss.... Hmm… Mwah…

Hmm… Camp is great, I love sleeping with you every night. Kiss... Oooh! You're so beautiful to me... Hmmm....

Gurlfriend, Kiss.... Kisssss..... Mwah… I want to sleep with you for the rest of my life!

[2.2] ARRIVING

JAS CAMP (Stud vacation resort)…

Okay, we're here Gurls. (The bus driver says) Your bags are gonna be brought to your dorm hall for you. You can go straight to the amphitheater for orientation.

Cool, let's go. I love holding your hand Jane. It makes it look like I own you and the other DOMs get jealous.

I don't care if they're jealous. I love holding your hand Mary because you're my Gurlfriend. Mwah…

Mwah… Oh! Wait, I forgot my JAS purse on the bus.

Cum on Jane! Hurry-up Gurl! I'm excited to meet all our Scout friends!

Okay! Got it! Mwah… Ja miss me? Mwah…

Haaaa Haa Ha… You were gone two seconds! Yes, I love you. Mwah… Never leave my side. Mwah…

Hey Nicky, hey Jean, (The Sissy-handshake involves shaking each other's exposed Sissy erect clits. When Sissies greet each other they involuntarily get erects for one another and often times the ritual makes them squirt Jizzies). Hey Lisa, Amy, hey Mary, hey Martha, how's it going? Ooooh!

Whoa! Big squirt Martha! I'm happy to see you to Gurl. Mwah…

This is great! I'm so excited about our last year at Junior Scout Camp. Ooooh! (Jenifer squirts one out, high in the air).

Hey Jane, everyone's squirting! Whooohooo… Hey Jennifer, Lisa, Dana, Martha, Tina, God-of-Cocks! All the Gurls from **Sissy-World**© preschool are here.

Hey Cathy! Annie! Hey Jane!

Oooh! (Annie, who has always liked Jane, squirts a load at her purposely). Sorry I got some Jizzzies on you. I had to squirt.

Wow! All of our Sissy school buddies are here, awesome! Hey where's Tammy?

HEY! WHERES ALL THE STUDS? (Tammy shouts).

Hey! Tammy!

Hey here's Tammy Pussa!

What's up Sissy Jane?

Annie do you think me and you will win the most cockage contest again this summer?

Yeah Jane! Of course we're B-Type Sissies! We're hot Bitches we'll do well I'm sure of it. And I know we'll do better than the DOM **D-Types** [1.1]. Jane what's your **Cockage**® now?

Oh, let me look, its 9,669 penetrations. Whoa! Gurl, awesome! Well at the risk of sounding derogatory or disrespectful, you're going to be ranked Fag by the end of JAS summer camp for sure.

I don't know Annie, I am feeling kinda slutty.

Oh yeah, easy! For sure you'll make Fag-Gurl this summer!

And hey, I don't take any insult about being called a **Fag-Gurl**©. In the new **MSES** [23.13] it's socially permissible and totally appropriate to call a Sissy-Gurl® a Fag.

Ahhhh... But the Sissy-Rights Amendment [17.30] says the slang word Fag is forbidden!

Yeah but that was only considered an insult by the Gay Cum-munity back in the old USA a few hundred years ago.

Cool! Because as sexually active JAS Scouting Gurls we don't wanna sound socially inappropriate. So hey! What's yours Annie?

Let me look Jane, I'm only at, 6969 (Annie scans her tablet for her Cockage® score).

Wow! Well, you might change your Sexual Activity Rating, your **SAR** [5] and make Fag this summer too.

Maybe, anyway we're way ahead of most Sissies our age. Yeah, me and you **Jane**, we're Sluts!

Ooooh! Nice **Gurl-Clit**® Kiss... Ooooh... Annie... (Annie's little prick is always at full erection when she's near Jane). Mwah...

 Yeah you like my clit don't you Bitch? Oh Jane, you know I've always liked you. Hmmm.... Kissss (Both of them are licking and slurping at each other). Gak, Guk… Suck... Slurp.

Ooooh! it feels so good, keep sucking my clit Annie Gurl! Aaaaagh! Yeah! Ooooh! I'm gonna pop a load! Ooooh! Suck it, (Jane holds Annie's head and guides her mouth) Ooooh you hot Sissy-Bitch! Aaaaagh! Mwah…

[2.3] INSECURITY

Mary feels her love for Jane is threatened by Annie…

JANE! (Mary struggles with insecurities about Jane's promiscuity. It turns out Mary's worries, in this case, are completely unfounded, Jane is whole-heartedly devoted to her one true Love of her life, Mary).

WHOA! Ouch! What the... Hey! Mary! What the HELL?

Cum with me Jane, (Mary grabs Jane's arm firmly and marches them both away from Annie and the rest of the Sissy Gurls). Why Jane?

Why What? Mary where we going?

Why do you always have to play? Huh? Jane, I wanna have a talk with you.

What! You wanna talk! Play! Yeah play! What did we cum to Scout camp for? I was getting a really nice blow-job from our friend!

Yeah, I know Jane! I'm your friend too!

Yeah Mary, you've always been my friend since I could remember having a friend!

And Annie? What about Annie? What's she your new SPECIAL friend?

Mary! Annie's a friend, OK! Just a friend, OUR friend!

Oh, sniffle... Just a friend huh? Sniffle... so... sniffle, so, so, are you gonna sleep with her?

WHAT? What the hell are you talking about? And why are you crying? Ahh... Ahh...Oh Mary! (Jane can sense Mary is about to have the very first melt-down of their relationship).

Sniffle, sniffle, bee... be, because... cause... I... sniffle... I... sniffle... I... sniffle... LOVE YOU JANE!

Oh God-of-Cocks Mary! Annie was just sucking my clit, that's it! We weren't making plans or anything. Hey, look at me, (Jane grabs Mary by her shoulders firmly and looks Mary in the eyes).

Jane are you mine?

Huh! I'm yours Mary and I always will be Gurlfriend. Mary, me and you, we're gurlfriends not just friends. You know this right?

You... u... u... Sniffle... u... sniffle, (Mary wipes her tears from her eyes). Sniffle... u...u… mean it Jane? Are you sure you love me? Sniffle, sniffle.

Oh Gurl hold me because, yes (hugs). Kiss... I love you Mary. And when we make love, it's not sex it's love making, Ok? Annie and I we were just having sex, not making love, Okay?

Okay... okay... Sniffle, I'm sorry Jane. Sniffle... sniffle... I just get so scared when I think about not having you.

You don't need to cry Mary. You'll always have me. Sniffle... Sniffle...

I love you Jane.

I know you do! Okay, Ok, stop crying. Now why don't you turn those tear faucets off and dry your eyes. Your mascara's running. Let's go back over to where OUR good friend Annie and the other Sissy Gurls are. And hey, I want you to apologize to Annie.

Ok Jane... Sniffle... Sniffle, I'll do anything you want me too, Sniffle.... Sniffle... Cause.... I love you.

Okay, I know you do. Are you alright? (Jane being much smaller than Mary is wrapped around her). Mwah…

Mwah… Yeah I just need to hold your hand. I get so scared of losing you Jane.

Mary, hey! Remember what my Mom said?

What?

Me and you, we're hooked-up. Mwah…

Mwah… Ha... haa... yeah Jane, me and you, we're hooked-up Sissy Gurls!

Yeah, right Mary, me and you Baby! Mwah…

Sniffle, haa... haaa... Mwah…

Yeah, there you go, that's my smiling happy DOM Gurl. Remember Mary, you're the DOM and I'm the Bitch,

Okay sweetheart. Mwah…

Mwah… Okay. (Mary forces smile)

Good, my beautiful DOM Gurlfriend is smiling and laughing again. Haa... hee... ha... ha, (The Gurls walk back to the other Sissies and Jane has her arm tightly around Mary's waist), me and you buddy. Mwah…

Me and you Jane! Don't let go. Mwah…

Back where the other Gurls are…

Hey Annie, sniff.

Hey Mary, why'd you guys run off?

Oh Annie, hey I'm sorry I just get emotional sometimes when Jane starts playing around.

Well Mary you know Jane.

Yeah, I know playful Jane alright. She'll have sex with anyone!

You got that right (Mary and Annie high five)!

Yeah I'm really sorry I broke you guys up before, sniff...

Hey (Mary and Annie embrace in a hug) cum here Gurl. It's Ok you and Jane are really tight. And Gurl, I would never cum between two Sissy-Gurls who are so obviously in Love! No way! I'm not a fool!

Haa... haaa... ha (Both Mary and Annie are laughing and hold each other). Heee... hee... Hmm… Hee... he… ha. Mwah…

Well, hey Annie maybe some night you can sleep with me and Jane? Cum to our bunk!

Sure, sure, I'd love to get some Sissy three-way sex on with you two.

Yeah, just some, make-up sex between good Sissy friends.

Sure Mary, I'll drop by your bed stall and then drop into your love-nest for some hot Sissy-Sex® with my sweet hooked-up DOM-Bitch pair of friends.

Yeah Annie, let's have some fun, me, you, and wild Jane!

Okay Mary! Catch yah later... Kiss... Kisss.

Ok, later, Oooh (Annie grabs Mary's ass tightly while saying good bye)! Nice ass Gurl! Kiss... Kissss... Hmmm. See you! (Annie winks and blows a kiss good bye).

[2.4] FO

Fucked-Out (FO) talk amongst the Scouts…

It might be gossip, but from what I heard every Friday for us last-year at camp Gurls, Studs® perform a ritual on us called Fucked-Out, an **FO**® [7.G1.6].

What's FO?

It's serious Whore® training for us mature five year old Sissy Gurls. A FO training is when we get screwed so many times we stop being aware of what's going on.

Uuugh, Cum on! I don't get it Cathy? What do mean, we stop knowing what's happening?

Well from what I've read and heard from my older Sissy sister, our ass-pussies get over-stimulated. And the neuro-chemicals in our body start to screw with our brains or something like that. And the same thing happens to the **Bonobo** [7.5] monkeys in Africa who we Sissies are genetically linked to.

Yeah Cathy, this is the same thing my Daddy told me. Because he got Fucked-Out® by our Holy Cockolic Church during his Sissy **Cum-firmation** [9.HS.6].

Wow! So you mean Sissies lose consciousness after being Fucked-Out?

It's called an **FO** and yeah almost, we just be cum semi-conscious.

Why?

Because silly Sissy-Gurl, you have so many orgasms you think the orgasm never stops.

Oooh! (Some Gurls find it so fascinating their rapidly rubbing her clit). Then what? Oooh!

Or something like that. Well then your body is in shock and your brain gets wacked-out. They say it's like being on drugs! But it's a sex high! Although you can get ad-Dick-ted to Cock, it's called **Cockoholism** [7.G5.2] is a disabling disease but treatable.

Has a Sissy ever died from a Fucked-Out ritual?

No dummy! Besides, it's against the **SRA** [17.30] law to hurt a Sissy after the, Sissy Rights Act (SRA) was passed. You're just gonna feel like you took a hardcore gangbang when you wake up the next day.

What I thought was really interesting in the article I read in **Sissy-Gurl**© magazine was the description of what happens after the Sissy has reached a semi-conscious state. It said the sex continues for hours after the Sissy is screwed out of her mind.

Wow! That sounds Awesome!

Yeah! So Cathy, the men just keep screwing us. And we have no idea what's happening. Just think of it as going to Cock-Heaven!

Yeah! But, when do they stop?

The article said they stop when the Sissy has reached the state of FO.

Okay but when does FO happen?

But Cathy, wouldn't it hurt the Sissy?

No because the Sissy is fine physically, just as sturdy as the monkeys we were created from. And besides there's always a paramedic team and a FO proctor administrating the event. It's just we can't remember too much about what happened to us when we wake-up the next morning.

Do we remember anything?

All we'll know is we were having a goodtime getting screwed as usual by a lot of big strong Studs. Then we black-out and when you wake up there's a gallon of Jizz leaking out of your really sore, Sissy-cunts and we have no idea how that much cream got into our screw-hole. This is when you realize. Wow! My Sissy ass took an FO the night before.

You Gurls want to hear a juicy orgasmic story about a real FO?

Sure Dana. Yeah tell us! (The Gurls are all a glee about hearing a true story).

My Non-Breed from Birth Transitioned SIT® Sissy uncle was telling us about the FO missions he was sent on in the military.

Wow! Your Sissy Uncle is in the military?

Yeah, he, I mean she, I mean he, was a he then…

Yeah, yeah Dana! We get it, what happened to your Sissy uncle?

She joined the Army's, Sissy-Corp, right after she finished the Sissy-in-Training, SIT [1.A2.4] program and was totally

Sissified. And she did several 69 day tours of duty on Mars before the US got band from the Red planet.

Ooooh! Cool! Wow!

Yeah! The US Army Corp of Engineers was building these huge tunnels for underground facilities on Mars. And they needed Sissies to provide labor compensation transactions, **LCT** [4.D-G2.27] and utility-sex for the servicemen.

They would send her out on **FO**® missions to these remote bases on the frontier of the Red Planet where there was nothing but lots of horny servicemen in need of compensation. She said her missions were only one week long, but she didn't remember anything after the first couple of days because she was engaged in an FO session the entire time. Except for when the soldiers came into the FO chamber once a day and hosed her out and the room down. After her hosting, a medical team of veterinarians would cum in and stick a big Vaganus® probing wand up her cunt to douche-out her fuckhole and did a PrettyPuss® test on her.

Wow! Sounds exciting! Did she sleep at all?

Yeah but only for a few hours a night, she said you're in a zombie state the whole time.

What was her Cockage?

She said she would take thousands of LCT penetrations per mission.

Wow! You have an awesome uncle.

Yeah she's awesome! She said after she reached the FO-State and she took her quote of pricks they just sent her back to the base she was stationed at.

Well how do they know when she's reached FO?

Oh, well a military type FO is different than civilian types. In the military it's all about the quote. She said it's not about if the soldiers can't get you to shoot jizz out of your Cockette anymore. The military FO is all about if you've taken your quote of pricks.

Wow! Like a fuck-machine?

Yeah! And also if she was too tired and couldn't suck anymore dick the solders just start slapping you around. You see in the military the Sissy Rights Act doesn't apply.

No way!

Yeah way! I mean it's just how the military is. You have no civil rights and rightfully so. Because, Sissies were designed to be just livestock, pieces of meat to be used as a cum-modity. Besides just like Cathy was saying, the Sissy gets dicked so many times they're in a mind numbing delirious state and in a constant orgasm so you just kinda black-out from the pleasure like a zombie.

So the abuse doesn't matter?

Not really! It really doesn't matter if the Sissy is abused. The Sissy's happy in a blissful orgasmic state of mind! You just lay there and thousands of soldiers do you! What can be better than that?

Wow! Dana your uncle's a real courageous Hoe! You must be proud of her!

Oh yeah my uncle's not only a Hoe, she's a real American Hero, a red, white and blue American Sissy! And I don't care what people are saying about Americans being imperialistic assholes at least we use our assholes for something constructive.

Oh yeah I agree, the phrase, American Asshole is actually a compliment to us American Sissies!

Okay so what happens afterward?

Well the Military doesn't mess-around! When she stopped sucking dick and they were done with her. They'd just throw her cum drenched, cream-filled body into a body-bag, zipped it up and toss her unconscious Sissy ass on a transport back to the main base. She would recuperate for two weeks before being sent back out on another FO mission to keep the troops happy and supplied with fresh Sissy-cunt for labor compensation.

Well, did she like it?

Oh Yeah! Are you kidding? She did 69 tours of duty on Mars. And she got all kinds of medals, decorations and rank advancement because she was brave enough to volunteer for lots of FO missions. Like she was awarded the Cock-n-Balls Medal of Honor, the Distinguished Vaganus Medal.

Wow, a real hero.

Yeah, I'm really proud of my Sissy Uncle **Prissy** she's so brave it makes me proud to be an American. She made officer rank, she's a Lieutenant but in the Sissy-Corp the rank is called

Princess. I'd like to join the Sissy-Corp and do FO missions someday just like her!

Yeah, me too. Well is she still in the Service?

No she was honorable discharged. She's a White House reporter for CNN now. Prissy Boye (EN08).

[2.5] ORIENTATION

JAS Camp rules…

Okay Gurls welcome to Junior American Sissy, JAS Camp! I'm Mr. **Fakku** (EN11) I'm your Camp-Scoutmaster. We have a lot of great activities planned for you this summer. I'll give you an overview here and for more details you've all been given a schedule and a description sheet explaining each activity. This includes how to prepare for the activities, what you're expected to wear and the Sissy training performed at each one of them.

Our camp is a Junior Sissy Camp (JSC-269) its eight weeks long and each week here at Camp there will be a new group of guests. All the thousands of guests are Studs. For you first year at Camp fragile little Sissy flowers, these Studs are all Sissy-Trainer Certified, **STC** [4.D-G4.3]. And all your parents have signed the permission form informing them of this. So the adults are allowed to have Sissy-Sex® with you young Sissies.

Now I know for some of you three and four year old Sissies, seeing such a large group of fully erect Studs for the first time can be very exciting, but let me remind you, at NO TIME is it permissible for you to have more than one prick in any one of your two holes. I mean, you cannot do a Double-Dick in your mouth or in your **Vaganus**® [14.O1.6]. It's one penis per hole! You got that?

Yes, Sir, (replied in a somber, low tone kiddy voice).

The daily schedule is as follows, you Sissies are all up and out of your bed stalls by 9:00 AM and your Stud-Daddies who Fucked-You-In® that night have to leave your bed stall no later than, lights-out at, 2:00 AM.

So, activities, some of the activities here at Camp are part of the United States Incorporated, National Sissy Training Program (**NSTP**), see Appendix D, [4.D-G1.30] in your Sissy Manual SM069 for details. And you'll be graded on performance during those activities.

The other activities are just based on giving you precious little nymphos some recreational fun things to do this summer. Like, Pool-Party, Party-Boat outings on the lake, Mock-Wedding-Orgies, Sissy Maid Training, Master/Slave Bondage, **Cow-Gurl**® Rides and Horse-Stud Farm tours, Booty-Call® at a real US Army camp, and lots more.

Oh! Let's not forget one of the favorite activities you Gurls do every night before bedtime, Daddy-Fuck-Me-In. And we all know how much you Sissies love getting fucked-in for the night. Because you little Junior Sissies can't live without a daddy dick, can you?

No Sir! (All the Scouts shout loudly).

And thanks to the modern miracle of genetic-engineering here in the good old USA Inc., you non-human children can take as much daddy as you want. (The Scoutmasters rubbing his crotch obviously looking forward to comforting the Gurls).

For you older Sissy-Gurls this is going to be a special summer for you as well. For you five year olds, it's your last-year here at Junior Sissy Camp. So for you JAS Gurls, every Friday, you will all be participating in an **NSTP**© [4.D-G1.30] sponsored training ritual called Fucked-Out otherwise known as **FO** [7.G1.6]. And again, for details go online or read your activities sheet given to you about FO Fridays.

The dress and hygiene requirements have not changed from last summer here at Junior Sissy Camp. Most of these requirements are National Sissy Standards specified in the SM069. So they must be followed by all Registered Sissies with no exceptions, (The Camp Scoutmaster looks sternly at Jane).

First, you Sissy Gurls still must wear eight inch platform, high heel shoes at all times. And I just want to make a reminder here, although they are not required, we encourage you little, soon to be professional **Whores**®, to wear either, knee-high socks or thigh-high lace-top stay-up stockings with your platforms (The Camp master looks sternly at Jane again).

Second, Cloths are optional, (He scowls at Jane), but let me remind you little Junior American Sissy's. Being naked is not always sexy and your training as a Registered Sissy is designed to make professional Whores® out of you someday. So a word to the wise for you little cum-gulping nymphos. Your focus as a Sissy should now and always be to make men horny. Here at Junior Sissy Camp we expect you to create male sexual arousal. In other words I want to see these Stud men vacationing here at Camp walking around with ragging hardons!

But let me make this explicitly clear to all of you Sissies. Just because I'm suggesting you dress provocatively, at no time are you to titillate the guests here at camp. When I say I want you to arouse them sexually, all I'm saying is to dress sexy. You're not here at camp to allure the men into lewd acts. Titillation is an illicit act and there's a law against Sissies acting like prostitutes and encouraging men to approach them for sex. Prostitution is immoral and illegal in the United States Inc. And so is lewd Sissy behavior. The Sissy Illicit Titillation Rule, **SITR** [15-69]. See SM069, Section 15.

The **SITR** is in your Sissy Manual. So in this camp, if a male Stud be cums aroused sexually it's completely a product of his own imagination. And it has nothing to do with a Sissy shouting out at the Stud, hey baby, you want some of this!

Haaa haa heee haa… (All the Scouts break-up laughing at the Scoutmaster shouting in a little girl voice).

I want to see Junior American Sissy Whores in my camp, not a bunch street walking HOOKERS!

Ok now back to your appearance. The platform high-heels, the authorized **FuckMe**® cloths, **SissyWear**® the perfumes, JAS scouting uniform, costume jewelry, your exposed tits, clit and ass, are all part of causing male sexual arousal. So, I want to see some hot sexy little Junior Sissy Whores strutting around the camp this summer in hot sexy outfits. We've provided a huge FuckMe® wardrobe and Gurly-accessories in your dormitories dressing rooms so there's no excuses for you being naked (he stares at Jane sternly). Unless of course the man or men strip your clothes off, but under no circumstance do the eight inch platform high-heels cum off. Like I said, they must be worn at all times, in and out of bed. Our Camp has one of the highest

Cockage® numbers of any Junior American Sissy Camp in the Nation, so let's keep it that way.

Third, Sissy Hygiene is extremely important! You must douche your man-pleasing loveholes at least three times a day. Once after waking up, again at midday and of course again before getting into your bed stalls and into your Bitch positions prior to, Daddy-Fuck-Me-In time at night. Oh and if necessary douching is required to freshen up your holes after a camp activity gang-bang, party, pulling-a-train, glory-hole training, etc.

Also, the Sissy must, I mean is required to test her **Vaganus**® with a PrettyPuss® tester after every time she douches-out with a **Douche-O-Matic**® [4.D-G1.23] machine. The **PrettyPuss** tester is a pussy hygiene tester. After sticking the testers probe up your love-tunnel and the tester makes the announcement to you, Booty-Call! then you'll know your Vaganus is disease-free, germ-free, odor-free and doable. You can find a PrettyPuss tester at all the Douche-a-Matic machines available to you in your dormitory shower-room. And another hygiene issue, I don't want to see any Sissy-Poop eating outside of the camps cafeteria. Your Gurly poop is collected on a daily bases to be served as a gourmet item to our distinguished camp guests, not snacked on by Sissy Gurls.

And remember, whether you know this or not, the men, the Studs here at camp, have all paid a lot of money to vacation at JSC-269. And they expect to have, fresh Sissy cunt to abuse, I mean to train while here on vacation. I won't stand for camp guests complaining about how their Sissy had a sloppy, cum-dripping, stinky ass cunt! So, again, keep those holes of yours FRESH! Squeaky Fucking Clean Fresh! YOU GOT THAT?

Yes Sir! (All the Gurls shout in tandem).

Jizz-Us, this guys an asshole (Jane whispers to Mary).

Ok next thing, day-trips. Like I've mentioned, we're gonna go on day-trips to some really cool places this summer. When we do you'll be required to wear your sexy mini-skirt JAS Scouting uniforms. And on some of these trips you young Junior Sissies will be exposed to things new to you. But not to worry, all of the training activities you'll be engaged in are all in the Sissy Manual SM069. These learning activities may include interaction with animals. But not to fear! You Sissies are also registered by the US Department of Agriculture as animals. So for example, a Sissy having sex with say a llama or a horse is just animal on animal sex and is perfectly normal. It happens in nature all the time. Cats & dogs, Giraffes... Whatever, see Scouting [16].

And all physical training with other animals by Sissies is specified in the US **Sissification**® Act as essential Junior American Sissy training.

The last requirement, and Jane I see your back at camp this year, Sissies must at all times wear a Clit-Cum Collecting-Sock®, no exceptions, and that goes double for Nympho B-Types like you Jane!

Busted! Hee... heeee... Very funny Mary, (Jane lightly elbows Mary while being embarrassed by all the other Scouts giggling about Jane's rule breaking).

Ouch! Jane!

Okay that's it! I suggest when you Sissies get to your dorm halls. Check if all your bags are there. And remember to put all your stuff in your stall closets assigned to you.

Hey Jane, I'm so glad your Mom fixed it so our bed stalls are next to each other.

Yeah, my Mom wants us to stay close, she thinks I'll be safer with my neighbor buddy, she has no idea how much we're in love with each other. Heee... heee... Mwah...

Yeah our Mom's don't know we're in love. Mwah...

Ok, listen up Sissies! One more thing after settling in, it will be lunch Cock-Milking® time and there's a Pool-Party activity after lunch. So do your midday douche-out of your pretty little Sissy pussies, pick-out a nice sexy Sissy swimsuit and put it on. Because right after lunch you'll be going to the pool-deck for the meet-n-greet, Pool-Party activity with our Stud guests.

But before you go, and this is advice especially for the younger JAS campers. The Pool-Party activity is a, Gang type activity and for the Sissies who haven't read the Sissy Manual cover to cover yet, a Gang-Type activity is when you, the Gurl® is handle two or more penetrations. And the maximum penetration at a Gang event is in accordance to camp experience as follows, first year campers a maximum of 30 penetrations, second year 40 and third year 50. Okay, you sweethearts get going and have a wonderful summer!

[2.6] DORMS

The Gurls unpack and freshen-up...

Jane you're doing a bikini?

Of course you know I like to show a lot of skin. Let me guess Mary, you're going to pick-out a one-piece?

Of course Jane, my Mom doesn't want me getting skin cancer. I love the **SissyWear**® swimsuits they have for us to wear, totally open in all the right places, exposed clit, lovehole and nipples, perfect! You know, it's ironic the only thing we're going to swim in is gallons of **Man-Cream**®.

Talk about Jizzies let's go milk some pricks I'm starving (Jane pats Mary on the ass).

Mary, check them out.

Oh yeah, you mean, **Nicky** and **Tina**?

Yeah. They're like us. They're always making-out and holding hands. They're hot together!

Yeah they're really cute. When I see Gurls together I think of us. Mwah…

Mwah… Hmmm, hot Sissy-Love is cute! Kiss… Hmmm… Sissy lover… kiss, (Mary and Jane are constantly rubbing each other's Clits). Kiss. Cum on lets go Jane.

Yes boss… Heeee heee hee. Mwah…

[2.7] LUNCH

Lunch at camp provided by the Stud® Soldiers…

Wow! Nice big dicks sticking out of the milking glory holes.

Oh yeah! They're huge, because of the nearby military base. That's where we're going for the **Booty-Call**® trips. The base sends all the Stud® Officers and Soldiers to get milked every day.

Oh, that would explain the ample size of these cum-hoses. Gak, Guk...Gek... (Jane practically swallows an entire shaft then gulps down a load). Hmm... fresh cream awesome! Slurp... Gulp... Slurp...

Half an hour later...

Well you done Mary?

Yeah I'm stuffed! Let's hit the Pool-Party!

Gulp... Gulp... Gulp Gak, Guk.... Yeah, that's it for me, my belly's full of milk. Tasty Man-Cream® milk.

Hmm... Yeah Stud-Soldier Jizz is super sweet! And Wow! Big loads! I choked on a few of them.

[2.8] POOL PARTY

Men with boners sipping drinks poolside...

Oh my Cock-God® Jane! This is a Pool-Party! Look at all of this potential **Cockage**®, there's hundreds of wealthy looking Stud® men here! I love summer camp! Okay, stay close Gurlfriend!

Hey Mary, lets hold each other and make-out, it makes men go wild when they see Sissies groping each other. We'll attract a lot of dicks that way and Sissy-Love isn't considered titillation! Kiss... Mwah... Lick... fondle me Baby! Hmmm... lick... kissss. Mary stick your ass in the air, it attracts men.

Honey, don't worry you're safe with me. I'm a **STC**, Sissy-Trainer Certified [4.D-G4.3]. And sweetheart I'm not going to hurt you. Hell, all the men here are STC.

Okay Sir. Gak… Guk… Slurp... (Mary is slurping on his long hard ten-inch dick and enjoying every inch). slurp.... Lick... Gak… Guk….

Ahhh… Good Gurl®. Oooh! That feels sooo good! Ooh! Oooh! Nice piece of ass (He grabs both of Mary's tender ass cheeks). Ahhh… You sure have a sweet ass Honey! Kiss... Kissss, (Mary wet kisses and makes-out with Jane intermittently while performing fellatio on the Resort guess). What's your name sweetheart?

I'm Mary Sir. Mwah… Mwah… Love you Jane. Mwah…

Ahhhh… Well you can call me **Bill** I'm from Texas. Mwah…

Now Mary if you want to know what a real man feels like inside of your lovehole, take Uncle Bill deep in your sweet little Sissy-Puss® of yours.

Gladly Bill, I'm lubed and ready to take you Sir! Please stick your hard man-tool in me while I make-out with my Gurlfriend!

Hmmm yeah push that sweet ass of yours up in the air and I'll give my ragging hardon to you sweetheart. Ahh… Yeah good Gurl, stay like that bent over for me (Mary has here ass up in target ranger thanks to the eight inch platform shoes). Aaaaagh! Wow! I went right in all the way up to my balls in one thrust. Slap... Thump... slap… Thump... Thump... (Mary reaches out for Jane who's facing Mary and also taking it doggie style).

Kisss... Mwah... I love you Jane Aaagh! Never let go Honey! Mary! Mwah... I'll never let go of my DOM! Aagh! Nagh!

Dam Mary! Something tells me you've done this before. Your hole is bucking back at my prick! Like a Dallas Cow-Gurl® Thump, Thump... Slap... slap. You know we won the NFL championship this year! Thump, Thump... Thump, Thump...

Yes Sir! The Dallas Cow-Gurls from Tex-Ass are the best team in the National Fellatio League, the **NFL**© [23.52]. My hole has been trained to want and need you!

Aaaagh! Slap... Thump, Thump... Talk about completion, you must be breaking a record in bed. Geeez what's your **Cockage**® [7.G5.4] total Mary?

Nah! Not really. I mean Bill, its 6969. This means my Sexual Activity Rank, my **SAR**® [5.E1.1] classified as being a **Fag**© Level Whore with less than 10,000 penetrations.

Thump, Thump... Thump, Thump... Oooh! My Cock-God! You keep your Sissy-Pussy busy! Take me you sweet little Sissy Whore! Slap... Slap... Aaaagh! Most human female cunts don't do it that many times in their life!

Aaaaagh! Yeah! Not half as busy as my Gurlfriend. Ahhh...

Thump, Thump... You sweet little Sissy Whore... slap... thumb... slap (Bill just keeps pounding Mary's wide, eager hole). Oooh! I'm going to pop my load Mary! Thump, Thump...

Give it to me Bill! Do Me! I'm a Whore! I was created to give men pleasure! Please Cum in Me! I won't get pregnant!

Jane, (Mary transfers the wad to Jane's mouth). Gak... Gulp... flap... gulp, slurp.... lick... kiss.... Ooooh! Hmm... snowballing is a little messy. Ummm... But, yummy tasting cream! Thanks Mary! My Sissy DOM® Gurlfriend. Kiss... Kissss (Sensuous wet, cummy, make-out kissing). Lick... Mwah... Gurgle... Gurgle...

Oh! Nicky, (Now Jane transfers the same wad into Nicky's mouth). **Snowball**! [4.D-G1.9] Whooohooo...!!!...

Slurp, lick kiss, Dana! Gurgle... Gurgle... (Nicky taps Dana on the shoulder). Gurgle... Gurgle... Here's a snowball open up! Jean snowball! Gurgle... Gurgle... (The preschooler friends pass around snowball wads of cum). Slurp... Lick, take it Martha don't swallow it! Guk, Gek... Glrck...

Gurgle... Gurgle... (The wad is so big now it won't fit in anyone's mouth). Take the snowball **Gurl**®. Lisa, open up Bitch! Good Gurl Tina, snowball load! Oh holy Cock-God! Cathy take it! Gurgle... Gurgle... Look at this scene we're all snowballing while dicks are screwing our loveholes! This Pool-Party is a Sissy fuckfest! Constant sex!

[2.10] AFTERWARDS

Four hours later, the pool party winding down...

Wow Mary! What a party I'm in Cock-Heaven!

Haaa haa ha...Yeah Jane, four hours of constant **Man-Meat**®, I love when they just keep stuffing us like that.

Yeah Mary, and all of our Gurlfriends faced each other in a circle, huddled together having fun putting on a snowball swapping show. It's so natural. We're just being our loving Sissy selves, having fun and attracting men to us.

Oh, I snowballed and made-out with all of our Sissy friends. Men love to play with a Sissy who makes-out with other Sissies! The men keep asking me for my Whorehouse number. I guess so they what? Can have another poke at us.

Wow Jane, you're so popular with the men! And we're both getting so good at groupsex. It's like something out of a Hentai magazine.

For sure, it was a great session, here, I'm gonna pull up my stats on my mini-tablet, Okay, I took, 69 in my bottom and 22 loads in my mouth, way over the maximum limit, cool!

Jane! You screw more than any Sissy I know.

Thank you Gurlfriend. Hmm... Kiss... Oh, I just love when Studs® take turns on me! I love men in me! Oh! I love COCK! Hmmm.... Kissss..... Kissss.... Mwah... (Mary exclaims out loud while tossing her arms in the air in a celebratory mood as everyone turns to see who shouted).

Hey let's go douche-out our loveholes and shower off. Then we can have a nice romantic nap in each other's arms before diner-time milking?

Okay Sissy Gurlfriend. Mwah... But I'd much rather prefer to eat all the sweet Man-Cream out of the **Vaganus**® [14.O1.6] of my beautiful Sissy DOM® before we douche. Can't let all those Jizzzies go to waste. Mwah...

Mwah... Ooooh! Lover you can always eat out my creampies. Then it'll be cuddle-time and spooning with my sweet Jane. Mwah...

Mwah... Sure, Mary, you're the only one I spoon with Baby.

Oh, I love you sooo much Jane, Kisss...

Love you too Mary! And I always will, kiss. Hey and you don't have to be jealous or worried about me having Sissy-Sex® with our friends anymore my Lover. Hmm.... Kissss. Mary, don't forget, I'm your **Bitch**® [1.A2.2] and I'm the only one sleeping with you. Right? Mwah...

Yes Jane, I only sleep with you. Oh Baby! I love you with all my heart, I'm sorry I got so jealous, kissss. Hey Jane?

Yeah Mary.

You know what a **DOM**® is right?

Sure you're my dominant love partner.

I mean, Jane did you have a talk with your Mom yet about DOM/Bitch relationships?

Well yeah my Mom sat me down and discussed it with me. The DOM in a Sissy relationship is the Sissy who has the bigger Clit and is more dominant over the other Sissy, the Bitch. Mary let me ask you a question, what do you think dominant means?

Well, the DOM, the dominant one, likes to be in charge of things. Like, where and when to go places and what to wear, or who to be friends with, stuff like that. And the DOM holds her Bitches hand not the other way around.

Mary, it's a perfect description. You left out the part about us being equal, but so did the guys who wrote the Sissydom Manual. And you know what Lover? I love not being the DOM Mary. Mwah...

Good Honey! Because I want you as my Bitch®. And Jane I don't think any less of you because you're submissive to me.

Well I'm glad, kiss... You love me, and Mary I could remember the talking you gave me about how neither of us had the decision to be a DOM or a Bitch, It was planned in advance by all the smart bio-engineers and social scientists in our government.

You're right Baby. My Daddy tells me all this stuff when he gets home at night from his Sissyology classes he's taking for his college degree. You see, parents are given either the patented D formula to breed a **DOM** [1.A2.1] like me or in your case your parents were given the B formula to breed a **Sissy-Bitch®** [1.A2.2] it's that simple.

He also sat me on his little Sissy love-probe and told me our Cunt-tree is run by very intelligent bureaucrats who will do things only for profit.

Huh! Mary, you mean anything for profit?

Yeah! And this means we'll have a wonderful life because when we grow-up and be cum US Federal Civil Servants working as Whores® we'll have all the benefits the human government employees have. But hey it's a free Cunt-tree, not just Sissies are be cuming wealthy! All patriotic Stud® citizens working for the

Federal government who practice, Standard Submissive Behavior, the **SSB** [4.D-G2.30] towards our government in the MSES® are prosperous too.

Well yeah! If you're not submissive and a profiteer you might as well not be an American!

Right! And all the fantastic drugs our government supplies us with like the **D** and **B formulas** [1] and the Mind Control **MCD** drugs [4.D-G1.28] are great. It's all part of the new America. It's a virtual utopia of designer drugs to bring the passive American citizenry to a more prosperous future in their minds. And quite frankly I don't know how you could control Americans any other way then by keeping them heavily sedated!

Oh for sure Mary! Americans are easily controlled by drugs or fake news propaganda on TV. But the real genius is the control of the world monetary system! The American creation of **Sissydom**® will lead to the future hegemony of the world's economic system as it had been many years ago.

Exactly! Eventually we'll preliterate the world with patented American Sissies causing a global ad-Dick-tion to **Vaganus**®.

Ah huh! This will give the USA Inc. total control of all financial markets and economies forever.

Yada, yada, ya… Mwah… Hey Professor Mary, thanks for the American economics lesson. But regardless of the total control our government has over us and someday the world, you know you're in control of this relationship right? So Mare, let out my leash a little bit Baby. Because I'll always cum running home to you lover.

Sniffle... sniffle... I love you sooo much Jane, cum here. Kiss....
Hmmm... (Hugs) Kisssss. Mwah…

Chapter 3: Elementary School

The year is 2238…

[3.1] DROPPING OFF

Is that all your wearing **Jane**? (Sandy remarks how scantily dressed Jane is).

Mom, there's a good reason why I have the highest **Cockage®** [7.G5.4] score in my grade.

But Jane, there's a difference between sexy revealing fashion and dressing skanky.

Okay and you should talk about style?

What? I'm classy not trashy!

Mom, you dress like Daddy, in fact you both dress like hookers.

Jane! You don't even know what a hooker is!

Yes, I do! We watched a documentary in school about the sex industry in America back a couple hundred years ago. And I know Daddy dresses like a slut because of his job. He's a Professional Sissy Whore, a **PSW®** [2.B2.4] but what's your excuse Mom?

Honey, don't be a brat and talk to your mother like that. You know Daddy always knocks me up. It's hard to look and dress perfect when I'm pregnant and holding down the fort at home, popping out Sissy babies.

Pleeeease... Mom! You hold down the dude you're riding!

Hey! I take care of you three Sissies. Mandy, stop suckling-on Sarah's clitty! God-of-Cocks! For a three year old she can't stop draining her little Sissy sister's balls. And then there's your Sissy-Breeding® sister Sue, who won't stop eating my vagina. Oh and let's not forget your whore of a father. I cook and clean, what else can I do Jane.

Mom! Haaa ha... You're kidding right? You know you don't cook! We're all either non-human mutated lab experiments or transitioned **SIT**® [1.A2.4] like Dad. And you and my sister are Sissy-Breeders. The only food we eat is bottled Man-Sperm, there is NO COOKING! Hell! We live in a Government sponsored Sissy Whorehouse® in the middle of a Stud neighborhood and we don't even have a KITCHEN! All we have is a refrigerator stocked with freshly bottled, flavored, Dick-Milk.

Okay! So I exaggerate a little! All the human moms talk like that.

Yeah, yeah... The humans cook and clean. But we're just a Whore® family! Our existence is bankrolled by the USA Inc. government. The more Sissies you and Dad pop-out the more money you make!

Jane! Where did you learn all this stuff?

In Modern Sociology class. It's no secret Mom! You human Sissy-Breeders were poor and this is why they make Sissy livestock babies, for the money!

Jane! That's horrible! Don't you dare thing Mom and Dad made you for profit! We love you and your sisters. Mwah… We're a perfectly normal American family.

Mwah… I guess… (Jane pouts). And cleaning, please Mom! We have a maid paid for by the Government. Juanita, she's a fantastic lover and has the sweetest tasting pussy. But the poor Non-Stud, NS lady, not only picks-up after us Sissies, she also cleans-up all the cummy mess in the sex-training rooms in our WHORE-HOUSE! We're a Sissy-family Mom! (Jane's having a little Gurls tantrum) There is nothing NORMAL about us! And if it wasn't for the Sissification® scientists, I wouldn't even EXIST!

Oh Honey, so we're not normal and Okay, I don't have the same housewife obligations and duties as a typical Non-Sissy Breeding housewife. But, all I want is to be as sexy as I can for my Sissy-Family®. Don't you want a hot sexy Mommy to cum home to and make love to Sissy-Gurl?

Please! I hate when you put on that, *get in bed with me* voice, (Mom is playing with Jane's clit). Geeeezzz… it feels so good when you stroke my clit. Ooooh! Ahhh…. I popped!

Wow! You popped a load sweetheart. Oh and you're all cummed up now! Oh you're a cummy mess Jane, let mommy lick it up!

Aaaagh Mom, I got to go (Jane opens the car door). Mwah…

Mwah… Love you Jane Gurl!

I Love you too Mom.

Put your sock on please!

Mom, hey I sorry, I kinda get upset about the whole Breeding thing. (Jane pauses with a smile on her face).

Ahhh... It's okay Jane. Kiss Mommy!

Mwah... And Hey I love your mini-skirt with your thigh-high lace-tops showing and your tight-top pushing your big tits up on display. It's really classy.

Mwah... Thank you Jane Gurl, I love you too. And Jane, you're just like all the other human girls, okay? It's just that you're a little different. It's not your fault. Mwah...

Sure Mom, if that's what you want me to believe, sure. (Jane smiles at Mom to appease her).

I'll pick you up later Sweetheart!

No Mom! I'm taking the bus home with Mary.

Ok see yah home Sugar-Puss! I'll give your Sissy coochee a nice licking when you get home. You can poop on Mommy's face!

Okay Mom! Love you...

[3.2] JANE & MARY

Jane where were you? You missed the bus. Mwah...

Mwah… Oh Mary it was great! Jon my Sissy Sexual Trainer, my **SST** [4.D-G3.1] was super horny and screwed my brains out with his magnificent foot-long this morning. And hey, heeee heee hee… I was glad I missed the bus.

Sounds great! My Mom makes sure it's pulled-out, I'm up and out for the bus every morning.

Yeah Mrs. Dune runs a tight ship at your house.

Yeah! My regimented Mom makes sure my SST® finishes my cooch training early to give me enough time to get ready.

Well your college educated Mom is super organized and on it! But my wild Mom is part of the problem. I'm usually fisting her while getting training from my SST.

Sounds like party. So, it's not all her fault?

Yeah I guess. Oh! Wait there's more! Then I had to listen to my Moms blah, blah, blah the whole way to school. Uooogh! (Jane puts her hands up to her throat to mock being choked by her mom's rants). Lecturing me about not wearing **SissyWear**® panties or a **Sissy-Bra**®. And oh, I should have douched-out Jon's cum load or let her eat it out of me before leaving home. And stuff like why a proper Sissy® always goes out in public with a slash of Snatch® perfume.

Wow! What did you tell her?

I told my Mom I like going, *la natural* without panties, because I always have cum dripping out of my Vaganus® anyway.

Ooooh! You set her straight. Jane, if I told my mother that, she'd cum down on me so hard. She'd make me do time-out. She's really sharp about improper Sissydom® standards.

Well your Mom, Mrs. Dune she's a proper Sissy-Breeder® Lady, she has class like you Mary. Mwah…

Mwah… Thank you my Sissy-Puss!

Yeah Mary, our friends always say, you're the Lady and I'm the tramp. I wanna be your tramp! Forever! Mwah…

Mwah… Yeah Jane but your Mom's really cool!

Oh yeah! Mary, I love my Mom. She's cool and everything, but her and my Dad, and your parents they're the old hippy Sissy generation who were in the transition phase of the Modern Social Economic System.

Oh the MSES®. Yeah, I guess you're right Jane. Our parents were radicals.

Yeah, yeah... In the streets protesting for Sissy civil-rights, fighting against inequality between the Sissy® and Stud® classes.

Right, right… They were the peace-love-dove generation, who got the Sissy Rights Act, the **SRA** [17.30] passed in Congress.

Yep! But our generation is the, Cock worshipping, screw anything in sight generation. We're a product of our parent's generation.

We're different Sissies than our parents are!

Dill-a-ling, dill-a-ling, dill-a-ling…

There's the first bell. I'll talk to yah after class Sweetheart. Mwah…

[3.3] HISTORY

USA Inc. Modern History…

Class, US modern history is an interesting topic for several reasons, depending on who wrote it. In your government issued textbooks the first chapter goes over the restructuring of the non-constitutional fascist United States government. This non-constitutional government lasted from December 23, 1913 to 2213. Three hundred years of financial slavery for the American people. It started with the passing of the, Federal Reserve Act, to its abolishment in the year 2213.

Also in this class you'll learn about, why our Cunt-tree uses penis size as a measure of social class status. Open your books to page 69, figure 6.9. Here we see a young Sissy® performing fellatio on the President elect of the United States during the inauguration ceremony. Class, now what can you tell me about class status by looking at this picture? Yes, Stevie!

Well Mr. **Penese** (EN11), I see a pathetic Sissy® faggot boy being the Whore he was breed and trained to be, privileged to service his Cunt-tries leader.

Yes, this is partially true. The Sissy is performing HER patriotic duties as a trained civil servant Whore® of the United States of America Incorporated. And notice class I refer to the Sissy in the feminine. Sissies are referred to as, her or she, unless of course they're ugly and look like a guy, for example, my mother-in-law, I digress.

Remember, Sissies are classified as females by the Bureau of Sex Classification, the **BSC** [4.D-G6.4]. Therefore it's considered rude and disrespectful to refer to a Sissy in the masculine, I mean calling them boys. Also, it is derogatory to describe a Sissy creature as pathetic.

And burn this to memory. Oh! And this is going to be on your chapter test. Sissies are considered a valuable national resource. And because of this, they are given our Nations fullest support and encouragement to live in our new MSES society. To live, free of all sexism, racism, criticism and other isms of any kind. Class, they're to be applauded for their contribution to the welfare of our Nation.

Mr. **Penese**, are the Sissies animals, livestock?

Yes they are. But despite pure BfB® Sissies being humanoid creatures, Sissies are government employees not objects. The Whore® jobs they have are the highest paying civil servant positions in our Cunt-trie. So show your respect for our brave Sissies.

Mr. **Penese**, you speak so fondly of Sissies, are you a faggot?

Ha... haa... hah... hee... hah... haa (The class laughs).

Quiet down class! No Jimmy! Haa ha... Very funny, NOT. You realize it's a crime to say the **F** word? Amendment thirty-four [17.34] which is punishable by castration, forbids the use of the *gay words*, And I dare not speak them here. You'll have to look them up in the Sissydom® manual.

And No! I'm not a Sissy either. Now mind you there is a difference. I do know the amendments of the United States of America Incorporated. In the Second **Cunt-Stitution**© [17], thirtieth amendment slavery is abolished for Stud and Whore Classes. And also Sissies are protected by the thirtieth amendment with the Sissy Rights Act, the **SRA**. You'll be learning all about Sissy rights and the functionality Human-Sissy Sex, **HSS** [7.G1.19] during this course. Including how the American Sissy Vaganus® was created for and will be used by our government to dominate the economies of the world in the decades to come.

For example the non-ratified first amendment of the Second US **Cunt-Stitution** Amendment 28, [17.28] states, one unit of money is equal to one unit of a male-orgasm or one **MO**®. Also refer to the Sissydom® Manual SM069, Section 12, [17.28]. Here HO means Whore®. And as you can see the sum of a HO and MO means more Cum-modity is produced.

$$HO + MO = increased\ productivity$$

This is how the framework for our current money system in our Modern Social Economic System is defined. Stated in the twenty eighth amendment, a **MO**® [12.L1.0] is a unit of worth, much as gold and silver once was in the United States many, many years ago.

Yes Jane?

Mr. **Penese**, when you say **MO**® do you mean when a man penetrates a Sissy during a Labor Compensation Transaction, an **LCT** [4.D-G2.27] or when they do a human female girls vagina?

Thank you Jane, I was going to get to that. One **MO**® unit is when a Non-Stud or **Stud**® male ejaculates his sperm into the non-impregnable **Vaganus**® of a registered Sissy®.

Ok, Mr. **Penese**, so when men have compensation sex with me, I'm collecting one unit of money with my Vaganus?

Yes, yes, yes! In a way Jane. But the system isn't that simple. For example, if a Stud® has coitus with a female vagina and the female is a Non-Stud female, he has money deducted from his account.

Huh! What?

Yes, our USA Inc. government discourages breeding with Non-Studs due to (1) the small size of a Non-Stud penis and (2) these impoverished women are kinda scanky. But wait! It gets even more complicated so I'll try to explain the system as best I can.

Let's go over some of the details here. One unit is given to the Sissy **Whore**® and one unit is given to the male who performed the, Labor Compensation Transaction (LCT) on her. The **MO**® is an equal distribution, but the amount of money paid to the Whore and the male who emptied his nuts-sack into her is different. And you can gain extra credit if you hand-in an essay on the pay ranking system found in Section 12, Appendices L and M of the Sissy Manual SM069 [12.L].

But suffice it to say. Because the government of the United States of America Incorporated has declared a Male-Orgasm or **MO**® is, when performed in a registered **Sissy**®, one unit of worth, than it is of course one unit of worth.

What da? Ha haa… Mare, are following this? (Jane whispers in Mary's ear).

Shhh… I know he's rambling. Jane, don't get us in trouble please.

For example, a unit of worth is similar to an old unit of money, say, gold or silver or even a US fiat dollar. The dollar used to be issued by a private central bank called the, Federal Reserve Bank a few hundred years ago before the fascist's destroyed the US dollar and took it off the gold standard.

Why did we go off the gold standard Mr. **Penese**?

Ahhh… It doesn't matter why Tricky Dick Nixon, a Re-Pubic-Cunt took us off. But back then as in all Empires, our military debt was not repayable.

The main point is, the US dollar was once used as a currency backed by real gold or silver. But you see Boys and Gurl-Girls the American empire, our government lost the Financial World War of 2069, the **FWW** [23.24]. So afterwards we lost all our gold reserves in war reparations to the Eurasian Union nations. This caused the United States to have a total financial economic collapse in 2069. And this is why we had to invent a new unit of money, the **MO**®.

And the Second US **Cunt-Stitution**© states, the new unit of currency is still the US dollar except this US dollar is special because it is created by the United States Government and not by some private money whoring fractional reserve central bank. So now the US dollar is worth one MO® unit of money.

What's that mean Mr. **Penese**?

Well, it means, all full-time working men are eligible to do man-work, which is defined as, ejaculating sperm from our penises into a transaction hole of a Sissy®. Our government pays the worker in US dollars backed by MOs. Those dollars are worth male-orgasms, one MO, per dollar. And if we want to buy groceries we use the US dollars to buy the products in stores.

I'm still confused Mr. **Penese**. Yeah me too... Me too... (The class is totally confused).

Okay well, you see class, when a man goes to work, say in a factory or office the employer does not give the man a pay-check at the end of the week. Instead the man has to go to an Official Whoring Station, a **WS**® [7.G4] or if the man belongs to the Stud Class, he can also go to a Whorehouse®. Then he would collect his pay by filling the Sissy Whores Vaganus® with his man cream. It's called the, Labor Compensation Transaction or LCT.

Mr. **Penese**, now I'm really confused...

Well think of it this way Kids, in America, a Sissies hole is like an ATM machine. And a Whorehouse® is like a bank.

Huuuh? I don't get it! Yeah me too! I'm still confused...

Ok, Ok, let's take a real world simple example. Last week I went shopping to buy a month's worth of groceries for myself. I chose to buy a case of FEMA Camp **Mystery-Meat**® [4.D-G1.21] spam which costs 80 US cents of a MO. So, this means I would have had to have sex with a Sissy at least one time to make the one dollar needed to buy the case of spam. At the store, I give them a dollar and they give me twenty cents back in change.

Mr. Penese how does the store know you have the money?

Another good question, I received from our government the amount necessary through the, Sissy Sexual Activity Auto-Accounting System, **SSAAAS** [4.D-G1.26]. You may have heard about it on the news. You see everyone has had a special undetectable antenna ring embedded under the skin of either a penis for boys or on the opening of the vagina for girls or around the opening of a **Vaganus**® and mouth for Sissies. Everyone nowadays has them implanted when they were born by a self-dissolving tape which makes your skin absorb the micro-transmitter antenna band around their penetration holes.

Why can't we see the ring Mr. **Penese**?

Like I said, it was embedded under your skin and the RFID's bio-micro-wire and bio-micro-chips are so small, no one can see them.

What does the wire do?

Well, the wire is an antenna it sends a signal to the government that a MO® event happened and it also records who the male was who had the MO and the Sissy or female who received the MO. It's very accurate and works flawlessly most of the time.

Mr. **Penese** I have a question.

Ok Mary Dune!

When you said, full-time working men are eligible to do man-work, what gives them the privilege to do man-work? Like what did they have to do to be eligible to perform the **LCT** [4.D-G2.27] on the Whore?

Great question Mary and I expected this kind of sophisticated inquiry from the winner of the Sissy-World Preschool Scholarship Award.

Thanks Mr. **Penese**.

There's a thing called a HOMO or Hourly Occupation Male Orgasm. This is one of the pay structures in the MSES which regulates how many dollars are given per work-hour done. And the necessary MO's, in other words, the man-work necessary to be perform on the Whore to acquire the dollars owed to a worker. Class your blank expressions are proof enough to convince me further explanation is necessary.

Now! I want you all to go to the back of your textbook and study the **HOMO** [12.L1.9] table in Section 12, Appendix L of the SM069 Sissy Manual.

Male Orgasm (MO)

Pay Rank (PR)

Pay per Hour in cents (PPH)

Dollar per MO in dollars (DPM)

PR	PPH	DPM
1	10	1
2	20	2
3	40	4
4	80	8
5	100	10

Ok class look at it this way. Say there's this hypothetical worker dude called whatever, Joe Blow, his PPH is 10 cents for every hour of work. Or 80 cents per 10 hour work day, so this amounts to four dollars for every miserable fifty hours of work per week.

So by looking up Mr. Blows PPH and DPM values in the HOMO table, can anyone tell me how many times Mr. Blow has to perform the **LCT** on the Sissy® to collect his pay for one week?

SM069, Sissy Pussy Pay per Penetration (SPPPP)

Yes, Miss Dune again because there are no other hand-up.

Mr. **Penese**, if the workers pay rank (PR) is one than the worker would have to ejaculate in the Sissy four times to get paid four dollars for one week's worth of work.

Very good Mary! It's obvious the gene mutation **D-Type** formula [1.A2.1] used to breed **DOM**® Sissies produces higher IQ intelligence than that of normal humans. Thank you Mary.

Mr. Penese, yes Jane!

Thanks for the explanation but, how cum I don't have any money if I screw so much?

Haaa...Oh Jane, haa... haa... hee. You're whore! Scank! Haaa... Haa... Haaa. Hoe-Bag! Tramp! SLUT! (The Stud boys in the class all erupt in a loud barrage of degrading insults).

Hey! Hey! Settle down everybody. No smart ass remarks! You Stud boys know better than that! QUIET DOWN!

Well Jane, it's because you're not thirteen yet. And that makes you a, Junior Sissy Whore or **JSW**® [2.B2.2]. Right now the money goes to your parent's bank account until you're the legal whoring age. When you turn thirteen you'll be a legal age and you'll be an, Associate Sissy Whore or **ASW**® [2.B2.3] and the money will be directly deposited into your bank account.

And let me make something perfectly clear here. For you under-age Sissy® Gurls doing your Whore training in your Sissy families registered Whorehouse® be very careful. You Sissies are extremely horny at all times, especially you, **B-Type** [1.A2.2] Gurls like you Jane. But the rules are the rules. You may not have sex with men or boys unless they have an official Sissy Training Certificate, **STC** [4.D-G4.3]. All of the faculty and students here at the Special Sexual Integration School 69 are Stud® class and have an STC.

Dill-a-ling, dill-a-ling, dill-a-ling…

Ok that's it for today! Don't forget to read the rest of chapter one section 6.9 on the Second US Cunt-stitution and the legalization of Sissy Incest for the test on Friday.

[3.4] COLLAR

Holy Sissy-Poop **Jane**! We're only eight years old. We'll be broke for another five years!

I don't care Mary, I love sex! I'd screw for free anyway. I don't care about the money.

Oh Jane, you sweet innocent thing. It's a good thing I'm the DOM and you're the Bitch.

You mean I'm your bitch-in-heat! Heee.... Heeee.... Mwah… And if you ever officially be cum my DOM, you'd better get a collar around my neck and put me on a tight leash because I need a man's prick up my coochee constantly! I mean, did you see those hot looking Sissy Gurls in history class?

Yeah Jane they were hot. (Mary gives Jane a disapproving grin).

Hell! Yeah! I wanted to get jumped by that one hot Bitch. But she had a DOM® Gurlfriend that pulled her away from me.

Yeah, I saw the DOM just yanked her leash really hard.

Huh! I felt bad for her Bitch, (Jane squirts a load out thinking about how cute the hot Sissy Gurl classmate was). Agh! Yeah! Jizz-Us! She was sooo cute!

Aaah! Geeez! Jane! Watch it! You almost popped your load on my new skirt! God-of-Cocks Jane! Put a sock on it! You squirt all over the place!

Sorry Mary you know me, I get excited.

Hmmm.... Yeah maybe I should use a collar and leash on my Bitch like the other DOMs do.

[3.5] BOYS

Recreational sex between classes...

Oh! Oooh! (Jane gets poked by a hardon). Hey! Nice man-tool **Jimmy** you wanna poke me?

Oh yeah Jane! You're a choice piece of ass Sissy-Gurl. And yeah I always want to screw you! You're hot Jane! Mwah...

Mwah… Yeah I know! Well, make it quick Jimmy we got class in a few minutes.

Oooh take it Bitch! Aaaagh! Mwah… Mwah… Yeah!

Oh! Nice dick Mark. (Mary says while checking her make-up in a compact mirror).

You want me to fill your hole Mary!

Ummm… No quickie for me dude. I have my favorite outfit on and just don't want to get it all Jizzed up. But Mark, Jane's mouth is free why don't you stick your probe in my Bitch. Jane's a **B-Type**® she always needs more prick.

Ok! Open wide Jane, your DOM told me I can fuck your face!

Mwah… Sure but make it quick you two. The last thing I want is to keep my DOM waiting.

Aaaagh! There you go Sissy-Gurl, filled your cum-bucket! Ahhh… Mwah… nice fuck!

Mwah… Thanks for the quickie Jimmy.

Aaaagh! I'm Cumming Jane! Spank! Ahhhhh….

Ouch! Mark! Not so hard on the ass. Mwah… Mwah…

Dill-a-ling, dill-a-ling, dill-a-ling, dill-a-ling, dill-a-ling.

Thanks for the Cummy snack Mark.

Sure Jane!

[3.6] SEX-PE

Sexual Physical Education (PE), Sex-PE class, your favorite!

Yeah Mary and it's two periods for us Gurls.

Yeah Jane, there aren't enough Sissies in the Integrated School yet so we get twice the **Cockage**®. This is definitely the best class besides Sex Awareness!

Yeah, if it wasn't for the, Piss-On-Me after the workout by all the Stud-Gurls, it would be perfect. I like **Piss-On-Me**®, it's this Anti-Sissy teacher asshole I can't stand.

Ok, Sissies mount your Benches and Studs line-up in front of the Benches you've been assigned. Stud® boys start getting those dicks hard. Yeah! That's it, jerk that prick! (The gym teacher is a real Sissy hating douche-bag). Yeah! Pull on your man-tool! Get those fuck muscles nice and hard!

You Sissy and Stud-Breeder® Girls get on your, **Eat-Me-Out**® benches and spread your legs, open those baby-making pussy lips wide. The Non-Stud (NS) girls who have declared a class **Opt-Out**® [13] to breed-out of their pathetic NS working class into a Stud or Sissy class can start eating out the Stud and Sissy Breeding cunts on the **Eat-Me-Out**® benches.

Wow! Mary, this guy is a real womanizing asshole.

And make sure you Stud-Breeder® chicks start drinking your gallon of water for the Piss-On-Me with the Sissies after class. Girls I want to see those gallon water jugs empty before we hit the showers.

And you Non-Stud boys who have declared a class **Opt-Out**®
for Breeding out of your NS working class into the faggot Sissy
Class, start fluffing up the **Stud**® boys waiting in line. You'll
need the blow-job practice if you're going to pass the Sissy
qualification exam.

Ok, is everybody ready, Ok! Wheeee! (The macho teacher blows
the whistle).

Go! Go! Go! Aaagh! Thump, thump... slap... slap... slap (The
sound of the boys balls slapping against the Sissies asscheeks).
Agh!

Ok next! Keep it moving Studs! We don't have all day! You
Sissy want-to-be faggots, doing the fluffing, I want you to have
the Stud ready to explode the second they penetrate those ass-
pussies.

Slap, thump, slap. Aaaagh! Next! Let's go people, faster! Slap,
slap. Ahhhh! Slap.... slap.... Agh!

Ok! Pump and go Studs! Screwing Sissies isn't love making it's
a sport. Slap... slap... Aaaagh!

That's it Johnnie quick and easy, in-and-out, pop-n-go! Let's go!
Next! Slap, slap. Are you Studs or Sissy boys? I want to see
some ass rimming here PEOPLE! Next! Slap... slap... (Cum
flying everywhere) Aaagh!

A while later...

Okay, nice that's all fifty of you Stud jock's, let's hit the showers
playtime is over! Jimmy! Don't you go missing anymore football
practice chasing Sissy cunt, you hear me BOY..!!!!...

YES SIR!

You Whores! Hit the showers, take your Piss-On-Me from the Stud Breeders, then shower, douche-out and get back here for the next class. Go! Go! Go!

Wow, what an asshole. The Physical-Ed teacher has issues.

You got that right Jane. It's do this, do that. Please, we're the ones doing all the work around here. They think training to be a professional Whore® is easy. Huh!

Mary, I think it's because we're gonna being Civil Servant Whores. That's why he has issues.

You think he's Sissy-Phobic?

Yeah! Don't you? Huh! He hates us!

Well I heard he's never given more than a C grade to a Sissy in his Sex-PE class. And he gives an A grade to all the Stud jocks.

Yeah he definitely has Sissy-Phobia.

Oh yeah for sure. I heard he only does a Sissy enough times to collect his pay. In and out of the Whoring Station.

No way! For real! What an idiot!

Yeah he's a jerk! Considering in a Whoring Station a Sissy® by law is required to perform recreational sex with Studs if the dude can afford it.

[3.7] SHOWERS

Piss-on-me shower play...

Hey Lisa! What's up!

Hey Jane! You wanna do it together? Mwah...

Mwah... Yeah, yeah... Please piss on me Stud-Girl?

Slap! Hmmm... Kiss Kisss. Yes, please piss on me Stud chick! I'm just a Sissy Gurl. Hmmm Kiss... (Jane makes out with her pisser Lisa), piss on me please beautiful! Aaaagh! Pissssss... Aaah! Pissssss... Pissssss...

Yeah! Open your mouth Gurl! Slap! Jane, if I had a dick I'd screw you so hard! Oooh! Mwah... Yeah, I had to pee so bad!

Give me every drop you Stud-making bitch. Mwah...

Slap! Oh hey! Slap me more Babe! **Lisa,** I love your golden showers Girl! I'm so into you! Kisss... Ummmm... Kisss...

Ummm... Jane! Huh! Wow! Way to go Gurl! You're so fucking hot Jane! Ummmm... Kissss... Mwah...

Yeah thanks for the humiliation Lisa. Mwah... Hmmm... Lick... kissss. Mwah...

Yeah it was great we make a good pissing team, kiss.

Well hey! There's a **Piss-On-Me**© contest at the Cum-munity center next month you wanna team-up and do it together?

Yeah sure! Sounds like fun! I'll call you. Mwah...

Mwah… Ok Sissy-Gurl. Hmm... Kissss... Ooooh, I wanna bed you down Jane hmm... kisss. I really like you. Ummm… Mwah… Mwah… Cum by my house tonight and sleep with me. Mwah… (Lisa, who is twice the size of Jane, is all over her).

Oh Lisa! I'm hot for you too. Mwah… But, I don't sleep around on Mary (Jane jumps up onto her lovers hips and whispers into the girls ear). Mwah…

Okay a threesome, cool! Mwah…

Haa haaa ha… Okay I'll ask Mary if she's up for it. Mwah…

Mwah… Later Stud bitch!

Slap! (Lisa slaps Jane's ass goodbye). Oooh! Kissss... kisss, call me!

Mwah… For sure beautiful. Mwah…

After all the pissing...

Uh! My belly's full of piss, yeah mine too, let's get out there on our benches before the Anti-Sissy Asshole cums looking for us.

Out in the Gym...

Ok! You faggots are late! Get on those benches NOW! Ok! Studs ready set. Wheeee…. (The whistle blows).

GO! Slap, slap, thump... (The boys are banging the Gurls) thump... Next! Slap. Ahhhh!

Next! Slap, Next! Slap. Aaaaagh! Next! Slap... slap.... Next! Slap. GO! GO! GO!

Half an hour later...

Aaagh! Next! Slap... Thump... Slap... Aaaagh! Next! HEY! Don't just stand there admiring it, screw it! Slap... Next! Slap!

Dill-a-ling, dill-a-ling, dill-a-ling, dill-a-ling...

[3.8] LUNCH

Elementary School cafeteria...

Lunch! I'm so hungry I can milk an army.

Hee... hee... Yeah Mary, you're biggest gangbang was 69 Studs and you're going to milk an army?

Okay, maybe not the whole army but I hear the US Sissy-Corp in the army is awesome!

Yeah, I'll talk to you later about it. I got to slurp down some milk. I'm starving!

Hey Miss **Donna**! (EN01)

Hey Gurls! I knew I'd run into you two at Special Sexual Integration Elementary School 69.

Yeah you're not at **Sissy-World**© preschool anymore?

Well I finished college and got my teaching degree in Sissyology. My work at the Sissy-World Preschool was an internship for my teaching credentials.

Oh, cool!

So, are you Gurls still making-out in the lunchroom?

Nah! We're over that Miss **Donna**! We're sleeping together now! Mwah…

Haaa… haa… ha… Okay! Sure why not. You two are like bookends. Well good to see you Gurls.

Yeah you too Miss Donna, see you third period for Modern Sociology class.

Oh Mary! That reminds me, are we good for Friday night? (Jane remember Whorehouse obligations).

Yeah, yeah… It's my place this week.

Okay, your house around eight.

Jane my Mom told me to ask you if you can make it over by seven thirty, because if we're going to do Whorehouse (WH) training together we have to be douched-out, in our **FuckMe**® cloths and on our Labor Compensation Bench, a **LCB**® [22.4] before the scheduled eight o'clock WH opening.

Oh yeah sure Mary. I can make it over early. I'll do my homework during my Sex Training session with my SST. I wouldn't want to miss whoring with you. Four glorious hours between eight and midnight of constant man-sausage, no way am

Mwah... Oh Jane, I would love being with you forever my wild Sissy Bitch. Hmmm... Kiss.... Kisssss.... Mwah...

Hey, are you gonna sleep with your Sissy Sex Trainer again?

Oh Mike? Yeah, well we have to sleep with our trainers every night, except at Sissy Summer Camp and on the weekends.

Maybe we can swap our sex trainers in bed again?

Sure! You like Mike?

Yeah, yeah... I like Mike, he lasts longer than Jon my SST.

Oh yeah! He last more than an hour! Well I like Jon because he's a little wider than Mike's dick and when he's finished with me and pulls-out, my stretched Vaganus® feels satisfied.

Oh yeah me too. When he pulls-out of me, my hole stays open for business. There's nothing better than having a well-fucked feeling! Listen to us! We're comparing the Cocks we use. Haa haaa ha!

Yeah he's so big and thick, when he trains me I feel like I'm being fisted!

Cum on get to your milking stations Sissy-Gurls! (Ms. Donna hurries them along).

Slurp... Gulp.... Slurp, Gak... Guk.... Oh fresh **Man-Cream®** I love Dick-Milk! Slurp. It's so awesome and good for you, slurp.

Dozens of gulps later...

Glrck… Guk… Gak… Oh! Miss Donna I'm full! Glrck…

Ok, ok… Mary sweetheart, if you've had enough and can't swallow anymore, leave it to me. Get up and off of your LCB® when you're done milking. I'll just stick the milking machine on his Stud® dick if you can't handle the full load. You Gurls remember we don't want a drop of Man-Cream to go to waste.

Thanks Miss Donna, I can't swallow anymore!

Ok Honey, good Gurl, here's a towel clean the Jizzies off your face. And head to the waste room. The bells gonna ring anytime now.

Dill-a-ling, dill-a-ling, dill-a-ling…

Geeeez… Jane I couldn't swallow another drop! I think it's the mix between the piss from PE class and the lunch Sperm.

Yeah I can't swallow as much on Phys Ed days either.

How many loads did you down? I'll look on my Sissy-tablet.

I love the pink tablet case your Mom got yah. It's so cute.

Okay! It says I just drank down sixty point nine loads of Man-Cream. Whohooo!

How about you Jane? Ah, wait... Ah... sixty-nine!

Whoa! Jane, you cum-guzzler Whore! How did you do that? You always take more than me, you wild Cockoholic!

Thanks Mary. Hey when are you going to make Daisy?

I'm working on it Jane, you nympho! But it's typical of the **B-Type** Sissy. You Bitch types always have more sex than DOM® types.

True! We were made from different formulas.

Dam! Jane, I'm always trying to catch up to your **Cockage®** number. I need another 6,900 penetrations to hit the 20,000, the **Daisy** mark.

[1] **Level**: Fag,   **Quantity**: 10,000
[2] **Level**: Daisy,   **Quantity**: 20,000
[3] **Level**: Trap,   **Quantity**: 60,000
[4] **Level**: Wild Flower, **Quantity**: 100,000
[5] **Level**: Blossom,   **Quantity**: 200,000
[6] **Level**: Princes,   **Quantity**: 500,000
[7] **Level**: Queen,   **Quantity**: 1,000,000

Mary, Trap is an even harder ranking to achieve then Daisy. I'd have to have 60,000 penetrations to have a Trap ranking. Yeah, the Sex Activity Ranking, **SAR®** [5.E1.1] gets harder the higher up in Sissydom® you get.

[3.9] SOCIOLOGY

Modern sociology in elementary school…

Okay, class, take your seats. We have a lot to do today. We're on chapter 6, section 9 of your Modern Sociology textbook page 69. Who can tell me, from reading their homework assignment in paragraphs 6 through 9 the following question?

Why are Gurls Whores and not female girls?

Uooh! Uooh! Miss **Donna** (Mary excitedly waves her hand).

Yes, Mary.

Ms. Donna (EN07), it's because, the patented **Sissy-Gurl**® cannot get pregnant.

Very good Mary! This is one of the reasons, who can tell me another?

Miss **Donna!**

Yes, **Philip**.

Because the girls with a vagina have to make Stud® babies.

Okay, this is most of it, who can expand on this?

Okay **Jimmy**.

Well, if the human girl with a vagina is out being a Hoe no one would be home cooking, cleaning and getting knocked-up! Haa... haa... ooh... ha... ha. (The whole class cracks-up laughing).

Ok, Ok quiet down class! Quiet down! It's not funny! I don't want to hear the expression **knocked-up** in my classroom anymore. The appropriate expression is, breeding. I wanna have a talk with you after class Jimmy.

Okay, actually what Jimmy said is true, but it's the way he said it that disappointed me. In modern life in the MSES® of the United States Inc., women do have the subordinate role again of being exclusively housewives, and under total subjugation to their Stud® husbands who own them. As they have been in the pass in the US and in other male-dominated Western Cunt-tries down through the millennium. This switch back to woman being controlled by men is just one of the wonderful things which makes the new United States of America Inc. such a culturally unique and progressive place to live in the world.

But who can tell me why woman are not allowed to work in jobs and also have the privilege of being subservient housewives to the hard working Stud® men in our Cunt-trie?

Yes Danny.

Because the Sissies have little dicks and the men with big dicks work harder than woman.

Ok, Danny, did you even read this section in your textbook?

Yeah, kinda.

Ok who else has an answer and has actually read the assignment? Yes, Jane.

Because, men work harder and produce more if there's a treat waiting for them after they work. And men can be trained by regulating how much reward is given for how hard they work. Just like monkeys, mules, rats, horses or dogs, men are morons and trainable. Like Pavlov's dogs. Men in American will work for sex. They're a bunch of idiots!

Wow! Jane you took the words right out of my mouth. Go on.

You see Miss Donna. Thankfully, American men are no smarter than an animal in a cage and this is regardless of how many college degrees they have or not. If you feed them they'll do what the master tells them to do, and woman, especially Sissy women, are much more intelligent than men and the human species for that matter. They're not fooled by the old stick-n-carrot trick like human men are. Having a Vaganus® makes us smarter and clever.

Exactly Jane, **A+** for you smart Sissy-Gurl, very good! I'm so proud of you! Ok, one more thing, try to answer the question I asked earlier. Why are Sissies whores and not human female girls?

Yes Jesse.

Miss Donna it's because Sissies are little boys with very small penises and don't work as hard as men with big dicks.

Oh Cock-God in heaven! Forgive these ignorant human children!

Haaa... haa... (The class breaks out laughing), haaa... heee... haa.... ha....

What is so hard about this topic that I can't get you guys to learn it? Please if anyone knows the answer please speak now! Yes, Mary Dune again.

Well the original concept of breeding Sissies to perform as Whores stems from the Sissy-Culture or what was sometimes referred to as queers, which is an improper categorized. And visa verse, the Gay-Culture has been confused with the genetically engineered Sissy Class. So the fact is Homo-Sis-Sapiens [18.0.1] are not part of the Gay Cum-munity.

Very good Mary. Continue.

Right, that out of the way. The Sissy cross-breed with the Gay-Cum-munity were the least utilized. I mean it was the least exploited combination of sub-cultures in the old United States. This was due to the fact that our old fascist government wasn't smart enough to monetize sex as worker compensation.

But thanks to the manipulative nature of the United States, it seized on the opportunity. And its traditional method of abusing passive groups by submerging them into debt was replaced with a similar criminality of enslavement through Vaganus® ad-Dick-tion.

These abusive tactics unfortunately lead to the eradication of the over-paid working middle class and also lead to the miraculous creation of a new improved version of the sub-culture called **Sissy**® **2.0** [18.0.1]. This non-utilized, weak, queer group was genetically **Transmuted**® into the present-day **Hono-Sis-Sapien** [18.3] genome. From which the non-human genome the Sissy aka Vaganus® were breed and ultimately mobilized into action as a work-force by the Trade Promotional Authority (TPA) also called Fast-Track, passage of a Cunt-gressional bill in the year, 2213 called the United States Sissification® Act.

Wow! Thank you Mary, I learned that stuff in college!

Miss Donna can I just make one last important point here?

Ahh Yeah Mary! Wow and you're an eight year old BfB® Sissy? (The teacher can't believe this young part monkey gurl is so articulate).

Yes Ma'am, like I was saying, although crafting the Sissification Act did not include negotiating with our trading partners, or for that matter, any debate in Cunt-gress. Its product, the American

Vaganus® creature, was intended to be distributed globally. The distribution across borders of American Sissies would need to be by covert actions. This is due to the fact that our trading partners all band the shipment of the Homo-Sis-Sapien genome animals to their Cunt-tries. Sissydom® has never been embraced by any nation other than the United States Inc.

Anyway by passing the Sissification Act, mutant hybrid Sissy humanoid animals were breed into existence with the implementation of the **Sissification**® Drug [4.D-G1] formulas B and D. These new abstractions of the Sissy class are capable of having many times more orgasms and produce more tit and clit milk than the average human female.

This scientifically mutated group, often referred to as Sissy® 2.0, provides the entire human male population of the United States Inc. with a paper-less, worker pay compensation as well as recreational sex while freeing the Stud-Baby making female population of our Cunt-trie to have the ability to produce stronger, longer cocked males to do productive industrial work and also defend our nation.

Now this is the correct answer to my question! Yes, Sissy's are the smartest students! There's hope after all. Okay, only one smart child in the whole class could answer my question and it was a Sissy® child. Thank you Mary Dune.

Dill-a-ling, dill-a-ling, dill-a-ling, dill-a-ling...

That's it guys! See you on Thursday and don't forget to read chapter 6, and answer questions 6 through 9, on, Sissy Breeding and the Non-Studs inability to work hard. Not so fast, Jimmy, a word!

I'll miss my bus Miss Donna!

Ok Jimmy, go but I got my eye on you boy! You **Opt-Out** [13] kids are always looking for trouble and dumb as a Non-Stud. Dam! If it wasn't for those idiots opting out to Breed into a Stud or Sissy class in society they wouldn't even be enrolled in a Special Integration School.

[3.10] BUS

Waiting for the bus home...

Aaaagh! Ok! Ok! William, pop your load and pull your dick out, I'm gonna miss my bus! Whoa! You Jizzed my skirtini dude!

You told me to pull-out Jane and I was in the middle of filling your hole. Sorry!

Ok! Mary hates when I get all Jizzed-up. Kiss, see you William.

Thanks Janie, you're the best! Sorry Janie... Mwah...

Mwah... Yeah I know. Thanks for creaming my skirt William. Geeeezy Weeeezy! I'm just gonna take it off and stick it in my backpack.

What's up Gurlfriend? Where's your skirt Jane?

Oh nothing, you know William has at me every day before our bus cums, but he showed up late today. Let's just get on the bus quick before we miss it. He ended up getting me Cummied up.

Wait Jane you're naked, except for your knee highs, platforms and training bra. Here, let's put my paisley scarf around your hips and Walla! Hippy Sissy Gurl skirt. Haaaa haa ha...

I love you Mary. Kisss. You're my true friend.

[3.11] RID

The Gurls rid all the boys home...

I'm so glad our families **Whorehouses** [7.G4] are on the same block.

Yeah me too **Mare**, we get to ride the school bus home together.

I love you Jane. Mwah... You're precious to me!

I love too Mare. Mwah... Let's get married?

What? Jane you know Sissies have to marry Sissy Breeding Ladies so we can breed more Sissy-Whores. It's a law.

Hey, but we're still Gurlfriends right?

Yes! Of course Honey. And we'll be best friends forever. My BFF. Kissss. Hey, when we grow-up we can do a Sissy-Promise!

Oh yeah, Sissies take vows to be a couple.

Yeah, Jane, we can take the **Sissy-Promise**®, look in the Sissydom® manual [6.A].

Mary get off the school bus and skip away holding each other's hands. Leaving a trail of semen which is freely flowing out from between their legs.) Mwah… See you Boys! Mwah… (The Gurl blow kisses to all the boys on the bus).

Hmmm… I'm hungry for **Sissy-Poop**® [4.D-G1.37] too! (Ummm sounds delicious!). Mwah…

Chapter 4: High School

The year is 2246...

[4.1] DRESS-CODE

The Gurls dressing-up in Lady Cloths...

How do Gurls walk in these stupid things? Six inch classic pumps! Dam! Why can't we just keep wearing our eight inch platforms? I've been wearing platforms since I was a baby and now that we're going to high school we have to wear proper lady shoes. I hate all these changes.

Yeah, but Jane we don't have to wear those stupid elementary school Hentai style uniforms anymore! With the pleated, plaid, mini-skirts and the open chest tops, obviously designed to make us look like slutty traps.

Right! So we can show our pert little Gurly tits. You know school uniforms are just stereotype outfits.

Yeah, I mean why wear a uniform if the style says, Hey I'm a school Gurl FUCK ME! It makes us look like porn stars.

Porn? What's porn?

You don't remember watching the documentary about the sex industry in the US back a couple hundred years ago?

Oh yeah! Female women sold their bodies for sex. It actually hasn't changed much, other than the sex industry is now owned by the US government and Sissies replaced woman as Whores®.

Ah Jane, you left out the part about the Stud® men get paid to fill our loveholes.

Oh yeah, sorry, minor detail! Haa... haaa... I'm just so glad to be a Sissy-Gurl® cum-bucket on the receiving end of the deal.

Yeah me too Jane.... Kisssss.... Well anyway, what are you wearing for the first day of high school?

I think I'm going to wear a peek-a-boo or cup-less SissyBra® with my nipples sticking out.

Ooooh Hot!

And a crotch-less panty my Mom bought me to wear for my Dad's birthday party.

Nice! Revealing but sexy nice, you gonna wear gloves too?

Oh yeah! Definitely, totally whored-up, with elbow high gloves with the lace cuffs. And thigh-high stay-ups, above-the-clit lace skirtini and of course, the mandatory six inch classic pumps.

Oooh! Bend over Bitch, my three inch DOM® clit is so freaken hard for you. I wanna do you right now Baby!

Oooh! Kiss... kiss, (Jane and Mary are constantly making-out) kiss... Lick... Kiss. Mwah...

I'm serious bend over! I'm going to pop a load!

Oooh yeah! Do me Gurlfriend! (Jane props her tiny little ass up in target range).

Ahhh Yeah! Take it! Aaagh! Oooh! Jane, yeah that's a good Bitch! I love the way I have you trained to bend over, good Gurl! Aaagh! Aaagh! Aaagh! (Mary rapidly plows her Lovers bottom).

Thank you Mary, Hose me! I love you! I'm your Gurl Baby! Fill me with your special Sissy-Cream®. Hmm.... Kissss... Ooooh! I love when you cream my coochee like that! I wish I could have your baby!

After recuperating…

Mary, what are you gonna wear?

Well you know my Mom?

Yeah, your hot foxy classy college educated Sissy-Breeding lady Mom who I've eaten-out a million times. Yeah sure! I know her.

Yeah haaaa haa ha… You know her. Funny, I mean she's a little bit too conservative on the dressing-up thing. So I have to wear something less revealing than you. I'm wearing, a real pretty white lace see-through top, a long paisley scarf with a see-through lace-bra, a suit blazer and a pearl necklace.

Ooooh high class! I can hear the Stud® boys whistling at you.

Yeah, yeah, I should be able to attract plenty Cocks. And of course my Mom picked out my outfit. For my bottom I'm wearing a just below the clit pink skirt with a pink **SissyWear**® lace panty with a matching lacy Clit-Sock®. And you know my usual lace-top stockings with garter-belt and the mandatory high school, six inch classic pumps.

Oh it sounds so adorable and totally you. You're always dressed as a classy lady, Mare. Mwah… If I had a big enough dick, I'd rape you right now. Mwah…

Mwah… Thanks Gurlfriend. You turn me on too Jane. Hmmm.... Kiss..... Kissss.... You turn everyone on Jane. Your **Cockage**® total is so freaken high, I'm jealous. Kiss... kissss... French me Bitch! Kiss... lick. All the Sissies are so jealous of your hot ass Jane... Kiss...

Suck my clit Mary, I love you! Dominate me Mary, slap me, I want to obey my sweetheart **DOM**®. I love you so much! Kisss... Kisss... Show me who the boss is Mary, slap my face. Make me your Bitch Mary! Spank and slap me. I wanna be owned by you. Mwah…

Slap! Ooooh! Kiss... Lick... (Mary lightly slaps Jane on the cheek). You're mine! All mine! Mwah… Oooh Jane! I love you Baby!

Harder! Slap me hard Mare!

Slap!

More Mary! Slap me again I'm yours. I belong to you Baby! I squirt Jizzzies when you slap me! Agh!

Slap! Slap!

Several orgasms later…

Thanks, Mary I needed that. Once in a while I just need you to put me in my place. (Jane buries her head in Mary's bosom). Mwah... I love when you slap me around. Mwah...

Well my little submissive Bitch®, all I know is you're going to get all the attention you need, because we're going to quadruple our **Cockage**® by going to high school. I know we're gonna have dicks constantly up our loveholes.

How much more?

I read online we can expect to be doing a minimum Cockage of several hundred or more loads per day!

Cool! I'm ready for this party. Mary, I'm ad-Dick-ted to penis and the sweet cream that cums out of them! I think I'm a **Cumoholic** [7.G5.1].

Baby, I'll be there for you if you ever need me, so don't worry. Kissss... If you ever need Cum-rehab I'll be with you. Through good times or bad, I won't let anything happen to you Lover.

But about school I read on the Special Integration High School's website the enrollment is several thousand students this year. And only sixty-nine or so Sissies are in attending. Some of the Sissies are non-breed from birth Transmute, **TM**® [2.B2.11]. This means we each have to take several hundred penetrations per day. And don't forget the admin and faculty. That's several hundred more.

Wow! You just described paradise.

Yeah but the Sissy® training distribution system at high school is different. It won't let you horde cocks like you did back in elementary school.

What do you mean?

If you start building up a reputation as a nice piece-of-ass, you'll attract more than your fair share of boys.

Yeah! Exactly my plan, Mare! Mwah... I want as many as I can attract to me.

Yeah well Jane, we know this will happen with you because you're such a hot Sissy-Gurl. With your long blonde hair and your perfect petite little sexy seven year old looking body! You're a cock-magnet!

Oh bummer! Well, Mary then how do we get more boys up our skirts?

You mean if you're wearing one? Heee... heee... Anyway, I knew you were gonna ask this question Jane. So don't worry Lover, I did some research Gurlfriend and this is how we can satisfy your eternal itch in your genetically modified, **B-Type** Sissy-cooch.

Cool! Mwah... You got my back. Mwah...

Sure I do! Mwah... So! We can volunteer for after school stuff and extra-sexual-curricular activities, like cheerleading, Sissy-Stud citizenship, band, glee club and stuff like that.

Cool! Cool! Cool! Mwah...

Mwah... Oh and also we're eligible for Cum-munity service projects through the high school, like Cum-munity Recreational Sissy Training and special Sissy career day fieldtrips to military bases, our state capitol and factories. They're all filled with lots of perverted corrupt Politicians, horny workers and brave Stud soldiers. And also trips to college campuses.

Whooohooo...!!!...

We're gonna have huge **Cockage**® numbers!

Oh, and don't forget, we've both turned thirteen and are legal Whoring age, so we can take penetration from the general public. And because we're in high school, every Saturday we have to volunteer at a Whoring-Station for a minimum of two hours. The best part is we can volunteer for our Whoring® duty at the Whoring-Station our Father's Whore at.

Awesome! Yeah, Station WS690C.

Right our Dads are both working as common Hoes at Whoring-Station 690.

Yep! Hundreds more cum-spewing man-sausages! Hmmm! More tasty treats for us young professional whore wannabe Sissy-Gurls!

Oh! And don't forget about **JAS** [16] camp and JAS Scout meetings!

Oh yeah! We can do all the really cool JAS scouting merit badges, Deepthroat, Cow-Gurl, Fisting, Squirting, Gangbang, Horse-Stud ranch.

Hey! Mary we never talk about college, maybe we can go to the same college together?

Oh Gurlfriend! Mwah… I'm not going to college without you but let's get through high school first. You'd love college, the **Cockage**® [7.G5.4] is like twice the amount in high school.

Wow! Two hundred or more loads a day! Holy-Poop! I'm salivating! Gimme! Gimme! Gimme!

Yeah! Haaaa haa ha… Calm down Jane, your mission in life is to swallow and screw! What am I gonna do with you? You're my penis-craving, sperm-hungry Sissy best friend forever. Mwah… Love you!

Well, hey our Sissy-in-Training, **SIT** [1.4] Daddy's get this kind of Cockage® as professional Whores®. And hey! They're always walking around with a smile on their face.

Yeah, yeah… They're happy. And they're not even pure breed from birth Sissies like us!

Right, we'll have a lot more opportunities then our fathers do because we're pure breed Sissies, **PBS**® [2.B2.10].

Umm… Hmm… Not queer faggots like our transitioned SIT® Dads.

Jane! Don't you dare let anyone hear you talking **gay-words** like that in public! It's illegal to talk naughty derogatory words.

Right, right… The thirty-four Amendment, **Profanity** [17.34]. Use of disrespectful accusations regarding sexual orientation is forbidden. I got it!

But you're right my lover. Being pure has so many benefits. Like I've never had boy feelings ever.

Yeah, me too. I never wanted to be a boy.

Right, or do a Gurl with my big three inch DOM clit. And this is despite having a tiny man-penis and a pair of miniature balls which won't stop producing Jizzies®.

Mary, I've always been a Gurl. I've always wanted men to do me. And even though I know I'll never be able to get pregnant like a real human girl, I still have feelings like I'm gonna be knocked-up.

[4.2] BEFORE CLASS

Getting to class in high school…

Hey Jane, I have to hit the boy's restroom and get some Studs to mount me before class.

Hoe! This is weird. My DOM Lady needs to get her twat serviced? Hmmm… Mwah… Enjoy!

Yeah well, I'm dry down there and I hate sitting through a class without a fresh Jizzzie load up my coochee.

Well I gotta get a fresh Clit-Sock® from my locker so I'll see you in class. Mwah…

Mwah… Okay! Save me a **SissySeat®** [4.D-G1.22] next to you.

Babe! We'll always sit next to each other, kissss. Oh! Mary in the boy's restroom if you take a load in your face can you save a snowball for me!

Okay Lover! Hmmm.... Kisss... Mwah…

[4.3] GANG

At the lockers...

Hey! Watch it! (Jane is bumped hard by several girls passing her). Dam, Ouch! Hey watch where you're going.

You got a problem? (One of the large husky girls shouts at Jane).

Hey! Whoa! (Jane, being a stick person compared to these girls, easily gets knocked to the floor).

You knocked me down! Dam it! Oh! Okay, wait hey I didn't do anything to you and I don't want to fight anybody!

It sounds like you got a problem, Bitch? (The larger than the rest gal says in a domineering voice).

What the… (Jane gets up off the floor) HELL? Hey stop pushing me, Ouch! Hey! HEY! Stop it! Leave me alone! (Now the whole gang, of butch looking girls, is pushing Jane around).

Really, six on one! Let go of my hair! What-the-fuck do you want? Ouch!

Slap, slap. (It starts getting physical).

HEY! Stop it! You're hurting me! What do you want?

Do you know who I am? (This chick is obviously the leader of the gang. Dressed only in black Goth style, black make-up, combat boots, tattoos, and lip and nose piercings).

Queen of the Domination Freaks?

Slap, Slap, Slap (Jane hits the floor again).

Stop it! Sniffle, sniffle... Ouch! Sniffle, sniffle... You're hurting me! Sniffle...

Huh! This little Sissy-Bitch cries like a little Non-Stud boy. Haaa... ha... ha (The Goth gang members laugh at Jane crying). Like a little boy! Boo hoo, hoo... Ahhh... Hah... haaa...

I'm Hilary. Hilary Clintcum! And if you're gonna be attending Special Integration High School 69 you need to know something. NO Stud goes up a Sissy twat without me knowing about it. You got that Bitch?

Sure whatever. (Jane isn't taking this arrogant witch seriously).

SLAP.... SLAP... (The leader pounds Jane's face with her hand).

Whoa! Dam! Stop slapping me!

SLAP.... SLAP... (The subjugation lesson continues).

OH! Ooouuch! Go way!

THUMP! (The leader kicks Jane in her tiny little nut-sack).

Ooooooh! You kicked me in my freaken balls! Ooouuch! SHIT! Aaagh! That hurts! Oooh! Ok, ok... NOT IN THE

BALLS! (Jane puts her legs together and cups her balls to protect her precious, little nuts).

I know who you are. You're Jane Goldberg you got quite a reputation. The highest **Cockage**® and the smallest clit of any freshmen Sissy here.

So what? No, no, no... (The Leader raises her hand to Jane as a threat to slap her again).

And your petite little fuckable B-Type body is the kind the Studs love to toss around and take turns with. You're just a fuckdoll. So it makes you the new hot little Bitch® the Stud boy's love screwing.

Yeah so what?

SLAP! (Jane gets trained by heavy handed tactics).

Aghhh! Okay, okay... What do you want?

I want you to remember this for your own sake my friend, I'm the Sissy Queen at this High School and never, ever, ever try doing any of my Stud® boys. You got that scank? (The Amazon size butch-type girl, is gripping Jane's face in one hand) Slap.

YES! Okay Yes! I get it!

Listen to me you gangbanging slut. The big foot-long Studs are mine! You got that?

Yes! Yes! Okay I get it! The big boys are yours.

You better get it, if you don't want me kicking you in those precious little Sissy nuts again! You can have any boy you want, but they better not be from my Stud stable of foot-long, (L12) boys. Let's go Girls! Oh! And Jane.

WHAT?

Have a nice day.

[4.4] RESCUE

Mary finds Jane in the fetal position on the floor…

Sniff... Sniff... (Jane's in tears). Sniff…

Jane what happened? Why's your stuff all over the place? And your face is all red! Cum on get up. (Mary helps Jane sit up against her locker).

Mary! This, this, this gang of big Girls just attacked me! Sniff... Sniff... Sniff... Sniff...

Oh Jane! You've got quite an imagination Gurl.

MARY! I just got kicked in the balls! Ow! They hurt.

Well, do you want me to massage your little nuts? Who'd you piss off this time, Jane?

NOBODY! I was just standing here, minding my own dam business, putting my stuff in my locker, getting a new Clit-Sock® out. And the next thing I knew I was pushed to the floor surrounded by this gang of these black leather wearing, tough Goth looking, Amazon sized Sissies! And their Queen sat on me and slapping the shhh...it out of me! Literally! Oh shit! I crapped my panties! Oooooh, dam it! Sniff... Sniff...

Oh God-of-Cocks Jane! Here let me help you up. Oh Honey, I worry about you Jane, are you sure they were Sissies?

MARY! I don't know! I've never seen Sissies that big before but I swear there was a violent gang of ahhh... I don't know what the hell they were! (Jane still in shock from the beating she endured isn't quite sure what they were). All I know is I saw up their skirts, they didn't have Cocklets. They had big man size dicks!

Hmmm.... Jane these Amazon Sissy bullies weren't real Sissies.

Huh? Well then what the heck were they?

Trans-Mutts® [2.B2.11].

What's a Trans-Mutt?

They're defective Transmutation® chicks. When the DNA gets screwed-up in the Sissy transmutation process the result is more like the guys who beat you up. They're very human in most ways, rude, violent, ignorant, greedy, and obnoxious.

Yeah, they were like humans, dumbass and violent!

They're a resemblance of the old US government. Nothing like us pure Sissies. Trans-Mutts are more Homo-Sapiens than Homo-Sis-Sapiens. But the government can't use them as Whores®, because they're not classified as animals by the US Department of Agriculture like we are. So most **Trans-Mutt**® gurls are just put back into the system as janitors at Whoring Stations.

Aaah! My nuts still hurt. Mary! I just got my balls kicked-in! Sniffle... Sniffle... (tears) ...Sniffle.

Oh, Jane Honey, come here, I love you, I'm sorry I wasn't here for you sweetheart. Hmm.... Kisss.... (Mary puts her arm around Jane's shoulder to console her). Oooh my poor sweet honey-puss.... Kisss....

Mwah… I'll be okay. Psssss… Crazy chicks with dick.

Jane, I would assume those mean **Trans-Mutt**® chicks are just territorial bullies, because they know you're a hot Bitch. Trans-Mutts are always jealous of Sissies and especially pure breed Sissies, **PBS**® like us. The street name for Trans-Mutts is just Mutts.

Yeah Mutts! Huh! The name fits. They wouldn't win a beauty contest, that's for sure.

True! But it's because they're a cross-breed, they're not Sissy or fully human. Like I was saying, Mutts definitely have more human traits than Sissy. Hell they're not remotely like real Sissies cause their clits and tits don't squirt or lactate voluminously like ours. And Mutts don't even have a **Vaganus**® so they're sexually useless and definitely unwhorable.

Right, you can't make a Whore without a Vaganus®.

As far as picking on you, they know by your petite little body and your tiny little clit you're a **B-Type**®. Created to be constantly on the prowl for penis. So they feel threatened because you're naturally promiscuous. The **Mutts**® know they don't have the seductive powers and pheromones of a purebred Bitch like you.

Oh Mary shut-up! My balls hurt! Kiss me. Mwah…

Mwah… Ahhh… Jane Honey, tell me all about what happen (Mary being parental, as usual, consoles Jane. She pats Jane on her back to calm her down). My poor Love bunny. Mwah…

They sniffle... sniffle... kicked my ass Mary! Punch!

Ouch! Jane, don't hit me. Okay, Okay. Just tell me what they wanted from you Honey?

The Sissy, Mutt Queen, whatever, sniffle... sniffle... just doesn't want me, sniffle... sniffle.... playing with any of the foot-long Stud® boys at school.

Okay Jane! This sounds like a perfectly reasonable request.

MARY!

Okay, so yeah, you do have an unusual desire to be screwed constantly by large penises.

MARY! What am I gonna do? You know the type of dicks who are attracted to me.

Yes Jane I do, LARGE!

Stop making fun of me! (Jane lightly punches Mary on the shoulder again). Sniff... Sniff... This is SERIOUS!

Oh sweetheart. Hey look at me, I love you. I'll always be there for you and always have been there for you. Kiss... (Mary kisses Jane on her forehead).

We've been together forever, since we were babies. Ever since our Mom's put us in a crib and we instinctively started suckling each other's Gurly-Clits like they were our Mommies tit nipple.

Yeah, we bonded forever Jane. I think of you as my sister and my Bitch®.

Mary, don't forget the part about us being Lovers. Snifff...

Mwah... Yes, my Honey-Bunny and Lovers too. Kiss... Kiss... Okay, well obviously I'll have to stay closer to you here at high school. Cum on Jane, let's go change your panties and go to the lunchroom before class and guzzle some Man-Cream®. This always makes you feel better.

What the **Man-Cream**® or you changing my panties? Mwah...

Mwah... Oh Jane (Mary throws her arm around Jane), both you silly Sissy Gurl!

After morning class...

[4.5] LUNCH

High school cafeteria...

Wow! The high school cafeteria is soooo big!

Yeah, and look at the milking stations, it's so different here at high school. Wow, and the pricks have access to us at both ends, cool! We're screwed while we milk dicks, awesome!

Yeah, I love my holes filled at the same time! It's like when boys take turns on us.

Good! Did you get enough Cream?

Yeah Jane, I got a cunt and belly full, what about you?

Yeah, Uooogh! I can't swallow anymore Jizz. And I love taking it at both ends! High school is Sissy heaven!

Jane, Jane, (Mary can't get Jane's attention, she's not responding while thinking about the way she was treated when feeding).

Yeah! Mary look at all of these magnificent hard Studs! Oh! My Cock-God! I don't want to go to class. Mary the dick-milk flows like a river here.

Jane we have a Sissy Hygiene lecture after lunch. With Mr. Asshemer.

Geeeez… What a name, Ass! Heee... hee...

[4.6] OPT-OUT

The Gurls discuss the social class system…

But hey you're right about the volume here, **Jane**. There's way more Stud® cum here because at an integrated high school they have the Non-Stud boys fluffing the Studs for us.

Whoa **Mare!** Isn't that considered gay-sex? Or Man-on-Man sex, MOM [4.D-G5.6] sex?

Yeah **Jane** it is for Non-Sissy boys. But if a Stud® man has a high enough Stud-Cock Ranking, an **SCR**® [5.E2.1] they can submit a form to perform Man on Man sex. I mean they don't let just any man mount a dude. It highly regulated.

Well, I thought gay-sex like that was illegal?

Yeah, yeah… It is but this is an Integration High School which has special rules. Here the Non-Stud students who have declared a class **Opt-Out** [4.11] to breed-out from the Non-Stud class into the Sissy class are just humiliated for their own good.

Huh! Okay explain the Opt-Out again.

Well the point is they need special training. Because it's like our dads did after their eighteenth birthday. If they're going to grow up and be transitioned into the Sissy Breeding Program, the **SBP** [4.D-G6.2], they might as well start to understand humiliation is part of a Sissies life.

Yeah! Tell me about it. (Jane is still holding her head from her lunch time incident).

I mean they're in high school which means they're older than twelve years old and can't do **Transmutation**® into Sissy humanoids. So it means these human kids just need to be placed in the **Junior SIT** program [4.D-G2.6].

Junior SIT? What the hell?

Yeah, it's in the SM06 **Sissydom**© Manual. Human kids between eight and eighteen whose families have declared an Opt-Out to Sissy class must enroll in the Junior SIT program. They can only do supervised oral training before they're eighteen and only with adolescent children never with adults. They legally cannot be penetrated or have intercourse sex by anyone till they're a legal age because they're humans.

Poor kids, they get to lick, kiss and suck other kid's dicks but they can't screw them! It's torture not training. It would drive me crazy.

Yeah the Junior SIT program sounds crazy.

Mary, I don't get the whole, Opt-Out thing.

Well it's like this Jane. Here in America our Government wants to get rid of the Non-Stud class altogether just like they eliminated the working middle class after the 2008 financial crisis.

Right, they created a debt-peonage which causes enslavement of the working population.

Exactly! You see my precious, the Non-Stud or what they used to call the middle class are now and were in the past unemployed and supposedly costing the government too much money to support with social services so they were and still are just being eliminated.

Sounds evil to me!

Yeah Jane, super-evil. It could be considered a financial genocide of an entire population. But our Government didn't kill them, they would never be that cruel, instead they just starved them out of existence or forced them to move into a **FEMA** [4.D-G7.13] zone, camp or to another Cunt-trie.

But ironically it's not the poor and middle class who cause the government to have less revenue. It's the government, the wealthy one percent and corporations, through unfair trade agreements, huge trade deficits, zero-interest loans for private banks and multi-national corporations. Those profiteers are importing products back into the US and paying no taxes.

Yeah! Or import tariffs on products produced in their overseas factories. Those factories used to be here in the United States. Oh! And let's not forget to mention the complete sale of our Cunt-trie to private bankers through the Federal Reserve Act back in 1913.

Wow Mary! Ain't we the junior socioeconomic, historian?

Haa... haa... Well Sissy-Puss I get voted class president every year for a reason. I state the facts. The wealthy bourgeoisie run our Cunt-gress and the Whitehouse. And I read all my Dads Sissyology textbooks. We're living in a Ponzi scheme.

Hey Mare I don't care who our government screwed in the past, it works for me because the Stud® students pop the second they put their pricks through the Glory-Hole and the tip of their rock hard dicks touch our mouth or pussy lips! Boom! Instant Cum load, after load, after load, it was like they opened the cum-valve and the Jizzies just kept flowing out of their sperm-hoses. And Mary, I really don't care if someone gets humiliated or financially impoverish as long as it's easier to guzzle more Man-Cum.

Oh! Okay I see, said the cum-guzzling opportunist! Heee.... heee... heee... Jane! What am I gonna do with you?

[4.7] PROTECTOR

Mary watches out for Jane...

Ouch! (Jane's rubbing her face which is still sore from being abused by some misogynistic asshole).

What's wrong Honey Bunny? (Mary, parentally always there for Jane).

Oh, it's nothing. My throat kinda hurts a little. I just hate when these macho assholes call me a Boy-Bitch, we're just a new breed of chicks-with-dicks, what don't they get?

Their just stupid Jane. Humans aren't the brightest creature on this planet.

Well, yeah men in particular are stupid this is a fact. Stupid or not, I do love the larger size pricks here at high school. They're definitely larger than the ones at elementary school. When I was feeding, the one teacher must have been at least a foot-long. And I gagged on it.

Wow! Jane? You gagged on a dick? That's a first!

Yeah! Haa haaa…. I know. Ouch! Ugh! Ugh! (Jane coughs).

Jane, are you alright? Let's go to the Nurses office.

No I fine. Mary you're right, you could put a snake down my throat. But this asshole reached his hand through the Glory-Hole grabbed my hair and pulled my head to him. He was slamming his prick down my throat so hard he was giving me a face-fucking not a Sissy feeding me. The god-dam idiot! My throats really sore. Ugh! Ugh!

JANE! Why didn't you tell me when it happened? You can file a complaint at the Principles Office!

It's Okay Mary. Ugh! Ugh!

Jane it's not okay! I don't like when men are rough with you! I'm not going to let (Mary stops Jane and looks at her sternly) these assholes hurt my Gurlfriend! There's a federal law against hurting Sissies.

Yeah I know the Sissy Rights Act, the **SRA** [17.30]. No Mary let it go I'm fine. It was just some idiot macho asshole there're plenty of good boys out there to feed from. Ugh! Ugh!

Okay! I'll file the complaint for you myself!

NO Mary! Ugh! Ugh!

Jane you're my Bitch®. I'm not going to let anything happen to you.

STOP! Just, just stop it Mary! If you file the complaint the teacher and his other macho asshole teacher buddies will make high school a living hell for us. Just let it go. I love you Mary and I know you care about me, but something's in this Stud-Sissy world just can't be fixed. Okay?

[4.8] PROPOSAL

Mary proposes the Sissy-Promise to Jane...

Hey, I'm sorry Mary.

I'm sorry too Jane. Kiss... Kissss. I don't ever want to argue with you but after the Trans-Mutt® gang beating you up, I'm just concerned and feel I should be doing more to protect you.

Oh Lover, I don't wanna be your pet, a liability to you.

You're not Jane! You know I care about you so much. I worry about you all the time. I don't want to lose you! You're everything to me! I would take my Sissy-Promise vows with you, this is how much I love you! Mwah...

Oh Mary, I'd vow to you too! Wait! I dream of promising myself to you! I've been wearing the Sissy Gurlfriend ring you gave me and I've never taken it off since you put it on my finger. Sniff... Sniff...

Oh Jane, you Sweetheart. Mwah...

Remember when we were seven years old and we took a walk in the park. Then you got down on one knee and asked me to be your Sissy Gurlfriend and I cried and cried tears of joy.

Mwah... Jane, you realize we're both legal Whoring age now?

Yeah Mary, we're thirteen, we're not jail-bait anymore. Hell, even Non-Studs can do us now! Uuugh....

Ooooh! Scary thought! Jizz-Us® I'd never let a Non-Stud up my DOM® puss. But what I was getting at is, being older also means we can take our Sissy-Promise vows with each other. And this means you can't have sex with other Sissies unless the DOM you're promised too gives you permission. And Jane you know how jealous I get when other Sissies play with you?

Mary? Are you **Sissy-Promise**® [6.F] proposing to me?

Yes Jane I am. Oh Jane! (Jane throws her arms around Mary).

Yes Mary? Yes! I do! I do! I do! I want to be your Bitch!

Jane will you be my Bitch?

Oh Mary, I love you! Yes I'll be your Bitch®, I'll be your Sissy Bitch forever! Will you be my DOM?

Yes, Jane! Of course I'll be yours! Let's take our Sissy-Promise (Jane and Mary compassionately embrace) vows (tears flowing from both Gurls) together!

Oh Mary! I Love you so much! Kiss.... kiss... Mwah…

Jane like I was saying, promising yourself to me means you won't be able to cheat on me, you realize this don't you?

Mary, I'm yours, I wear your ring, I'll wear your collar, obey you and I'll never sleep with another DOM. I have a great Lover and I don't need another in my life.

Good because, I've already filed the papers.

Oooh you sneaky! Haaa haa ha… Mwah…

Yes and we'll have to announce it to our folks about getting Sissy Promised®. Hmm.... Kisss.... Oh! And Honey.

What? Mwah…

I even bought a collar and leash for you. Hmmm…

Ooooh! You smartass! You knew all along you were gonna propose to me!

Of course I knew darling, after all, I'm the DOM® and I do most if not all the thinking for us. Oh... Kiss.... Mwah…

[4.9] ASSHEMER

Sissy hygiene meeting and the SSSM…

Ok, lunch is over for you Sissy-Queers! I'm Mr. **Asshemer** (EN15) and there'll be no free time after lunch today for you freshmen. I need all of you Sissies to follow me into the milking stations locker-room for a brief lecture on Sissy Hygiene.

Mare do you think he's going to probe us with his man-tool?

Huh! No he sounds seriously evil. He won't probe us because he knows how much we would enjoy it! Hee... hee.... heeee....

In the locker room...

After my talk with you cum-factories, you're going to douche-out your dirty cum dripping cunts, clean yourselves up like normal semi-human beings and get to class! But first I need to remind you young freshmen wannabe Whores you must wear a Cum-Collecting-Sock here at school at all times with no exceptions. Those are the rules!

Oh! We're definitely gonna get probed! Hee... hee... heeee...

Miss Goldberg? (Asshemer looks at Jane with a penetrating look).

Huh? What?

Jane Goldberg right?

Yes Sir! (Jane replies just to pacify Asshemer).

Miss Goldberg! I was given your academic history file by the Principle and notice I'm not holding anyone else's file.

Yep! (Jane is almost looking for trouble).

I see on your school records you love to spray the walls of the schools you attend with your Jizzies. First at, **Sissy-World**® preschool and then again at, Special Sexual Integration Elementary School 69. Do you have an explanation for this misbehavior?

Heee... heee... hee... #$%@&! (Jane cusses under her breath).

Shhhh… Jane, stop it (Mary whispers in Jane's ear while nudging her in the rips). He's not being funny or joking.

But judging by your giggly laugher, you obviously think the topic of uncontrolled discharge of your Sissy-Cream in public places is hilarious.

Ahhh…. Kinda funny… Heee... heee... hee...

Well, Miss Goldberg! I don't care how funny you think this is, or what you do at home! I don't care if you're sleeping with your Daddy, I don't care if you're Jizzing on your brothers and sisters while they sleep! I don't even care if you're creaming in your senile grandmother's breakfast cereal bowl!

Wow! Doesn't sound very concerned. Heee... heee... hee...

I have one piece of advice for you Goldberg, put a SOCK ON IT! (Asshemer bellows out the command). And keep a sock on it! If I catch you without a sock on, what's got to be the smallest little Sissy-Clit I've ever seen in my life, you're going to be in detention forever and banded from extra-sexual-curricular activities! You got that FAGGOT!

Sure. (Jane can't believe how big a douche-bag this guy is and just shakes her head).

Okay, what was I saying? Oh yeah! So, basically we don't want to see your Sissy Jizzies all over the place.

Mr. Ass Hemer?

Yes? The little blonde with the pigtails.

What if our collecting sock is full?

This is an excellent question! You can get a new clit-cum-sock for free at the Nurses Office. They'll even help you remove the old one and replace it with a new one.

Yes! You, the almost naked little slutty gurl in the front. What's wrong with you people? You don't have the decency to wear cloths!

Sir, can we drink the cum-loads from our socks?

Yes, of course! Follow the rules for proper cum disposal at all times. There are instructions about cum disposal in your Sissy Manuals, version SM069, in Section 4, reference **SSSM** [4.D-G2.9].

Appendix D, Government Programs, Systems,
Sissy and Stud Sperm Management (Program)

Which I'm sure, now that you're all high school students and are a legal Whoring® age, you have read thoroughly, cover to cover.

Remember, there's a Federal Law against wasting Stud or Sissy sperm. The Sissy and Stud Sperm Management law, the **SSSM**. Non-Stud sperm on the other hand, is trash and should be flushed down the toilet! Non-Stud middle-class folks are not USA Inc. citizen, therefore they're Sperm is worthless.

Wow! Mare, this guy is really a douche-bag. (Jane whispers).

Now, about the Cum Disposal rules in the **SSSM**. If a Federal Inspector cums to our school and finds a Cum-Sock®, male condom or so much as one Stud or Sissy sperm cell anywhere but up a Sissies Vaganus® hole, we could be severely fined for a cum disposal rule infraction.

So look! There's no need to toss Cum-Socks® in the trash. If you go to the Nurses Office you can have your sock removed. And if you're too full to drink down your own collected sperm the Nurse will transfer your Jizzzies properly into a special refrigerated storage container to maintain cum freshness. In fact there's always freshly bottled dick-cream available at all times in the cafeteria partly due to all the saved **Cum-Sock®** Jizz.

Ok now another issue, Cum-Sock® breakage. This is something which happens frequently around here. Because let's face it, you Sissies are cum factories. Your bodies have been genetically modified to produce extra cum ejaculations for two good reasons. One is to promote successful Sissy **Breeding** [4.D-G3.27]. And number two, to enhance the sexual experience for the men the Sissy services.

You Whores® have so many orgasms and produce so much Gurl-Cream® we just want you faggots to know eventually you're going to pop a sock full of Sissy-Goo. And when this happens remain calm there's no need for,

DRAMA! (Asshemer shouts).

And again we know you little sexually precocious Sissy-Whores are drama queens! So, STAY! CALM!

Mare he's the Cum-Police! Hee... hee...hee... we're doomed!

Sheeesh... heee... shheeeeesh, (Mary signals to Jane to be quiet by tweaking Jane's exposed nipple).

Ow! He's going to cut our clits off! Hee... hee...

Shhhh… Jane be quiet you're going to get us both in trouble.

Now you Sissies cum so much and so many times a day, you typically on the average, are carrying around a pint of Jizz in your Cum-Socks, weighing about a pound. What's that about half a kilo? So Sissies are walking around with a pound of cum dangling down from their poor pathetically small Sissy-Dicks. And let me make this perfectly clear here, a Cum-Sock is NOT a male condom. A real man's condom is way too big and would never fit on a tiny little Sissy clit.

And this is why the Sissy clit socks are specially designed for size and for large volumes of Sissy goo. The maximum daily cum volume for Sissies of your age is about six point nine fluid pints per day, which is a lot of Jizzie goo. The socks are engineered and made of very strong material so you can carry extra volume for long periods of time.

But don't wait till you're walking around with a big ball hanging from your mini-dick. I'm the official **Clit-Sock**® Patrol Officer on this school's campus. So, don't let me catch you little faggots running around swinging a big ball of Jizz from your little cum nozzles. With this much ejaculation, a Sissy should change her sperm collecting sock at least six to nine times a day.

And we all know a typical Sissy can have orgasms at any time. I could remember… (Reminiscing moment).

Oh fuck he's gonna tell us a story, gag me! (Jane rolls her eyes).

…and this is before they passed the Sissy and Stud Sperm Management law. I was standing at a bus stop one time with a whole bunch of you little fags and suddenly for no particular freaken reason, they all started spewing cream out of their clits. Holy fuck-cream shit! Sissy goo all over the god-dam place!

Hell and the really weird part of it was they weren't even masturbating or anything! All it took for them to pop was for some smartass Stud® kid walking by to whip out his long ten incher and twirl it around a few times at the Sissies and BOOM! Gobs of Sperm flying through the air, all over the jizz-fucking-place. People ducking out of the way! Let's face it. Sissies are just a bunch of cum fountains.

So I know from personal experience, it doesn't take much for you Sissies to pop off a load. For example,

Oh shit another story, shoot me now! (Jane agonizes).

You little queer faggot's can be passively sitting there at your **SissyDesk**® [11.K.2] with the seats probing wand stuck-up your hole during a class. Then of course your queer mind starts to wander off. You slip into some weird, twisted erotic day-dreaming when your eye catches your teacher's large, beautiful, voluptuous tits which are begging to be nuzzled on. And without even touching their tiny little cum nozzle, an involuntary reaction happens, BAM! You can't hold the load back anymore and the Sissy squeals like a little gurl. They pop loads right there in the middle of class. So these are just some of the ways how cum socks fill up, really, really, fast and for no apparently good reason!

Now if you're in a situation of a large cum ball dandling or you find yourself sockless, just go to the Nurse's Office and avoid a compromising situation. Or if you think you can handle more cum in your belly and I know you fags drink gallons of this shhh...it! Un-strap the cum catching sock, take it off, right there in class in front of your classmates and guzzle down your own Jizzies.

Let me make this clear. Sissies do not have to be ashamed of eating their own cum out of a collecting sock which had been hanging painfully between their legs. You're a Sissy faggot. Just empty the dam thing!

Mr. Asshemer? Mr. Asshemer? (Jane raises her hand).

Oh! Ms. Goldberg! Wow, this is unexpected. You actually have a question?

Yes Sir. Isn't speaking gay-words punishable by castration? The thirty-four Amendment, **Profanity** [17.34].

Haaa haa ha... You little wise-ass Whore! I'm a US Federal Government employee! I don't need any god-fucking-dam permission to break the law!

Now, where were we? Oh yeah! We all know the non-Sissy student's make fun of you, wait for it I'm gonna say a *gay-word,* QUEERS. They disrespect you, piss on you, face-fuck you, cum on you, slap you around, gently I hope and humiliate you. But you can always report the incident to the principal's office at any time if they physically harm you in any way. It's a Federal Law, Sissies cannot be physically harmed. And the Sissy Rights Act, the **SRA** [17.30], is always enforced here at, Special Integration High School 69.

But about the sock problem, just listen to some good advice developed over the course of years of dealing with Sissy mishaps. First, if you do pop a sock inside the school, in a classroom or maybe in a hallway, somewhere that has a relatively clean surface,

DON'T PANIC!

We suggest you get on your hands and knees and lick up your own cum load off the floor with your tongue. Because we all know it's a shame for a Sissy to waste a good cum load, right? And yeah this may seem humiliating to you, but remember, you're a trained Sissy® and Sissies are engineered and breed for humiliation. So, there's no shame in licking your own Jizz up off the floor like an animal!

And remember, you're American Sissies and despite your human appearance you Sissies are classified as animals not humans. So you should be proud to be considered a citizen of the United States Inc. which is the only Cunt-trie in the world that promotes Sissydom®. This makes the USA Inc. the only place where Sissies can humiliate themselves with the same pride and dignity their own government does.

Whoa! Where's he going with this? (Jane scratches her snatch).

I mean sure the US Government is humiliated like a Sissy Bitch by the world enforcing economic sanctions on the United States but hey, we were just intervening in other Cunt-trie for profit, we weren't trying to democratize them or anything!

Geeez! What-the-hell is he talking about? Jane, you were right, he is an asshole. (Mary whispers).

Mare, I take it you don't like this idiot.

Oh! This guy's a wacko! How did he go from licking-up cum wades to the USA Inc. government? Oh wait! It's a related topic, heee... heee... heee... Unbelievable!

Hey! I don't believe it, his voice, he's the idiot who face fucked me at lunch. Mare, This teacher's a deceitful Sissy hating bigot!

Well anyway, secondly, if you think the surface where your sock broke is not hygienically safe to lick, ask a faculty member to call a Non-Stud janitor to clean it up. And make sure you get a new sock on your cum-hose.

Dill-a-ling, dill-a-ling, dill-a-ling, dill-a-ling...

Okay, that's it, thanks for listening, clean-up and get to class. And Goldberg, I'm watching you punk!

[4.10] MSES

Modern Social Economics class...

Ok, class. I know you're all freshmen here at, Special Integration High School 69. So, well cum to your new school. I'm Mr. **Cockum** (EN15) and you'll be studying Modern Social Economics, the **MSES** [21.4] in this class. Yes?

I think I'm in the wrong class.

Ok, you're free to go. Ah what class are you supposed to be in?

Sexual Discovery.

Oh! It's in room 69 with Miss Clitenormous.

Okay, what is, Modern Social Economics? Yes the DOM in the power suite.

It's about the economic system which was created after the collapse of the United States dollar as the world reserve currency.

Exactly, let me guess. You purchased your textbook early and read it during your summer break?

Yes, cover to cover Mr. **Cockum**.

You're Mary Dune aren't you?

Yes Mr. Cockum.

Well thanks for signing up for Modern Social Economics Mary. I understand you were awarded the highest scholastic achievement award at Integration Elementary School 69.

Yes Mr. Cockum.

Teacher's pet (Jane whispers under her breath).

Shhh.... Quiet down Jane.

He... hee... heee…

I'm warning you, stop it. (Mary always the disciplinarian).

Why don't you just go up there and blow him!

Sheeesh....

Yes, Modern Social Economics is a system created after the financial collapse of the US government and subsequently the dollar as the world reserve currency. Also was the result of the pursuing losses by the United States in the Financial World War, the **FWW** of 2069 [23.24] and also the Pivot to Asia War, the PAW [23.6]. So after the Financial War there was NO money in the US treasury. And there hadn't been for decades due to the US Empire giving up the gold standard. Now Class, currency is not money and I'll speak more about this later.

[4.11] GREAT DEMISE

So let's first cover some of the not so pleasant history of the old non-incorporated United States. As a result of centuries of private banking greed, the states of Washington, Oregon, California, Alaska and Hawaii along with most of our gold reserves were given as payment to the governments of the Eurasian Union for debt we owed them as war reparations. This dark moment in history is also known as the American Economic Disparity **AED** [23.45] era.

In the last two hundred years of American history after the FWW we had, the Great Famine, the Great Plague, Great Censoring and Great Exodus. After those horrific events came the, Trans-Anal Trade Investment Partnership, the **TTIP** [23.56] conflict which lead to import trade laws against importing the American patented Vaganus® by all nations.

Then the New Industrial Revolution or just NIR, which ensued after the TTIP conflict. The NIR was made possible by the talented scientists acquired, captured, kidnapped, imprisoned or detained by the United States through the valiant efforts of the US Immigrant Army, or USIA. This army was made up mostly of Central and South American prisoners from the conquest of the Americas by the United States in 2069.

These captured foreign scientists, later to be Americanized, were seized, oddly enough, during the intellectual conquest of our befriended and allied nations in Western Europe. This opportunity happened in part by the global fiat banking industry. Actually the Europeans (EU) became militarily impotent and economically insolvent by their involvement and dependence on the US dollar as their reserve fiat currency. So basically the EU was held hostage.

On a positive note, the NIR has brought us, Nano-Steel which is stronger than steel, but light as a feather! It can be made to grow into any shape, through the miracle of molecular biology. Then, there was the discovery of, Anti-Gravity Levitation or (AGL), Dark Matter and Dark Energy were both harnessed for near-light-speed space exploration.

These newly captured, I mean acquired inventions and discoveries lead to the attempted but regrettably failed invasion of the Eurasian Union colonies on Mars. This was the last imperialistic effort sponsored by the old United States using the antiquated military Space Force **USSF** [25.30].

So after the demoralizing defeats of the US Space Forces by the Eurasian Union the claims by the US of sole proprietorship of the planet Mars were declared void. The Red planet since then has been placed into the stewardship of the Eurasian Union. The US is excluded from the rich resources gained from the exploration of Mars. This includes the vast gold deposits and other precious metals found there. But our Cunt-tree doesn't really need gold anymore because the USA Inc. has embraced Sissydom® with the creation of the new economic system called the, Modern Social Economic System, or for short, the MSES©.

God-of-Cocks Mare! I'm so sick of hearing about the warmongering this Cunt-tree did before the creation of **Sissydom©**.

Yeah Jane now wars will be fought in bedrooms. As the USA Inc. penetrates into the Sissy-less Cunt-tries with the proliferation of Vaganus® a new monetary value will emerge. No one will need gold anymore!

Right, like the new world order slogan we hear nowadays,

World Economic Domination through Vaganus Addiction

Aaaagh! I squirted! Sorry!

Geeeezy Weezy Sissy-Puss, calm down Gurl.

The USA is prohibited from ever attempting to establish a colony on the newly colonized planet. For the Trans-Anal Trade and Intercourse Partnership, the **TTIP** [23.56] conflict reparation, economic sanctions were initiated against the United States Inc. Seriously, the assertions of the USA taking hostile actions against non-aggressive peaceful Eurasian nations! I mean they didn't ask the United States for permission to settle on the Red Planet! What do they expect would happen!

These sanctions I mentioned are due to the alleged US war crimes and crimes against humanity over the last several centuries. These outlandish accusations claim the private FED banker supported US oligarchy raped and pillaged the non-nuclear weapon defended nations.

And also the European Allies during the TTIP conflict & the NAFTA confrontation. I mean it's preposterous! We were merely barrowing vital resources from our Allies by force, in a friendly way, where there was a minimum of collateral damage. Besides the **TTIP** conflict only happened because our allies in Europe rejected the American Sex-Trade & Investment in Sissydom®. Similarly the Trans-Pacific Penetration (**TPP**) treaty [23.57] didn't work for the same reasons! The Asian Cunt-tries didn't embrace Sissydom®.

But regardless of these misguided nations not cooperating with the USA Inc. our new and superior social economic system, the MSES© plays an important role in the development of products and systems. And seriously they were born from the many agonies of conquest and the glory of our defeats. The stupendous discoveries and inventions, for example, the patented American **Vaganus**® [14.O1.6], is merely one of the many bi-products. The Sissies hole is nothing more than an ATM machine.

Mare what-the-fuck is so glorious about defeat? This guys a freaken moron!

And don't forget this class because it will be on the final exam. They are all American inventions. They were discovered by American Scientists despite the scientists being captured citizens from allied countries in Europe and from China. In reality the USA Inc. did these smart guys a favor by forcefully indoctrinating them into Sissydom® and the MSES here in the greatest Nation on Earth! I mean, where else in the world can you get an unlimited supply of free Vaganus!

Mary what the hell is, Trans-Anal Trade?

Shhhh…. Jane I have no clue what he's yapping about.

Yeah me neither, this guys a babbling idiot. And saw him wearing one of those **MAGA** [23.40] hats, so how smart can he be? Heeee heee hee…

[4.12] LCT

Labor Compensation transaction (LCT)…

Ok, now that we have all those unpleasant things out of the way, let's move on to the new socioeconomic system, the MSES. One of the most significant and essential changes made by the implementation of the MSES and the creation of Sissydom here in the United States brought changes for, worker compensation through a new money system. It also has formed a new improved social class system which reshaped society in the USA Inc. You see class, prior to the Second US **Cunt-Stitution** [17], look it up in, SM069 Manual, Section 17.

In the MSES we had a two social class system here in the US. One class was the top 1 percent comprised of the wealthy government aristocratic and money whoring, Neo-Cons along with their pimps the Wall-Street bankers. The other class was the poor and destitute or what has been referred to as the new, Niger-Class or Neo-Nig class, the **NNC** [22.28] which makes up the remaining 99 percent of the United States Inc. population regardless of color of your skin. So yes! Our working middle class is the **New Nigers**, no one or race excluded. Get used to it!

And class when I refer to people as Niger I'm referring to the new definition of the word not the old racist one. The new Niger includes anyone from any race or culture who is living in abject poverty. Mind you, the working middle class were made extinct by the greed of American banks and the Corporatocracy. The one percent had all the money and the impoverished ninety-nine percent had only hopes and dreams, nothing tangible. The Neo-Nigs, middle-class were shit-on by the one percent Uber rich and rightfully so, considering the wealthy contributed vast amounts to the construction of **FEMA** [4.D-G7.13] detention camps.

Partly due to the corralling of the useless masses into these camps we now have a vastly improved system developed by the wealthy and powerful in our Cunt-trie, it's a social miracle! It's a financially equal system for everyone with Whore and Worker Classes having an equal distribution of wealth and opportunity. And these two social Classes of the MSES form the core structure for our national agenda of making the United States a world superpower once again by setting up puppet regimes throughout the world to embrace Sissydom. And class the word Intervention is not a dirty word in America!

Intervention to an American means, the Unites States Inc. is simply trying to help the other needy, Sissy-less, Vaganus-less Cunt-tries in the world. We're just helping them share their wealth and prosperity with us. I mean, the USA Inc. through **Vaganus**® and Cock-Worship is more intellectual, morally correct and definitely more liberated sexually. So naturally the global proliferation through Sissydom® is totally justified. This is due to the fact the USA Inc. is the only incorporated Cunt-trie in the world who could pull it off.

I mean, hypothetically through the use of the USA Inc. federally owned Hollywood Propaganda Corporation, **HPC** [21.B.17]. We could conceivably accomplish complete Sissification® of other populations. You see class, by the benevolence of the United States Inc. and through their acceptance of Sissydom as their economic salvation, Sissy-less Cunt-tries would merely be lead to be cuming blissfully subordinate to our great nation!

Oooh! I pop a **Jizzzie**® load (Jane is a B-Type and is typically squirting off a load).

Shhhh... Quiet down Jane we'll get in trouble.

Sorry, but he's such a rambling ignoramus. Ahhh.... My Gurl-Clit® is always squirting when **Sissydom**© is mentioned. Aaaagh!

Yeah me too, my tits are lactating... Aaagh! I'm getting hot-flashes about this domination stuff.

Well class, I'm glad I straighten out this misconception. So to clarify the new social-economic system, it can be broken-down into two parts; Worker-Stud and Whore-Sissy. It's a simple system and in this class we'll be studying the complexities of this new social class system in detail over the cuming school year. Ok here's a good question. Who in the class can tell me why we have two groups in our economic system? Yes Mary.

Well Mr. **Cockum** (EN04) to start with, our old antiquated economic system, needed to be changed because our Cunt-tries government was taken over by private bankers and big business. Then they printed our money into a hyper-inflation which bankrupted our nation making it insolvent as all fascist movements do.

Then, like all other empires, the United States imploded economically from within. Finally, through desperation, the US Government used Sissy® people to coerce Americans to work for the government or government sponsored businesses by providing pay compensation sex. This is what Fascist do. They take advantage of the working middle class or in this case, defenseless Sissies and poor working people. You see, after copulating with the Sissy, the workers bank accounts are credited for purchases of, food, shelter and frivolous expensive luxury consumer goods like toilet paper and warm winter clothing, etc. These luxuries are all manufactured in Count-tries not controlled by the USA Inc. In other words, in the Vaganus-less, economically thieving Cunt-tries in Eurasia.

Also in our new modern economic system workers are paid in **MO**.

I'm sorry Mary, can I interrupt you here? Class, Mary is referring to **Male-Orgasm**, **MO**® [12.L1.1]. Go ahead Mary.

Well the workers are paid in MOs by the employer, which are typically businesses owned by the USA Inc. government, then the worker penetrates the Whore to exchange the MOs for dollar credits.

In conclusion Sissies are used as if they were farm animals for labor compensation. I'm sorry they're non-consensually used as, Federal Civil Servants by our government. This incorporation of Sissies into the economic system was necessary because the workers did not trust their own government anymore. So the use of Sissy® people to coerce the American workers into going to work again was justified. The Whore® class is a sub-culture which was constructed to be the US Governments bartering system. In other words, our Sissy ass-pussies are lawfully exploited by our Government because it created us. Meaning, the Sissy Gurls® are the Whores and the pimp our benevolent Government. And I'm proud to be an American Whore® serving my Cunt-tree. I want and need American sperm dripping out of my government owned Vaganus®

Applause... Applause.... Applause... (The teacher and class applaud). Thank you Miss Dune. Well done Mary that was a very exact and simplified explanation of the MSES. Expanding on Mary's explanation, in our Cunt-tree we have two classes in our society. One Class, the Workers are 100 percent human Non-Sissies. And in this social class we have two sub-classes, a Stud-class and an inferior Non-Stud-Class. Where **Stud**® class [1.A1.1] members are all males with penises of eight inches or greater in length. Non-Stud class male members have penises less than eight but larger than three inches in length. For clarification of penis sizes let's all turn to the back of your textbooks to the Sissy Manual. [1.0]

Ok, so who besides Mary can tell us about the social taxonomy and what it means to us as a society?

Ah, the young Stud® looking fellow in the back.

It means, BIG DICKS RULE! Yeah!

Whooohooo... !!!...

Ooh! Yeah! Whoo hooo! Dam Right! Studs Rule! Hey! Calm down, everybody! (The Studs students whoop it up).

That's enough! I don't want outbreaks like this in my class. Just settle down! Everybody, back to your seats.

Okay, who else can give a reply? Yes, you!

Well, some people who were born a particular way are made to do certain things and others different things.

Okay, this is going in the right direction, but is everything equal for everybody in the MSES?

Yes, the young **B-Type** [1.2] Sissy next to Mary?

Mr. Cockum, how long is your dick?

Ho! Hoe Bag! Sissy-Bitch in Heat! Hoe! Slut! Scank! You Hoe! Ho! Ooh!

Settle down!

Slut! Scank! Hoe! Cum-Toilet! Fuckhole!

Settle down! That's enough! (Mr. Cockum shouts). Calm down! You Studs, everybody settle down now!

Miss what was your name?

Jane, I'm Jane Goldberg Boosh, but my parents didn't want me to be associated with the **Boosh** family [3.C1.c.6] because President Boosh my great, great, great, great, great grandfather was convicted and hanged as a traitor for master-mining the 911 government sponsored false-flag event. So they change my name to just, Jane Goldberg.

Well regardless of your social position or history, I want to have a word with you after class young lady.

Mr. Cockum I'm going to answer the question if you give me a minute of time.

I don't know why (Mr. Cockum smirks). But okay, I'm a very fair guy, but I'm warning you Jane, this better be good, don't press your luck.

Thank you, Mr. Cockum.

Okay, I asked you your penis size because, size matters in our modern socio-economic system. For example, you have a job working at an integration high school as a teacher and there's a requirement rule about what social class a teacher can be from.

Ok, I see where you're going with this, continue.

So I know you're Stud classified because (1) you're a teacher and (2) you are required to have a penis eight inches or longer in length. It's like this for everything. Your Penis Official Length Certificate, your **POLC** [4.D-G1.3] needs to be long if you want a good job and don't wanna end up living in a FEMA camp.

Very good Jane, continue (Cockum admires Jane specificity).

Teachers, managers, senators, proctologists, engineers and administrators, the President of the United States are all Stud® Class. And in the military, Officers are all from the Stud-Class. So there is an inequality in our society in the year 2246. In factories only Stud classified men are promoted to management. Most colleges only accept Stud and Sissy students. In other words, for those in the Worker class, the bigger and longer their penis the higher up the socio-economic ladder your family goes. The bigger car, the bigger house, higher quality Whores to **LCT** [4.27] with. And it's like this in the Whore class as well.

Even in the sub-class of Sissy. Size-wise, the smaller the Sissy-clit, the less opportunities there're for the Sissy. For example, the DOM® type Sissy often referred to as type D-Type Sissy, who have the largest Sissy clits, can own the subordinate B-Type. But the Bitch® type can't own a DOM. And the DOM can have as many Bitches as she wants in a for-profit-harem.

Well Jane, despite the bold beginning of your answer, it was the answer I was looking for, good job, but next time, please just ask the person what social class they're from.

Thank you Sir (Jane winks and blows a kiss at Cockum). Mwah...

Huh! (He winks back). Okay, so going on what Jane just told us, is there an upward economic mobility in our modern society?

Yes the young man in the front here.

Yes there is mobility, despite the Neo-Capitalist running the USA Inc. The details are in the Manual SM069. The working class has always been decimated by the wealth acquire at the top of society. I think they call this the, Rot-at-the-Top, the **RAT** [23.47].

Class! This is known as the American Economic Disparity, the **AED** [23.45]. After **Cock-Mas**© [9.I4.4] we'll study this period in American history. Okay, go on, continue.

My family was a Non-Stud class family for many years, until my great-grandfather shagged, excuse me, I mean breed with, a Stud® Baby-Maker woman, my great-grandmother and from that breeding on the males in our family all had eight inch or larger pricks. Now my Dad is a factory manager and we live in a nice house which is close to a really cool Whorehouse and stuff.

Thank you?

James, my name is **James Munchonet** and I'm proud my family breeds with and is in the Stud Class!

Well congratulations young man. He's right class; Americans can improve their station in life regardless of their family history. But it depends on your selection of which class you breed with. A Non-Stud family can do what's called a, class Opt-Out or a **COO** [13] where the Non-Stud wage-earning working family, sometimes called the NS family, breeds with a class member who they have selected to move up in class too. Typically if a Non-Stud family all have small penises, they might choose to Opt-Out and shun the Non-Stud women by breeding with a Sissy-Breeder® woman. You see, so everything is equal in the new United States Inc.

Dill-a-ling, dill-a-ling, dill-a-ling, dill-a-ling....

Ok, don't forget to read chapter six, section nine of your textbook, Whoring-Stations why they're part of the new American banking system, see yah on Thursday.

Let go of my hand Mary, I want to talk to Mr. Cockum.

Jane Lover! You haven't had much luck today let's just go before you get into any more trouble.

Mare, I just want to tell him thanks for trusting me to finish my response.

Okay, I'll be right outside the classroom door if anything happens. Be careful Jane.

Okay, what could happen? I give him a blow-job. This will only take a minute or two or three depending on if I can fish his huge dick out of his pants. Heeee heee hee…

JANE! (Mary, being parental, rolls her eyes).

Hey Mr. **Cockum**, thanks for letting me finish.

Hey no problem Jane, but in the future please try not to say stuff that gets the Stud boys all up in a rage, or you know, up as in hardon up. Those Stud-Boys are all on the **PED** [4.D-G1.8], the Penis Enlargement Drug and have an extremely high level of testosterone. The slightest comment about sex sparkers them off.

Sure Mr. **Cockum**, sorry about that.

So Jane?

Yes Mr. Cockum?

How longs your clit?

Yeah our Whorehouse® number is, WH33969R. So, Mr. Cockum you can mount me anytime.

Well, I'll definitely stop by and have a poke at you Jane. You're a hot little piece-of-ass. Mwah…

Mwah… Yeah, I know, (Jane brushes her hand over Mr. Cockum's erection). See yah Stud (wink, wink, Jane playfully skips away).

[4.13] COLLEGE TALK

Oooh.... Mary, Cockum has a huge prick! Ahhh… He's a freaken dream!

Whoa! JANE! You Jizzed on me! Dam-it, now I gotta go change my blouse! Where's your sock? Calm down Gurl.

Sorry, you're jealous?

No! Yes! God-of-Cocks©. You act like you don't get enough up your coochee. When **we** get to college we'll get probed constantly!

Hmmmm.... you said **we**.

Huh! I always say **we**.

I love you Mary. Mwah…

Mwah… Oh! Jane cum here and hold me.... Mwah… Kiss...I love you too sweetheart. We'll always be together lover. Kiss...

In college? Are we gonna go to college together?

My dear Jane. You & me forever! Yes we're going to college together, but first, let's survive high school. Hmmm.... Kiss.... Kisssss.... Mwah...

Continued in EN03, Chapter 1....

=== THE END ===

Review Request & Suggestion

Thanks for purchasing this book or bundle (four book set). Please leave a review on Google Books, Amazon or Audible. Also to help our readers or listeners, we strongly suggest downloading the Empty Nation manual **SM069** to assist with the complexity of the story from any one of the following.

Audible.com, free after purchase as a Product Summary

Amazon.com, (low price) ASIN: 1719912866

Google Play Books, (free) GGKEY: X02BGY24G4K

The Official Sissydom Manual SM069

The National Sissydom Association (NSA)
A subsidiary of USA Inc.
All rights reserved, copyright 2020
Revised: 01-09-2020

SM069-06 Description

The Sissydom manual version SM069-06 encompasses details from years 2213 to 2259. This manual is intended to be used by United States Inc. citizens for the sole purpose of clarification of the procedures, laws, rule, codes, regulations, probing, documents, exams, rating, ranking, classification, drugs, qualifications and behavior of all parties participating or remotely involved in the United States Inc. MSES (US-MSES).

TERRITORIES

This manual also applies to all occupied territories under control of the USA Inc. Including but not limited to all of Latin America (LA) including countries in both Central & South America; refer to the LA-MSES.

SAR

Special Administrative Regions (SARs) enjoy a higher degree of autonomy under the "one Cock, one Cunt" concept developed by President Tramp. There are currently two SARs, Mexico located in the Central America and Canada in North America. Both were turned over to USA Inc. control after the NAFTA war in 2169. Both SARs mentioned here implement the LCT system.

Persons living in a SAR are NOT and never will be citizens of the USA Inc. Also neither is allowed to cross into the USA Inc. at any time (visas are not available) unless the border-crossing is for a female surrendering her rights and becomes a host-mother at a Sissy Farm Breeding facility.

MSES AFFILIATES

Although the following Cunt-Trees are not controlled territories or SARs of the USA Inc. they are dependent and liable to the USA Inc. monetarily. This pretty much means, the USA Inc. can squeeze their balls at any time to induce compliance.

IN-MSES (India)
RU-MSES (Russia)
IS-MSES (Islamic)
AU-MSES (Africa Union)
SE-MSES (Southeast Asia)

These Cunt-Trees are all implementing the MSES LCT system of payment (aka the new SWIFT system). For local rules and regulations consult the specific sections in this manual (section not available yet).

RULES

The rules and laws stated in this document are lawful and can be used in a court of law to defend and protect only the rights of United States of America Incorporated citizens. The USA Inc. governing body (Government) and any and all of its proxies or entities, owned, contained, endowed, funded, imprisoned, underwritten, confiscated, authorized, financed, detained, sanctioned, annexed, blockchained, begotten, empowered, captured, incorporated, forfeited, convicted, subjugated, forsaken, subsidized, sponsored, abandoned, franchised, promoted, controlled, conquered, incarcerated, entitled or restrained by said Government or its affiliated corporate members are fully relieved of any and all liability of wrong doing created by adhering to the laws, rules and regulations stated here in this SM069-06 document. Amen.

Please download the current manual for further details in Series...

About the Author

What Is It Press is the publisher of the Empty Nation Series. As far as the author is concerned, we know very little about the *Sue Yan Nish*. We know she is Chinese and lives somewhere in China. Although her location changes frequently. We receive cryptic messages form her telling us only that the manuscript is finished and where we need to retrieve it from. We leave her compensation in a small box in the same place the manuscript was left for us.

Contact Info

The following addresses are ways to get in touch with the author Sue Yan Nish.

Author Bio:
https://www.amazon.com/Sue-Yan Nish/e/B07GW252V1

Emails:
sueyannish@outlook.com
sueyannish@gmail.com

Website:
https://sites.google.com/view/empty-nation/home